I fell asleep the moment my head hit the pillow—awakened what seemed like hours later by a chorus of voices shouting in Italian just outside my door. I cracked an eye to squint at the ceiling, then reached over to hit the illumination bar on my travel alarm: 1:06. Okay, I knew Italians were night owls, but this was a public building, and some of us wanted sleep!

I crawled out of bed, shrugged into my Laura Ashley dress, and staggered across the room, thinking fierce thoughts. I threw open the door. "Would you people *please*—"

The corridor was empty.

I looked left. I looked right. I stepped farther into the hallway and peered down the staircase. The voices I'd heard echoed up from the lobby. But they weren't the voices of rowdy Italian night owls. They were the voices of a half dozen uniformed police gathered around a woman whose lifeless body lay at the bottom of the stairs.

My eyes froze open in horror.

And she was wearing my new stretch denim corset dress with the bra straps!

* * *

Turn the page to read critical raves for Maddy Hunter's bestselling *Passport to Peril* mysteries . . .

Top O' the Mournin'

Hilarious and delightful. . . . I found myself laughing out loud and wiping away tears (of joy) as I quickly flipped the pages. I can't wait for the next trip!"

—*The Old Book Barn Gazette*

"A delightful cozy that is low on gore but rich in plot and characterizations. There is plenty of slapstick humor. . . . The mystery is well constructed and the supporting cast yields a number of suspects. . . ."

—The Best Reviews.com

"No sophmore jinx here . . . very funny and full of suspense."
—*Romantic Times Bookclub Magazine*

"WARNING: Do not munch on Triscuits or anything covered in powdered sugar while reading this book! I nearly choked from laughing so hard. . . . There was belly laughter, or at least a chuckle, on each page. This is the most fun I've had in a while."

—*The Mystery Company Newsletter*

Alpine for You

"I found myself laughing out loud. . . . The word 'hoot' comes to mind."

—*Deadly Pleasures*

"Light and witty. . . . While we're all waiting for the next Janet Evanovich, this one will do perfectly."
—Sleuth of Baker Street (Ontario, Canada)

"A debut with more than a few chuckles. . . . *Alpine for You* is one to cheer the gloomy winter days."

—Mystery Lovers Bookshop

"A very funny and promising start to Hunter's *Passport to Peril* series."

—*Romantic Times*

"If you're looking for laughter, you've come to the right place . . . sure to provide giggles and guffaws aplenty. Hunter's confident voice and her compelling first person narration . . . mak[es] Emily a complete person with pluck and purpose and personality. The writing style is breezy and accomplished. . . . First-rate entertainment!"

Cozies, Capers & Crimes

"Move over, Evanovich, there's a new author in town. . . . One of the best I have read for a long time. . . . Hilarious. The characters are an absolute hoot."

—*Under the Covers*

"Delightfully fresh, with a great deal of humor."

—Creatures 'n Crooks Bookshoppe

"As funny as anything by Katy Munger, Janet Evanovich, [or] Joan Hess. . . . The laughs started on the first page and continued, nonstop, to the last. . . . This one gets five stars. It's a winner."

—Blackbird Mysteries

"A compelling heroine, an intriguing hero, and a great scenic tour. I'm impatiently looking forward to the next one."

—*The Old Book Barn Gazette*

Also by Maddy Hunter

Passport to Peril mystery series

ALPINE FOR YOU
TOP O' THE MOURNIN'

Published by Pocket Books

maddy
HUNTER

A *Passport to Peril* mystery

Pasta Imperfect

POCKET BOOKS
New York London Toronto Sydney

This book is a work of fiction. Names, characters, places and incidents are products of the author's imagination or are used fictitiously. Any resemblance to actual events or locales or persons, living or dead, is entirely coincidental.

An *Original* Publication of POCKET BOOKS

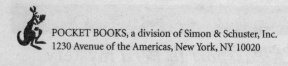

POCKET BOOKS, a division of Simon & Schuster, Inc.
1230 Avenue of the Americas, New York, NY 10020

Copyright © 2004 by Mary Mayer Holmes

ISBN: 0-7434-8291-3

First Pocket Books printing August 2004

10 9 8 7 6 5 4 3 2 1

POCKET and colophon are registered trademarks of Simon & Schuster, Inc.

Cover design by Min Choi
Cover art by Jeff-Fitz Maurice
Interior design by Davina Mock

Manufactured in the United States of America

For information regarding special discounts for bulk purchases, please contact Simon & Schuster Special Sales at 1-800-456-6798 or business@simonandschuster.com.

DEDICATION

To my buddies, Tony and Herm, who made
Italy so delightful . . . twice!

With love~
mmh

ACKNOWLEDGMENTS

"Everything comes to those who wait." Careers have their ups and downs. My writing career collapsed in the early nineties. For the next decade, I struggled to put two words together in the same sentence. When I finally finished what I considered to be the defining work of my career, no one wanted to read it. But I waited, and persevered, and waited some more . . . and then everything changed.

My universe is peopled with friends and family who believed in me even when I found it difficult to believe in myself. If not for my connection to them, I still might be struggling to put two words together. I offer my deepest thanks to all of them, and to the following people:

To Pam Johnson, for her kindness and generosity in introducing me to her amazing agent.

To Irene Goodman, a.k.a. "the amazing agent," for the phone call that began, "I love what you've written. I want to represent you."

To Herm Kuhn, Sue Hubbard, Margaret Dohnalek, Marge and Jim Converse, Sharon Gasser, Barb Schuler,

Micki Harper, Linda Kuhn, and Minda Danner, for buying my books in bulk and giving them away to their friends like pieces of penny candy.

To Margaret Kaufman, for her extra footwork and picture-taking in Florence, and to her companions, Virmati Hitchings, Lisa Wax, Tinker Zimmerman, and Merilee Obstbaum, for becoming part of the research team.

To Terri Bischoff and Linda Vetter, owners of Booked for Murder, for their enthusiasm in promoting a local mystery author.

To Johanna Farrand, for the tongue-in-cheek cover copy she so cleverly pens.

To Jeff Fitz-Maurice and Paolo Pepe, for their artistry and imagination in designing my dynamite book jackets.

And most especially, to Christina Boys, my extraordinary editor, for her unflagging encouragement, ultra-efficiency, eye for detail, uncanny ability to know what needs fixing and how to fix it, and on a more personal level, for her grace, thoughtfulness, laughter, and breathless chats. You are a special gift in my life—a gift that was well worth waiting for.

Maddy Hunter

Pasta Imperfect

CHAPTER 1

There are lots of things you can't do in Rome.

You can't leave your belongings unattended without fear of having them ripped off. You can't talk in the Sistine Chapel. You can't exit the Colosseum the same way you entered. You can't buy a ticket aboard a bus from a vending machine that's out-of-order. And you can't take pictures in St. Peter's Basilica.

Don't get me wrong. You can *try* to take pictures of the towering marble columns, the gilded arches, and the dazzling mosaics, monuments, and altars. The Vatican encourages all kinds of photography. But the thing is, everything is so big inside the basilica, you have to stand really far back to get your shot.

Like Tuscany.

"How do you s'pose they keep the floor in this place so shiny?" Nana asked as we stood near the monstrous holy water stoups in the nave of St. Peter's.

I marveled at the acres of gleaming marble that stretched before us. There was only one way to keep this floor looking as polished as an Olympic ice-skating rink. "Zamboni," I concluded.

Nana sighed with nostalgia. "Your grampa always wanted to drive one a them Zambonis. He said watchin' that machine resurface the ice sent chills up his spine. I never had the heart to tell 'im it wasn't the Zamboni what give 'im chills. It was his underwear. Cotton briefs don't cut it at a hockey game. You gotta wear thermal."

Nana stood four-foot-ten, was built like a fireplug, and despite her eighth grade education, was the smartest person I knew. To kick off the first day of our Italian tour, she was dressed in her favorite Minnesota Vikings wind suit and wore a Landmark Destinations name tag that identified her as Marion Sippel.

I never wore a name tag, but all twelve seniors in my tour group knew me as Emily. Emily Andrew—the theater arts major who'd gone off to the Big Apple to become a serious stage actress, even landing a minor role in *Joseph and the Amazing Technicolor Dreamcoat*, only to return home to Iowa after my husband ran off with the dreamboat who donned Joseph's dreamcoat every time the lead actor was under the weather. Life has a way of turning lemons into lemonade though. I applied for an annulment, which returned me to "virgin" status in my mother's eyes, and I found permanent employment at the Windsor City Bank as the well-paid coordinator for its Senior Travel Club. I arrange day-trips throughout Iowa during the year and holidays abroad through national tour companies. Then I get to accompany the group as an official escort. It's a dream job that suffers only one major drawback.

People keep dying on me.

Nana assessed the floor with a critical eye. "You s'pose the floor's as slippery as it looks? This would be a bad time to fall and break my hip."

Unh-oh. I'd had a feeling all day long that some calamity was about to happen. It was like a ripple in the order of things. A disturbance in the force. Ever since my eerie encounter at an Irish castle last month, I'd flirted with the idea that I might be possessed of some kind of sixth sense, but to be honest, I hoped I was wrong. Living through disaster was bad enough. Being able to predict it would be right up there with tooth extraction by rusty pliers.

"The floor only looks like ice," I assured Nana, checking out her size five sneakers. They weren't Nike or Converse but appeared to be some off-brand she'd bought at Wal-Mart for ten bucks. She might be a lottery-winning multi-millionaire, but she still knew how to save a dime. "Do those have latex bottoms?"

She shuffled her feet, making a loud, squeaking noise. "You betcha."

"You're all set then." But I suddenly realized I was hesitant to let her out of my sight. "Do you ever have feelings you can't explain, Nana?"

"Female intuition," she groaned. "Awful thing. I'm glad I don't get them intuitive twinges much anymore, and when I do, it's usually gas." She fixed me with a fretful look. "You're taller'n me, Emily. You see George anywhere out there?" She glanced around to see who was within earshot before whispering close to my ear, "Him and me have big plans these next two weeks . . . if we can steer clear of *you know who*."

George was George Farkas, an Iowa retiree with a pros-thetic leg, a great sense of direction, and an expandable body part that was reputed to be of mythic proportions. He and Nana had developed the hots for each other on our trip to Ireland, but they hadn't wanted to raise eyebrows back home, so they'd kept the relationship under wraps.

They'd been thinking of this trip to Italy as an extended date, until the unthinkable happened.

My mom got talked into coming along.

Nana went up on tippy-toes and in her best imitation of a periscope in search of enemy vessels, scanned the cavernous depths of the basilica. "You think I've lost her? She's been stickin' to me like denture cream ever since we left Des Moines. I swear when we get back home, I'm gonna strangle your father."

Dad had meant well. When Nana's assigned roommate, Bernice Zwerg, had to cancel her reservation to undergo emergency bunion surgery, he'd suggested my mom take her place. "It'd give you three girls a chance to spend some quality time together." I'd been a little frightened by the idea. Nana had nearly swallowed her dentures. I'd had to perform the Heimlich maneuver just to get her breathing again.

Nana wrung her hands beside me. "How's a mature widowed lady s'posed to carry on a serious flirtation with a fella when the woman's *kid* is taggin' along?" It didn't seem to matter that the "kid" in this case was fifty-eight years old. I guess the theory was, once your kid, always your kid.

"There's George," I said, spying his bald head, tartan plaid shirt, and chino pants at a second holy water stoup across the way from us. I pointed him out and aimed her in the right direction. "Remember to guard your pocketbook."

She massaged her oversized bag with a reverent hand. "We don't have to worry about no criminal element in St. Peter's, Emily. This is the safest place in all Italy. It said so in a travel guide your mother checked outta the library."

"Well, be careful anyway."

Mesmerized by the sparkle and glitter in every corner of

the basilica, I dug my Canon Elph out of my shoulder bag and spun in a slow circle, dazzled. Wow. I studied the holy water font in front of me. In my parish church back home, holy water was dispensed in a metal container the size of a soup bowl. Here, it was dispensed in a marble shell the size of a man-eating clam and supported by two cherubs whose heads were as big as wrecking balls. I pondered the cherubs. Weren't they supposed to be itty-bitty creatures with tiny little wings?

Obviously, I'd been confusing them with Tinkerbell.

I wormed my way through the crowd, looking for a shot that would capture the essence of the basilica, and soon found it in the ceiling above me—a gold-toned mosaic of a wave-tossed boat jammed with apostles. Outside the boat, a haloed Jesus stood atop the water, his hand extended in an obvious attempt to prevent a prayerful Peter from sinking to the bottom of the Sea of Galilee. Aha! This was perfect. It had everything. Raw drama. Human emotion. Bible-based special effects. I took aim with my camera.

I couldn't fit all the apostles into my frame.

I changed the setting on my camera to panoramic print. I could fit all the apostles into the frame now, but I was faced with another *teensy* problem.

They no longer had heads.

Okay. So maybe I wasn't getting any great pictures of the world's most famous basilica, but on a brighter note, think of all the film I was saving!

I continued to wander, my shoulder growing numb from the sheer weight of having to shlep my bag around. But I was an escort. I needed to carry a lot of essential stuff. Over-the-counter medications. Itinerary information. Pocketknife. Sunblock. Address book. Post-it notes. Maps. Cosmetics. Cell phone. The bank had decided to spring for the cell phone to spare my having to battle Italy's notoriously bad phone system in case of emergency. It was a really good one, too—the kind that could handle transatlantic as well as local calls. I was carrying my passport, money, and credit cards beneath my clothing in a neck wallet that the tour company, Landmark Destinations, had sent out to all its guests. They suggested this was the only sure way to protect currency and travel documents from the pickpockets and purse snatchers who preyed upon summer tourists.

At a side altar mobbed with people, I saw a glossy white sculpture perched high on a plinth behind a glass enclosure—a depiction of Mary cradling the lifeless body of her Son. Around me, shutters clicked, lights flashed, film whirred. I could feel a palpable kind of energy as people pushed and shoved their way to the front, but I expected their excitement was fueled less from the idea that they were staring at the marble masterpiece than by the fact that this seemed to be the only statue in the whole basilica that could fit inside the frame of a thirty-five-millimeter camera.

I whipped my Elph up to my eye and zoomed in. I poised my finger on the shutter button.

"There you are, Emily." I froze at the sound of my mother's voice behind me. "Have you seen your grandmother? I've been telling her to stay close by me so I can protect her from being crushed to death by the crowd, but she keeps disappearing. I'm afraid this can only mean one thing." She let out a woeful sigh. "Her hearing's gone. First thing when we get back home, I'm calling the Miracle Ear people."

My mom stood an inch over five feet and was as soft and round as a pigeon—kind of like a Midwestern version of Bette Midler. She had a moon face, round blue eyes that crinkled at the corners, a cap of wavy salt-and-pepper hair, and a fanny pack that bulged at her waist like an Igloo cooler. I looked nothing like my mom. I was taller and thinner, with an unruly mop of shoulder-length dark brown hair, cheekbones you could actually see, and enough fashion sense never to allow a fanny pack anywhere near my waist. Neither Mom nor I had inherited Nana's bulbous nose or Alfred E. Newman ears. Sometimes you just luck out.

Mom glanced beyond me, riveting her attention on the glassed-in altar. "Oh, my goodness, Michelangelo's *Pietà*. Did you know I have a photo of this very statue from the 1964 New York World's Fair? You have to get a picture of that, Em. Here. Give me your bag so you can maneuver a little better." She grabbed my shoulder strap with one hand, gave it a tug, and let out a surprised gasp when it broke loose from her fingers and fell to the floor with an echoing *thunk*. I stooped down to grab it.

So did she.

"You must feel so bogged down toting this thing around, Em." She gave the breathable nylon fiber a possessive pat. "Why don't you let me carry it for you?"

I manacled my hand around the strap. "You're sweet to offer, but I can manage. Besides, it's too heavy for you."

"Heavy? This little bag of yours? Really, Emily, it's light as a feather."

Sure it was. That's why it was sitting on the floor.

"Think how much nicer it would be for you if I carried it," she continued. "Imagine the wonderful things you could do if your hands were freed up."

I gave her an expectant look. "Like . . . ?"

"Well . . . you . . . you . . ." She shot a quick look around her. "You could bless yourself. And with Vatican holy water! I bet the water here is much holier than it is back home."

This was so like my mom. It was bred in her bones to want to make everyone's life better, to be generous to a fault, to be responsible for everyone's happiness. But she always ended up going overboard, like putting whole heads of lettuce on a sandwich when a single leaf would do, or arranging the cold medications in your bathroom in alphabetical order during the commercial breaks of TV shows. She'd been on a tear about alphabetizing stuff ever since she'd started volunteering at the local library. Dad was doing his best to keep her away from alphabet soup, but it was a constant worry for him.

"Here's the scoop, Mom," I reasoned, trying to "out-nice" her. "You want to show Dad what the inside of the basilica looks like, don't you? If you're saddled with my bag, you won't be able to take pictures yourself."

She crooked her mouth slightly and spoke in an undertone. "Maybe you haven't noticed, Em, but most of the statues around here are the size of forage silos. Who can take pictures? Besides, I read an article in *The Catholic Herald* that hinted it might be sacrilegious to take photographs in places as holy as this." She gave my arm an encouraging squeeze. "But don't let that stop you. If you didn't read the article, it probably won't count as a sin for you."

I hung my head and moaned. When Mom got an idea in her head, she could make the much touted "dog with a bone" look like a slacker. I wasn't a wuss. I mean, I could deal with rabid killers, runaway horses, and Irish ghosts, but dealing with my mom was a whole different dynamic. Through the years my family had learned there was only one sane thing to do when she got like this.

Give in.

If I didn't, I'd be engaged in a tug-of-war over my bag that would continue until it was time to leave, and then I'd get *no* pictures.

I raised my hands in surrender. "Okay. You win." I stood up, hoisted my bag off the floor and looped the strap over her head and shoulder. She looked up at me with an exuberant smile lighting her little moon face.

"I'm so happy you're letting me do this for you, Emily, but do you suppose you could do me one small favor before you leave?" She lunged for my arm. "Could you help me straighten up? My knees have frozen solid on me."

Five minutes later, with her joints thawed and circulation restored, she was ready to be on her way. "Remember," I instructed, as I shielded her arm over my shoulder bag, "this place might be the safest place in Italy, but don't tempt Fate. Hold the bag close to your body and keep your hand over the zipper. Everything I own at the moment is in that bag."

"That was such a shame about your luggage, Em. I know they'll find it quickly though. I said a prayer to St. Anthony."

Everyone's luggage had arrived at the Fiumicino Airport, except mine, which had probably ended up in Rome, all right, but the one in Kansas. The Fiumicino Airport officials assured me they would track my bag down and rush it to my hotel; but just in case it was missing for longer than twenty-four hours, I wrote down names, badge numbers, and phone numbers. I threatened to contact the American embassy. Rome was the fashion capital of the world. If I ended up having to wear Nana's little lace-trimmed sweatshirts and polyester togs again, I'd create a commotion that would leave Alitalia Airlines begging for the kinder, gentler days of Attila the Hun.

I checked my watch. "Okay, we have ten minutes before we're due to regroup at the front entrance." We actually had a half hour before we were scheduled to meet our Landmark Destinations guide at the door, but Mom operated on Iowa time, so she needed to be at least twenty minutes early to be "on time." "Any questions?"

"Just one. Do you have any idea where I should start looking for your grandmother?"

The main altar of St. Peter's Basilica is an oblong of white marble that sits beneath a soaring bronze canopy. Four black-and-gold corkscrew pillars the size of giant sequoias support the structure. I snapped several pictures of the sculptures atop the canopy, then, as I framed my next shot, heard a *click, click, click, click* of stiletto heels on marble. "Hold up, Emily," a voice echoed out in a throaty whisper.

I glanced over my shoulder to find a tall, glossy-haired brunette hustling toward me. She had the face of a madonna, the body of a supermodel, and a sassy style that turned the heads of most men. Her legs were long and tan, and she wore a sexy white minidress that fit like a coat of spray paint. She was all sleek angles, graceful curves, and exact proportions, except for her feet, which were big as snowshoes. Her name was Jackie Thum. Before she'd had sex reassignment surgery to become a woman, she'd been a guy named Jack Potter, and I'd been married to him.

"I'm so glad you told us about the dress code here," she said, straightening the flutter sleeves that fell from her shoulders. "If you hadn't, I actually might have worn something totally inappropriate today."

I wondered what she'd consider more inappropriate than white spray paint. I regarded her arms. Oh, right. Spray paint without sleeves. "Out of curiosity, how did you get your minidress past the clothes police at the front door?"

"I sneaked in with a flock of nuns. The dress code guys

were so busy arguing with a macho gorilla in a muscle shirt and running shorts that they never even noticed me." She removed what looked like a writing pen from her knit shoulder bag, held it to her mouth, and began speaking into it. "If you're visiting religious sites in Italy, check to see if there's a dress code. Bare arms and hairy legs aren't permitted in the church proper of St. Peter's; however, the clothes police might let it pass if you're planning to play bingo in the basement." She snapped the tape recorder off. "They play bingo here, don't they? It's a Catholic church. What Catholic church doesn't play bingo? Can you imagine the haul? I mean, this place can accommodate sixty thousand."

She held her minirecorder up for my perusal. "Doesn't this rock? It's the perfect gadget to help me chronicle your every move. I'll be James Boswell to your Samuel Johnson."

Ever since Jack had become Jackie, she'd been searching for her new niche in life. After ending up on the same tour in Ireland with me last month, she'd decided she might like a job like mine, so she signed up for this tour of Italy in the hopes of recording the dos and don'ts of the successful tour escort. I tried not to let it go to my head, but it was kind of flattering.

Jackie flashed me a smile that suddenly turned to horror. "Eh! Where's your shoulder bag?"

"Mom has it. She wanted to free up my hands so I could bless myself."

"You gave your shoulder bag to your mother?" Her brittle tone made it sound as if I'd given away my firstborn. "Jeez, Emily, that was brave of you."

Unh-oh. Was St. Peter's no longer the safest place in Italy? Was Nana's information outdated? OH, GOD! Was the travel guide Mom checked out of the library the 1952 edition of *Frommer's*? I swallowed slowly, a cold sweat prickling my forehead. "Why was it brave?" I asked hesitantly.

"Because you can get picked up by some really hot Italians in St. Peter's. You need to keep your cosmetic bag handy for those critical lip gloss touch-ups."

I waited a beat before thwacking her on the arm with the back of my hand. "Jack! You're *married!* What are you doing looking for men?" She'd eloped a month ago with a Binghamton, New York, hair designer named Tom whose specialty was corrective color and infliction of the choppy cut on unsuspecting heads.

"I'm married, Emily. I'm not dead."

I rolled my eyes, thinking if I came down with another case of stress-induced hives, I was going to kill her.

"Okay," she said, consulting a paper in the side pocket of her bag. "I made a list, and the next 'must see' in the basilica is"—she turned around—"this way." She banded her hand around my arm and dragged me half a mile down the center nave. We stopped before a mammoth five-sided pillar to regard a bronze statue of a fuzzy-haired man with a beard. "St. Peter," said Jackie. He was seated in a marble chair beneath an ornate canopy, one hand raised solemnly like Al Gore in a vice presidential debate, the other clutching a set of keys. I'd read someplace where the body of the statue might originally have been that of a Roman senator, with the haloed head and hands soldered on later. I had to compliment the Italians. St. Peter looked pretty darned good considering he might have been pieced together like Robocop.

"We need to get in line so we can kiss his toe," Jackie instructed.

I remembered back to my grammar school catechism and wondered what kind of spiritual reward we might receive for paying homage to this great saint. Partial indulgence? Plenary indulgence? In the days of the old Church, the faithful accumulated indulgences like frequent flyer miles and could use them to get out of Hell free. You didn't hear much about indulgences anymore. Wasn't that always the way? You just get locked into a great reward system and *boom,* all the perks expire.

"What significance does kissing his toe have?" I asked.

Jackie shrugged. "I thought it was the Italian version of kissing the Blarney stone. Hey, look. There's some of the people on our tour up near the front of the line. You see the tall guy in the rose-colored polo shirt? Silver hair. George Hamilton tan. Big bottle of water in a harness over his shoulder? That's Philip Blackmore, executive vice president of Hightower Books. They tell me he's a legendary marketing genius. He's supposedly the one behind Hightower's switch from literary to more commercial fiction."

It was Hightower Books who was sponsoring this two-week holiday to promote its unprecedented venture into the historical and contemporary romance market. The theme of the tour was Passion and Pasta and it provided an opportunity for romance fans and unpublished writers to rub shoulders with established writers, editors, agents, and other publishing luminaries. Guests were promised exciting excursions to historic venues as well as daily lectures from the experts on how to write a best-selling romance. My group of Iowans weren't particularly interested in the romance market, but when a slew of cancellations in the main tour occurred a couple of months ago, Landmark Destinations needed to fill up the empty seats, so they offered me some great discount prices, and I'd scooped them up.

"And you see the woman standing to the right of Blackmore?" Jackie continued. "The one in the floral muumuu with the horn-rimmed glasses and Cleopatra hair? That is none other than Marla Michaels. *The* Marla Michaels."

I gave the woman a quick look-see. "Who's Marla Michaels?"

Jackie stared at me in disbelief. "Emily! Do you live under a rock? Marla Michaels. *The Barbarian's Bride? The Viking's Vixen?*"

"Oh. *That* Marla Michaels. The world renowned"— there was only one occupation I could think of where barbarians and Vikings would be commonplace—"opera singer."

Jackie threw up her hands. "Marla Michaels is only the most famous historical romance diva in the world! Hightower lured her away from her old publisher by offering her a very lucrative contract that includes theme park rights and extended author tours to exotic places."

"She's a romance writer? How was I supposed to know that? I don't read romances." I cocked my head and smiled coyly. "But it seems one of us does. How do *you* know about her?"

"The seminar last night? She gave a talk? She autographed books? If you'd been less interested in complaining about your missing luggage and more interested in the theme of the tour, you'd know about her, too."

"Right. You read romances, don't you, Jack? Oh, my God. I bet you were reading them when we were married! That's why you were sneaking into the bathroom so much in the middle of the night. You weren't treating your athlete's foot. You were reading bodice rippers!" Wow. He'd kept a lot of things hidden in the closet back then.

"Are you guys in line?" I heard a chirpy voice inquire behind me.

She was one of ours—a flaming redhead in her twenties who was snapping gum like a kid snaps rubber bands. The wording on her name tag read, *Hi! My name is Keely*.

"You're on the tour!" she said, aiming a finger at Jackie. "I recognize you from the seminar. I would kill for that leather bustier you were wearing last night. Can you believe this? Marla Michaels and Gillian Jones in the same room together?"

"Gillian Jones?" I asked tentatively. "Another romance writer?"

"I'll say." Keely popped a bubble, then sucked it back into her mouth. "Sixty-four weeks on the *New York Times* Best-seller List for *A Cowboy in Paris*. Eighty-six weeks for *A Cowboy in Sydney*. The reviewers said books about cowboys wouldn't have global appeal. Boy, were they wrong. She's the most successful writer of contemporary romance ever."

"She's standing behind Marla in line," Jackie pointed out.

Gillian Jones was waifishly petite with platinum hair cut close to her head and huge cactuses hanging from her ears. I suspected the oversized earrings might be her trademark. The Lone Ranger's was a silver bullet. Gillian's was desert vegetation.

"Marla and Gillian supposedly hated each other for a lot of years," Keely explained, "but now that they've signed on with the same publisher, I've heard they've become the best of friends. I want to learn so much from them. I don't mean to brag, but I've won every regional First Chapter contest ever offered."

"That's great," I enthused. I had a hard time writing postcards, so I admired anyone who could actually win a contest for putting words on paper. "But you're unpublished at the moment?"

"Prepublished," she corrected. "Unpublished gives the wrong impression."

Right. I guess it would give the impression that . . . you're not published.

"But I'm this close"—she flashed a quarter-inch space between her thumb and forefinger—"to getting published."

"Have you had any nibbles?" Jackie asked with girlish excitement.

"Not exactly." Keely blew a bubble the size of her head, then had to use her fingers to shove it all back into her mouth. "I need to complete the manuscript first, but finishing up should be a piece of cake."

"Are you close to the end?" I asked.

"Real close. Only thirteen chapters to go."

Thirteen *to go*? I couldn't imagine the fortitude it took to sit down every day and grind out page after page of fiction. I regarded her with even greater respect than before. "How many chapters have you written so far?"

"One. But like I told you, it's award-winning." She blew another bubble. I gritted my teeth. If she did that one more time, I might be forced to grab it out of her mouth and stick it in her ear. "What I really need is an agent," Keely confessed. "That's part of the reason I'm on this trip. Gillian and Marla's agent is here, so I need to impress her big-time. I'm hoping if she reads my award-winning chapter, she'll like it well enough to represent me. Her name's Sylvia Root. Ever heard of her? They call her 'the barracuda.' High-powered. Ruthless. *Cojones* the size of Jupiter. She's every author's dream. And by the way—" She reached into her pocketbook, pulled out a business card, and handed it to me. "I run an online romance writers' critique service, so if you ever need help with your novel, e-mail me. I offer special rates to people I've met."

I skimmed her card. *Romance Solutions. Become a published author. Manuscript critiques offered by award-winning writer, KEELY MACK. Reasonable fees.*

"Whoops," said Keely, "there's my roommate. Gotta run. She wants to explore the grotto where all the popes are buried. She has this obsession with dead people. She wants to break into the market with the first zombie romance. Isn't that a kick? She'll probably start a hot new trend."

Good reason to stick to nonfiction.

The queue to reach St. Peter moved quickly. I kissed his little bare toe, then pondered what other part of the statue I'd be kissing if the early Romans had worn wingtips instead of sandals. "If kissing the Blarney stone imparts the gift of gab," I commented when Jackie and I were through the line, "what gift do you suppose kissing St. Peter's toe imparts?"

"I don't know, but if you start speaking in tongues, I'm outta here."

After oohing and aahing over the magnificence of Michelangelo's dome and Bernini's sunburst, we snapped some photos of the gilded lanterns surrounding St. Peter's tomb and headed back toward the entrance. "Hi, Jackie," gushed two blonde women wearing Landmark name tags.

A minute later a spit-polished man with a trim beard nodded at Jackie. "Ms. Thum."

I slanted a curious look at Jackie. "How do all these people know you?"

"It's called networking, Emily. Isn't that what a good travel club escort is supposed to do? I attended the seminar last night, introduced myself to all the guests, and the dividend is—" She shot me a toothy smile. "They remember me."

"Of *course* they remember you! You were wearing a leather bustier!"

"If you lower your voice, I'll let you borrow it some-time." She sidled closer to me and spoke in a whisper. "That man who just acknowledged me? He's apparently a *real* biggie in the industry. Gabriel Fox. He's a senior editor at Hightower and is supposed to be editing both Marla and Gillian. Boy, I wouldn't want that job. Can you imagine the egos? Anyway, they call him 'the book doctor.' If there's anything wrong with a book, he's the guy who's supposed to be able to fix it. But you know what I don't get?"

I could see the red-and-green umbrella of our tour leader bobbing conspicuously in the air near the front entrance. "What don't you get?"

"All these wannabe writers are all in competition with each other, right? So how come they want to help each other so much? I mean, you should have been there last night. It was a lovefest! When a guy's in competition with you, he stabs you in the back and steamrolls you into the pavement. When a woman's in competition with you, she becomes your best friend! It makes no sense to me."

"Maybe you need to boost your estrogen level. It might improve your understanding." I spied everyone in my group huddled around a baseball-capped Duncan Lazarus and his umbrella. Grace and Dick Stolee, Helen and Dick Teig, and Lucille Rassmuson—all of whom had gained a ton of weight since our trip to Switzerland last year. The Severid twins, Britha and Barbro, who were absolutely identical except for one characteristic, which they stub-bornly refused to reveal. Nana and George. Alice Tjarks, the former voice of KORN's agricultural report, with her new camcorder. Osmond Chelsvig, with his double hear-ing aids and bigger camcorder. And Mom, listing like the Tower of Pisa beneath the weight of my shoulder bag.

"Estrogen, smestrogen," Jackie sniped beside me. "Women act really weird sometimes. And to think of all the money I spent to become one of you. I should demand a rebate."

Even before we could blend back into the group, Duncan stabbed his umbrella in the direction of St. Peter's Square and led the charge out of the basilica. I checked my watch. Three o'clock exactly. Duncan must be from the Midwest. A wave of humanity followed him out the door, but I worried about the head count. Not everyone on the tour was from Iowa. What if someone was late getting back? *Uff da*. It wouldn't be a good scene if we accidentally left someone behind.

"Why is he walking so fast?" Jackie fretted, as we emerged into blinding sunshine. "He has old people on this tour! And young people wearing extremely sexy but *very* impractical stiletto slides that make their feet look at least three sizes smaller." She clattered down the ramp that funneled tourists into the square and stopped short when she noticed something on the service road that flanked the ramp. She motioned to me furiously. "Emily, you've gotta see this. An honest to gosh Swiss guardsman."

I scurried over, cringing at the idea of having to wear blue and gold striped balloon pants with a matching doublet and spats to work every day. I knew the guards formed a small army that protected the pope, but I figured if they expected to be taken seriously by an invading force, they might need to rethink their uniforms. I mean, that's why GI Barbie wore fatigues instead of spandex, right?

Jackie snapped a picture of the pike-holding sentry standing before his little guardhouse. "Emily, would you take a picture of me standing beside him? Maybe Tom can hang it up in the salon to show his clients what I'm up to these days."

I glanced back toward the entrance of the basilica. I didn't see any Passion and Pasta people lagging behind, but waiting a few minutes for stragglers probably wasn't a bad idea. I didn't remember seeing Keely leave with the crowd. Her red hair wasn't exactly hard to spot. Could she still be snapping gum in the grotto? I could be a big help to Duncan here. In fact, if I could prevent some tour guest the agony of getting left behind, I'd be a real hero, which would kind of make up for my not attending the seminar last night and introducing myself to the immediate world.

"Okay," I said to Jackie. "Hand over your camera."

I kept one eye on the front of the basilica and one eye on Duncan's umbrella as Jackie scooted down the ramp and up the service road toward the guardhouse. She said something to the sentry, who ignored her completely, then posed close beside him and smiled up at me. "Pizza!" she yelled.

CLICK. I listened to her camera rewind itself. "You're out of film!" I yelled.

"You gotta take one more for insurance!" She fished inside her shoulder bag and brandished another cartridge in the air at me. "You want me to throw it to you?"

I gauged the distance between the guardhouse and me. Unh-oh. Not a good idea. Given her recent sex change, she probably threw like a girl. "I'll come down and get it!"

Casting a final look behind me at the basilica, I hurried down the ramp. The rest of the group was filing helter-skelter through the nearest columns and emerging onto what looked like a street beyond where the bus would no doubt pick us up. I jogged toward the sentry house, reloaded Jackie's camera, and snapped a shot of her standing on the other side of the guardsman.

"Thanks, Emily." She retrieved her camera. "You want me to get a shot of you with Mr. Personality?"

I waved her off. There was only one man I wanted to have my picture taken with, and he was in Switzerland.

As we hotfooted it back down the road, Jackie threw on her sunglasses and looked perplexed as she glanced around her. "Where'd everybody go?"

I pointed to our right. "Through those columns."

Jackie stopped short. "Hold up. I want one last picture of the square. Have you noticed that the square really isn't square? Why do they call it a square if it's an oval?"

"Jack! Come *on*! Everyone's gone. They're probably on the bus already!" I hurried toward the shadow of Bernini's columns and passed through the relative coolness of the roofed colonnade, ending up on what looked like a residential street. But as I paused on the sidewalk, I noticed a minor problem.

Fifty-three people had come this way, right?

I looked left at the deserted street and sidewalk. I looked right at the deserted street and sidewalk.

So if fifty-three people had come this way, WHERE WERE THEY NOW?

CHAPTER 2

*C*lick click click click. "Ten seconds!" Jackie complained as her heels clacked on the pavement behind me. "You couldn't wait ten seconds while I took my picture?"

"They're gone!" I cried in a semipanic. "How can they be gone? They were here a minute ago. I *saw* them!" The street dead-ended to my right, but to my left, it intersected with a noisy artery of traffic about a block away. I ran to the opposite sidewalk and peered down a long pedestrian walkway that tunneled beneath the main road and emerged on the other side.

Empty.

"Where's the bus?" Jackie called out to me.

Fifty-three people could *not* disappear into thin air! I squinted toward the street, where small, angry cars chased after each other. That had to be where the bus was picking us up. I gestured wildly in that direction and took off at a dead run.

Click click click click. Jackie pulled abreast of me halfway down the street, a throwback to her high school track days when she'd laced herself into running shoes instead of satin corsets. "Emily . . ." she gasped out beside me, "why are we running like this?"

We skidded to a halt at the traffic-jammed street running perpendicular to us. I looked left. I looked right.

No bus. No group. No nothing.

"They've disappeared," I choked out, numb with disbelief. "They were here a minute ago; now they're gone. How is that possible? HOW CAN THEY HAVE VANISHED?"

Jackie dug a tissue out of her bag and mopped her throat, looking curiously left and right. "Gotta be alien abduction. I bet it happens a lot more than people realize."

"I *knew* something like this was going to happen. I *knew* someone was going to get left behind. But it was supposed to happen to someone else! It wasn't supposed to happen to me!"

Jackie's face lit up. "Female intuition! That is *so* cool. I'm dying to have my first flash of female intuition, but it hasn't kicked in yet. I hope I don't have to wait too long though. I have zero intuition at the moment. It's like being a guy again." She balled her tissue into her fist and regarded me hopefully. "So, now what?"

I was racking my brain to recall what my *Escort's Manual* said about getting lost when I suddenly realized why I couldn't remember. There *was* no section on getting lost. The topic was considered unnecessary because, unlike directionally challenged people in the rest of the civilized world, Iowans didn't *get* lost! Ever!

"Should we call someone or something?" Jackie prodded.

"We should, but . . ." I took a deep breath and spoke in a rush of words. "My address book and phone are in my shoulder bag."

Jackie lowered her head and stared at me over the tops of her sunglasses. "Good one, Emily. What about a public phone? Call your cell and when your mom picks up, she can tell you where the group is."

I bobbed my head a little sheepishly. "I uh . . . I didn't memorize the number."

"You WHAT?"

"I said, I DIDN'T MEMORIZE THE NUMBER! Why should I? I wasn't planning on calling myself!"

"Oh, this is lovely. Just *lovely*." Her hand flitted to her face where she massaged her temple with long-suffering fingertips. "Good timing. My female intuition just kicked in, and you know what it's saying? It's warning me that we're going to be wandering around here forever. Like . . . like the Robinson family in outer space!"

"Didn't they eventually get back to earth?"

"Did they? I must have missed that episode."

I checked my watch. "Okay, wherever everyone is, this was the last stop of the day, so I suggest we just hop into a taxi and meet the bus back at the hotel."

Jackie straightened up, seemingly electrified. "Meet them back at the hotel? Take a taxi? Right. I . . . I hadn't thought of that yet." She opened her arms and crushed me to her chest. "I knew you'd think of something! You're so clever, Emily."

That's what I've always loved about Jack. Consistency. I wiggled out of her embrace and straightened the bodice of the Laura Ashley sundress that fell modestly to my ankles and buttoned up the front—not my usual style, but it had been perfect for traveling eight hours on a plane yesterday. I glanced down the street, wincing at the roar of car engines, the buzz of scooters, the screams of irate drivers. Ireland had been chaotic. Rome was insane. "We need to find a taxi stand."

"We can't just flag one down?"

"Duncan mentioned it's almost impossible to wave down a cab in Rome."

"Why?"

"He didn't say why. He simply said it was."

"We'll see about that." Hips swiveling, chest out, she sashayed toward the street, scanned the lanes of traffic, then without warning, raised her arm in a kind of *Heil Hitler* salute and stepped off the curb into the path of an oncoming car.

"JACK!" I covered my eyes with my hands.

Tires squealed. Rubber burned. Horns blared. Terrified, I inched my fingers apart and took a peek.

Jackie stood before a miniature white car, a sultry smile on her lips, her stilettoed foot perched on the front bumper. But this wasn't just any car. It had a little sign on the roof. It was a taxi!

The driver laid on his horn and yelled something out the window. Jackie motioned me toward the car. "Emily! Will you get *in* before he decides to run me down!"

I opened the door and jumped into the backseat. "*Maleducato!*" the driver screamed at me, followed by a string of Italian that didn't sound too flattering. A cigarette hung from the corner of his mouth, a half inch of ash threatening to fall off. He wore a slouch cap that sat low on his forehead and a stained white shirt with sleeves rolled to the elbows. His forearms were dark, hairy, and bulged like sacks of seed corn.

"Hi," I countered, offering him a two-fingered wave. "You don't happen to speak English, do you?"

He projected his right fist in the air and slapped his elbow with his left hand—a rather subtle gesture that I took to mean, NO! I caught his eye in the rearview mirror and flashed a conciliatory smile. He glared at me, using his forefinger to slash an imaginary line across his throat from ear to ear. Oh, this was nice. All the taxis in Rome, and we had to get the one driven by Vlad the Impaler.

Jackie scrambled into the backseat and collapsed beside me. "There," she said breathlessly. "That wasn't so hard, was it?"

Not if you were a six-foot transsexual in stiletto heels. The rest of us could have a slight problem.

I gave the driver the name of our hotel in my most precise Italian, then fell backward as he gunned the engine and charged across two lanes of traffic. He drove with one hand on the wheel, one arm out the window, and one eye ogling Jackie in the rearview mirror. He wove left. He wove right. He thrust his head out the window to yell at a passing bus, then outraced a pack of scooters in a competition to be first across a bridge. The G force pinned me to my seat. Scenery sped by in a blur. I realized everything I'd heard about Italian drivers was true. They were rude. They were short-tempered. They ignored speed limits and signs. And considering the lunatic way they maneuvered through the raging disorder in the city streets, they had to be the most skilled drivers in the world.

Jackie angled her head away from the glare of the rearview mirror and whispered behind her hand, "Why is he leering at me like that?"

"He's Italian. I think they're all programed that way."

"How come he's not leering at you?"

"I'm not wearing white spray paint."

We took a corner on two wheels and shrieked to a stop in front of a building with curved ironwork fronting the second-story balconies and lots of black window shutters. "Albergo Villa Bandoccio Maccio D'Angelo," the driver announced with an emphatic wave of his hand.

I peeked at the building through the car window. I sidled an uneasy look at Jackie. "Do you remember balconies on our hotel?"

"Nope."

"This is the wrong hotel, isn't it?"

"Yup."

EH! "Excuse me." I tapped the driver politely on the arm and enunciated slowly so he could understand me. "Is there another hotel by this name somewhere else in Rome? This isn't where we're staying."

"Albergo Villa Bandoccio Maccio D'Angelo," he repeated, pounding a hand on the meter to indicate the fare owed him.

"I can *see* what the name of the hotel is," I fired back. "The problem is, WE DON'T HAVE A RESERVATION HERE!"

"*Figlio d'una madre infame!*" he spat, making a supplicating gesture to the heavens. "*Figlio d'un cane! Disgraziato! Figlio della miseria!*"

"You're doing a good job, Emily," Jackie exhorted. "Keep talking. Maybe you can piss him off a little more."

"*Figlio di puttana!*"

Jackie stiffened. "Unh-oh. That's not good. *Puttana* is not a word you want thrown at you."

I narrowed my gaze at her. "How do you know that?"

"Well, since you asked. I've been dying to tell you, but I wanted to wait until the right moment to surprise you." She curled her hand around my forearm with giddy enthusiasm. "I took a crash course in Italian right before the trip, and you'll never guess! I discovered I have a real flair for languages! My instructor said I had the best ear ever for picking up conversational Italian. When I was a guy, I couldn't even conjugate verbs. Now, I'm speaking Italian! Does that rock, or what?"

"You speak Italian?" I asked jealously.

"Like a native." She whipped her sunglasses off and studied the marquee above the hotel's front door. "Do you suppose you got the name wrong?"

"I *know* this is the right name. I memorized the names of all our hotels!"

"Okay. Let me see what I can find out. *Scusi,*" she said to the driver, followed by a string of Italian that wowed me. I beat back my envy as I listened to her. How could she have learned a foreign language in such a short time? But I refused to let her skill make me feel inadequate. I mean, I knew a little French and a little Norwegian. A knowledge of two foreign languages was pretty decent. Three, if you counted Minnesotan.

When she finished speaking, she shook her head. "He says this is the right hotel."

I heard a digital tone from the front seat followed by a gruff, "*Pronto,*" as Vlad answered his cell phone. Jackie threw open her shoulder bag and pulled out a book that mirrored the colors of the Italian flag.

"Maybe you reversed the order of some of the words," she suggested as she paged quickly through her phrase book. "It happens."

I regarded her bag, pricked by an unlikely thought. "You don't happen to have a copy of our itinerary in there someplace, do you?"

"Of course I don't have a copy of our itinerary. I'm on a tour. I'm not supposed to know where I'm staying. That's why *you're* here."

"*Si,*" said the driver into his phone. "*Ciao.*" He replaced the phone in a little holster attached to the dash, then pivoted around in his seat, rapid-firing a steady stream of loud, plosive words at us. He slapped his meter again and made a "gimme" gesture with his hand.

"What's he saying?" I asked out of the corner of my mouth.

"I heard the word *lire,* but I'm not sure about anything else."

I snapped my head around to stare at her. "How can you not be sure? I thought you spoke Italian like a native?"

"It's like this. I'm pretty sure what *I'm* saying; I don't always know what *they're* saying."

UNH! I buried my face in my hands and bent forward, banging my head against my knees.

"Emily? Stop that!" She grabbed my shoulders. "What are you trying to do?"

"Kill myself. Slitting my wrists would be quicker, but Mom has all my sharp objects with her."

"I have a fingernail file." She rummaged in the side pocket of her bag. "Whoops. Make that an emery board. That won't do you much good."

I looked up distractedly, noting the long row of digits on the driver's meter, then higher, where the holster for his cell phone hung on the dash. Phone? EH! I grabbed Jackie's arm. "Ask him if we can borrow his cell phone."

"Hel-loooo? You don't have any numbers. You can't even call yourself!"

Maybe not, but I knew one number that was bound to get some results. "Would you just ask!"

"All right already. Jeez." She turned to a page in her phrase book and smiled sweetly at the driver. "*Scusi, signor . . .*" She pointed at the cell phone and proceeded to unleash a flood of halting Italian that caused the driver's eyes to light up beneath his sagging lids. I'd heard Italians were extremely generous, but this guy seemed so excited to have someone else use his phone that he looked as if he was about to spring into handstands. He plucked the phone out of its holster and thrust it at Jackie, a broad smile creasing his unshaven face.

"*Che corpo*," he rasped, his eyes roving her body, his tongue roving his lips. "*Vorrei leccare il sudore della tua pelle.*"

"What's he saying?" I asked, as she handed me the phone. I hoped this phone was equipped with the right chip to connect me with another country. If not . . . I pushed away the thought and punched in the number while Jackie flipped frantically through her book.

"It must be an idiom. He's either saying his testicles are the size of cabbages or he's telling me I'm fat. If he's telling me I'm fat, he can kiss his tip good-bye."

At the other end of the phone line, I heard a torrent of static that was suddenly interrupted by the welcome sound of a man's voice. "Miceli," he answered in his beautiful French/German/Italian accent.

"Do you know the name of the hotel where I'm staying in Rome?"

A pause. "Emily?"

"I e-mailed you my itinerary. Remember?" Ever since his injury last month, he'd been battling migraine headaches and slight memory problems. He could recall all the major stuff, like the fact that his name was Etienne Miceli; he was a Swiss police inspector; he'd met me nine months ago when I'd visited Lucerne; he was in love with me. He was just having a hard time with minor details, like remembering that he wanted to marry me.

"I remember perfectly, darling."

"I'm going to hand the phone over to someone. Would you please tell *him* the name of the hotel?"

I shoved the phone at the cabbie, who responded to Etienne with a, "*Si? Si. Albergo Villa Barduccio Mastrangelo? Ah, si!*"

"What'd I tell you." Jackie eyed me sternly. "You gave him the wrong name."

"Hey, I was close!" The driver pitched the phone back at me and peeled out of the parking area. I pressed the phone to my ear. "Hi," I said to Etienne. "Thank you so much."

"Was that a test?"

"Yup. And you passed." I lowered my voice to a sultry whisper. "I wish you were here so I could give you your prize." I heard a clamor of voices in the background on his end. "Are you at the office?" He was such a workaholic, I wouldn't be surprised if he was nosing around the department in an unofficial capacity. Officially, however, he was on leave until his migraines disappeared.

"Actually, darling, I'm in northern Italy. Campione. Visiting my cousin. We're celebrating my great-aunt's ninetieth birthday. I thought I told you."

"Nope. You must have told someone who looks like me." His doctor assured him that his memory and headache problems would be only temporary. I was keeping my fingers crossed that he was right. The voices in the background reached a crescendo and erupted into excited cheers. "Your relatives sound like a rowdy bunch," I teased. Had to be the Italian side of the family—the gene pool responsible for Etienne's black hair, classic style, and awe-inspiring . . . hardware. I hadn't had a chance to try out the hardware yet, but I remained hopeful.

"They're complete strangers." He laughed. "They're cheering someone on at the roulette table. I'm at the local casino, trying my luck at *chemin de fer*. Did I forget to tell you the odd thing that's happened in the last month?"

I guess he meant *other* than the fact that he'd forgotten about his intention to pop the question. "Have you thought about writing things down? Making lists? It works for some people."

The cabbie growled something over his shoulder at Jackie.

"I seem to have developed an uncanny ability to maintain a mental picture of what cards have been played at the gaming table, what cards are left in the deck, and what my odds are of being dealt the card I need. I think it's called, 'being in the zone.' "

I thought it was called "card counting." I'd come back from Ireland hot-wired to sense disaster; he'd come back a card shark. Go figure. I watched Jackie scroll her finger down a glossy page of her phrase book and stab a word with her highly lacquered nail. "Are you making any money?" I asked, as the taxi swerved suddenly, slamming me into the door. Horns blared around us. A scooter zoomed past, nearly clipping our front bumper. I covered my eyes with my hand.

"I've only just begun, but I have a modest number of chips in front of me at the moment. The betting limit in Lucerne is five Swiss francs, but in Italy there's no limit, so as they say, if I play my cards right, I could make a killing."

Or be wiped out. Unh-oh. I was getting a bad feeling about this. "Tell me again why you can't come down to Rome?"

"The Jubilee year, Emily. There's not one room left in Rome. I did try."

And sharing my room was out. Not with Mom on the tour. "What about a rendezvous in Florence?" If he didn't lose all his money, he might even be able to spring for the train fare.

"*I nani mi divertono nel circolo!*" Jackie fired at the driver.

A pause at the other end of the phone line. "Where are you, darling?" Etienne asked, a humorous lilt to his voice.

"In a taxi."

"Who's with you who just said, 'Dwarves amuse me at the circus'?"

"That would be Jackie. She's demonstrating her flair for languages."

"*Non sei spiritoso!*" the cabbie fired back, gesticulating wildly. "*Come sei sciocco! Sei proprio scemo! Ma vorrei leccare il sudore della tua pelle!*"

"Did you hear that?" I whispered into the phone. "Can you translate?"

"He's telling her she's not funny, she's tasteless, and she's really stupid, but he still wants to lick the sweat off her skin."

"Hold on." Jackie posed one finger in the air as she consulted her book. "Okay, he adores my spirit, he loves my taste in clothes, and . . . he thinks I have killer legs." She smiled like the Cheshire cat. "I might give him a tip after all."

"*Figlio di puttana!*" wailed the driver, jamming on the brakes.

" 'Son of a bitch!' " said Etienne.

"What's wrong?" I winced into the phone. "Did you just lose all your money?"

"I was translating what your taxi driver just said. What's happening there?"

I peered out the front windshield at a major commotion surrounding a building that looked vaguely familiar. Cars. Trucks. Sirens. People clustered in knots on the sidewalk, pointing fingers at the upper stories.

"That's it!" cried Jackie. "That's our hotel!"

Unfortunately, it was on fire.

"The fire started in the kitchen and spread from there," Duncan announced to us three hours later over the bus's loudspeaker. Duncan Lazarus stood a couple of inches over six feet, had shoulders like a lumberjack, thick, sun-streaked hair that was a hint too long, and a voice that resonated with calm authority. I suspected his early ancestors might have played the gladiatorial circuit in Rome or resided somewhere atop Mount Olympus with the other immortals. "You're all aware this is Rome's Jubilee year. Unfortunately, that makes it difficult to find accommodations for fifty-five tourists anywhere in the city, especially on such short notice."

A low hum of discontent spread through the bus as we headed north on the Autostrada, watching cars the size of windup toys roar past us in the outside lane. It had taken a couple of hours for people to recover from the shock of their luggage, laptops, and powerpoint presentations becoming charcoal briquettes, but to their credit, all the guests had made use of their neck wallets, so no one needed to replace either passport or credit cards. A handful of people had lost their daily meds in the fire, but they'd followed Landmark's instructions to carry scrip for all their prescriptions, so they'd already replaced them in a pharmacy near the hotel. And since the structure had already been fully engulfed in flames when the tour bus pulled up, no one in the group had been injured, but my knees still felt a little gimpy at the thought of what might have happened if the fire had started later in the day rather than earlier. The bright note here was that we were moving on to our second city and everyone was still alive! Was I on a roll, or what?

Beside me, Nana flipped through some fresh photos taken with her Polaroid OneStep. "See this corner window that's engulfed in flames?" She slanted the picture toward me. "That was my room. It was a pretty nice one, too." She heaved a dejected sigh. "I spent a fortune on naughty bloomers for this trip, Emily, and they all went up in smoke. I didn't get to wear my reptile print Dream Angels teddy even once, and it looked real good on me. Slimmed my hips right down to nothin'."

I stared at her, wide-eyed. "You bought a reptile print teddy?"

"What? You think the leopard print woulda been better?"

"Given our housing problem, we'll be leaving Rome and traveling to Florence a couple of days early," Duncan continued. "We've located a hotel within walking distance of the famous Holy Mary of the Flowers Cathedral, which the Florentines refer to as the Duomo, and by a stroke of luck, it can accommodate everyone until we move into our assigned hotel in Montecatini. The upshot of this is, you'll be treated to a much more intimate tour of Florence than you ever expected, and I give you my personal guarantee that you won't be disappointed. Florence is a great medieval city. More manageable than Rome. It's a walking city, with less traffic and noise, fewer fountains, and incredible bargains on gold and leather goods."

"What are we supposed to wear while we're there?" Gillian Jones yelled out. "In case you need a reminder, our clothes are toast!"

Duncan flashed her an indulgent smile. "The miracle of insurance. Once we reach Florence you'll each be given a stipend of six hundred thousand lire to replace some of the items you lost in the fire. And when you fill out a more detailed insurance form, you'll receive the full replacement cost of all your belongings, so I suggest you start thinking 'shopping spree.' "

"Six hundred thousand lire?" Nana said, tittering with excitement.

I deleted the three zeroes and divided by two to calculate just how much. "Three hundred dollars."

"That's a lot a money. If they got a Super Wal-Mart over here, I'm thinkin', new wardrobe!"

"We'll be making a comfort stop at an Autogrill about seventy kilometers up the road," Duncan continued. "Their dining facilities are excellent, so we'll plan to eat dinner there this evening instead of Florence. In the meantime, if anyone's thirsty, I have bottled water and soft drinks in a cooler up here beside me. On the house. And please, don't hesitate to let me know if there's anything I can do to make your trip more enjoyable."

"Such a polite young man," Nana cooed.

The aisle suddenly filled with guests making a mad dash to the front of the bus. Apparently, watching a hotel burn to the ground made people really thirsty. I turned in my seat, spying my mother several seats behind me sitting with Alice Tjarks. "How did you convince Mom to sit with Alice instead of you?" I asked Nana.

"It didn't take no convincin'. She volunteered. I let it slip that Alice was packin' the deluxe travel edition a Scrabble. Every letter of the alphabet. Magnetized. It was too big a temptation to resist."

I shook my head. "You're bad, Nana. Tell me, were you able to avoid her in St. Peter's?"

"Barely. I seen her bearin' down on us, so I grabbed George and pulled him into a confessional. Woulda made my monthly confession while I was waitin' there, too, but the priest couldn't understand me."

Okay, so maybe Nana had a *teensy* problem with double negatives, verb agreement, subordinate clauses, and tense formation. She was still perfectly understandable, wasn't she? "What couldn't he understand?" I asked gently.

"English. Turned out to be a Polish confessional."

I smiled. "How did George feel about being inside a

confessional? That's a once-in-a-lifetime experience for a Lutheran."

"He didn't seem real impressed, dear. He thought it was a phone booth."

I heard the loud report of snapping gum beside me and groaned inwardly as I looked up.

"Hi again!" said Keely as she passed. "Remember me? From the basilica? Say, weren't you the one who missed the bus back at St. Peter's? Where were you anyway? Seems we waited at that bus terminal for you forever."

"You waited for me? That was so sweet!" I narrowed my eyes. "What terminal?"

"The underground bus terminal. You know, down the pedestrian walkway and left at the tunnel that intersected it halfway down."

"There was a tunnel?"

"A real nice one," said Nana.

My mouth sagged open. "How was I supposed to find a bus that was underground?"

Keely gave me a squinty look. "It might have helped if you'd stuck with the group. Hey, this is my roommate." She grabbed the arm of a young woman with short spiked hair and a bolt through her nose.

"Amanda Morning," the girl said, shoving a piece of glossy paper shaped like a flame at each of us. "I'm handing out my bookmark to everyone. It won first prize at the Southwest Regional Romance Lovers Festival."

I read the print copy aloud. " 'Passion's Flame. The sweeping romantic saga of a lovely young woman thrust into a vortex of danger and desire . . . and the one man who could awaken in her a sweet fire that would not stop burning. On sale soon wherever books are sold.' "

"This is the sixth time I've won the contest for best bookmark."

"Six books?" I marveled. "Wow. You must have your own section in Borders."

"Well, I haven't actually written anything yet, but I bought a really expensive computer system so I can begin. And Keely's promised to help me."

Which was bound to assure her of at least one chapter of award-winning prose. "But shouldn't it go the other way around?" I quibbled. "You write the book, *then* you design the bookmark? Kinda like, pillage then burn?"

Amanda quirked her mouth to the side and glared at me, her nostrils flaring around the silver bolt in her nose. She looked angry enough to do something really menacing—like sneeze. "I can tell you're not one of us. You non-writers just don't get it. There was a contest! If you want to be a writer, you have to enter contests."

Nana stared up at her with curiosity. "Do you ever get sinus infections, dear? They must be a real nuisance for you."

Amanda kept talking. "Saying I've won six *consecutive* contests is going to look really impressive on a cover letter to some publisher."

I didn't want to appear naive, but I wondered if actually writing the book would appear even more impressive.

Keely elbowed Amanda out of the way and directed her to Duncan's cooler at the front of the bus. "Publishing's changed a lot since I won my first contest. It's not about the manuscript anymore; it's about who you know. And I'm going to know a lot of people by the end of this trip." She blew a bubble the size of a grapefruit and sucked it back into her mouth with a pop. "Hey, look who else is in line. Fred!"

She clapped the shoulder of the man standing next to her and swung him around to face us. "Fred published a biography of his cat two years ago through a vanity press, so he's an honest-to-gosh author, aren't you, Fred?"

Fred was small and stooped and looked like an advertisement for J. Peterman in his safari shirt and pants. On his head he wore a matching cloth hat with a floppy sunblock brim that he was making no attempt to remove. Either he didn't want to ruin the look of his ensemble, or he was afraid some ornery ultraviolet ray would eat through the solid steel of the bus's roof and zap him. Considering all the holes in the ozone layer, I guess you couldn't be too careful these days.

"Some author," Fred said in a timid voice. "They told me I was going to make a bundle. They said the demographics indicated that elderly women *love* to read feline biographies. But what I ended up with was a storage shed full of books I can't distribute and a big fat debit in my checking account. I've gotta hand it to the little jeezers. They delivered the books just like they promised, but they didn't tell me that bookstore people refuse to handle the self-published stuff. You gotta do it yourself. Out of the trunk of your car!"

I suspected that could be pretty dicey, especially if you were stuck having to drive a subcompact. "Were you able to sell any?"

"Four. To my mother. She said they were a huge hit in her assisted living facility. People were clamoring for them in their little library there. But I'm not letting the hype influence me. I'm switching to romances. According to what I've read in *Publishers Weekly,* they're the backbone of the whole industry. That's where the money is, so that's where I'm headed."

"And here's another one of the gang," Keely interrupted, shooing Fred along and latching on to the arm of a sun-baked blonde with muscles like Popeye and a complexion that reminded me of dried tobacco. "Brandy Ann Frounfelker. She's from California. A professional body builder. Can you tell? But she actually wrote a romance and got it published online."

"I thought the e-publishing phenomenon would take off like gangbusters," Brandy Ann said in a soft, wonderfully refined voice. "It hasn't happened though. I've been soliciting more traditional publishing houses, but once I tell them I was published electronically, they don't want to have anything to do with me. It's as if e-publishing is a dirty word. And let me tell you . . ." She slowly clenched her hand into a fist that was the size of a car engine. Ropes of muscle bulged beneath her skin. " . . . it's starting to piss me off."

Keely's face disappeared behind a bubble that grew bigger . . . and bigger . . . and—

Brandy Ann turned suddenly and caught the bubble in her fist. "That's very rude." She yanked the wad out of Keely's mouth and crushed it in her hand.

Oh, yeah. I liked this woman.

KREOOOOO! Feedback screeched out over the loudspeaker system at a pitch that could cause eardrums to pop. KREOOOOO! "I—" *kreooooo* "—I hate when that happens," asserted a voice that wasn't Duncan's. "If you would all return to your seats, I have an announcement I'd like to make."

Keely and Brandy Ann grunted with frustration and headed back to their seats. I boosted myself high enough to see a man in a rose-colored polo shirt with silver hair and a George Hamilton tan standing in the aisle at the front of the bus. Ah, yes. The bigwig Jackie had pointed out in the basilica.

"For those of you who don't know me, please allow me to introduce myself. My name is Philip Blackmore, and I'm the executive vice president and associate publisher of Hightower Books, the company sponsoring this tour. Please accept my apologies for this unfortunate calamity that has befallen us. One never expects disaster to strike while on holiday."

"He's never traveled with us before, has he, dear?" whispered Nana.

"I understand the inconvenience of having to travel without any of your belongings," he continued in a sympathetic tone. "I know this is the kind of event that can ruin a vacation, but I want you to know that Hightower Books is committed to doing everything possible to salvage this tour and make it the most memorable trip of your lifetime. To that end, I've been in contact with our company president, who has authorized me to make amends for this catastrophe in a way that is sure to delight all of you who have ever imagined your name in print."

Nana leaned close to my ear. "That means, he don't wanna get sued."

"Drumroll, please," Blackmore said, grinning at his own cleverness. "Ladies and gentlemen, Hightower Books is proud to announce an opportunity for all aspiring writers on our tour. A contest!"

Squeals from the front. Squeals from the back. There was no denying it. The word "contest" created as much pandemonium among romance writers as the word "embargo" created among Iowa grain farmers.

"To the person who submits the most marketable synopsis of a book-length romantic novel, including the first five pages of a proposed first chapter, we are offering a single book contract for publication of said book, *and*"—he paused for dramatic effect— "a cash advance of ten thousand dollars."

Screaming. Yelling. Cheering. The woman in the seat in front of me leaped into the aisle and began to boogie.

KREOOOOOO! "I knew you'd be excited," Blackmore said pleasantly.

"Who's going to judge the contest?" someone yelled out. "You?"

"I'll leave the all-important task of judging to a panel of three people, two of whom have devoted more years to the publishing industry than they'd care to admit. Sylvia, would you stand up so people can see you?"

Three seats down from me on the left, a fiftyish woman with puffy features, mousy hair, and a gray jacket that bagged around her like an off-the-rack elephant leg stood up and waved to the passengers. "I'm sure you're all familiar with the name Sylvia Root," Blackmore enthused, "founder and president of the acclaimed Sylvia Root Literary Agency. Please observe her nose, because it's reputed to be the best one in the business for sniffing out best sellers. If Sylvia takes you on, you can be assured of literary stardom. And who knows? The next sensation of the publishing world could be seated right on this very bus."

Oohs. Aahs. Sporadic clapping.

A nod of Blackmore's head, and Sylvia slumped back into her seat. "Our second judge is a senior editor at Hightower Books and present editor of both Marla Michaels and Gillian Jones. You probably don't know him by name, but the publishing industry wouldn't be the institution it is today without his scrupulous knowledge and talent. A touch of his red pen, and he can turn any writer's work into a literary masterpiece. Gabriel Fox."

The man from the basilica with the spit-polished appearance and beard stepped into the aisle close to where Blackmore stood, sketched a bow, then sat back down. From this short second glimpse I caught of him, I judged him to be in his mid-forties with the kind of wiry body that smacked of either good genetics, long-distance running, or the Atkins diet.

"I've not appointed our third and final judge," Blackmore confessed, "but to ensure a fair mix on the panel, I'd like to open the position to someone whose interests are as far removed from the publishing industry as humanly possible. I know we have some tour guests from America's heartland traveling with us. A group of seniors from Iowa, is that right?"

"You bet!" shouted Dick Teig. Hoots. Whistles. Scattered applause. "The only one of us not old enough to join AARP is Emily!"

"Would any of you be willing to act as the third judge on our panel? I realize you didn't sign on to the tour to participate in our program, but let's face it, Midwesterners like you, and Jane Pauley, and—" He stirred the air with his hand, struggling to produce another name. "—and Jesse 'the body' Ventura are known for their forthrightness and homespun values, and I need the input of a person whose opinion I can trust to be fair and unbiased. I'm not being overly dramatic when I tell you that your participation could change someone on this bus's life forever. Do I have any volunteers?"

Hands shot into the air all over the place. The Teigs. The Stolees. Osmond Chelsvig. I scanned the bus. *All* my group was volunteering. Even Nana. Whoa! This was a switch. Normally, they were so preoccupied with being punctual that they devoted most of their vacation time to checking their watches and queuing up at the bus a half a day ahead of time. Philip Blackmore had read them like books. They might have homespun values, but that didn't mean they were immune to a little well-placed flattery.

"Well, this is wonderfully encouraging," Philip said,

obviously delighted with the number of hands inviting him to *pick me, pick me.* "I didn't expect so many volunteers. But your willingness creates something of a dilemma for me."

"No dilemma about it," insisted Osmond Chelsvig, who slowly unfolded himself from his seat and stepped into the aisle to issue instructions. Osmond was still president of Windsor City's electoral board despite advancing age, arthritis, double hearing aids, and the fact that he was the only person outside of Massachusetts who'd voted for George McGovern back in '72. "We gotta be democratic and do this by secret ballot. Listen up now. Remove your name tags from their plastic casings." He extracted his and held it in the air. "Then maybe that fella back there who's dressed in the Jungle Jim getup will be good enough to collect them in that hat of his and bring them up to the front of the bus."

I assumed he was referring to Fred, unless there was another person on board who was operating under the mistaken impression that we were touring Africa instead of Italy.

A round of applause erupted as Fred reluctantly removed his hat and made his way down the aisle collecting Iowa name tags.

"And the winner is," announced Philip Blackmore a few minutes later as he removed a name tag from Fred's hat, "Margaret Andrew!"

Hoots and hollers. A gasp of surprise from Mom. "Oh, my goodness!" I heard her exclaim from the back. "I feel so honored. I've never won anything in my life!"

"Where are you, Margaret?" asked Blackmore, peering down the aisle.

"Right here!" She stood up and put her hand on automatic pilot, waving to the crowd like a chubbier version of the queen of England. Oh yeah, this was going to be an evenly judged contest—the winner determined by a literary barracuda, an editorial golden boy, and a woman whose idea of truly gripping fiction was *The Runaway Bunny*.

"I'll meet with judges and contestants later at the hotel to explain how the contest will be conducted," Blackmore said, "but let me urge all of you who will be submitting stories to gather your thoughts and commit them to paper as soon as possible. I wish you all the best of luck."

"How long are you giving us to do this?" someone called out.

"Three days," Blackmore replied.

"Three days!" people whined in unison.

Blackmore stood his ground. "The winner will have to prove to me that he or she can work quickly and meet a deadline. A writer needs to be talented as well as organized and efficient to meet marketing demands. Three days, ladies and gentlemen, and at the end of that time, one of you will most assuredly be on his or her way to joining the ranks of the rich and famous."

I could feel the electricity in the air as Philip Blackmore returned to his seat. I could hear the anxious twitters and agonized sighs of would-be contestants as they congregated in the aisles. And as the miles passed, I saw the looks they exchanged with each other shift from adoration to suspicion, and their lips curve from smiles into sneers.

Oh, yeah. This boded well.

CHAPTER 3

A traffic accident in a tunnel outside the city limits kept us in gridlock on the Autostrada for hours, so we arrived in Florence after dark, which seemed a good thing since my instincts told me that the district where the *Hotel Cosimo Firenze* was located might not stand up too well in the glare of the noonday sun. The hotel itself appeared nice enough. Plain edifice. Victorian globe lights attached to the building. Crisp awning overhanging the entryway. Potted plants flanking the doors. It was the other stuff that threw me. The cars parked tailpipe to fender on the narrow sidewalk. The sea of garbage cans piled at the curb. The lack of streetlights. The cachet of spoiled meat and rotting fruit polluting the air. The rubbish lying in the gutters. I guess Florentines prided themselves on retaining the ambiance of their humble medieval beginnings.

We filed through a nine-by-twelve lobby that was crammed with vinyl-covered sofas and chairs straight out of the 1950s. Newspapers lay strewn across a small coffee table. A table lamp was set up for reading, but it was missing a shade. A flight of narrow, enclosed stairs led to the upper floors. Philip Blackmore cupped his hands around his mouth and addressed us as we squeezed into the lobby area.

"Could I have your attention before you all rush off? In about fifteen minutes I'd like to meet with all potential contest entrants and judges in the lobby." He eyed the space disdainfully. "Such as it is. It's getting late, so please try to be punctual."

Oohs. Aahs. An undercurrent of excitement.

A night clerk slouched on a stool behind the front desk—a huge slug of a man with a stubbled jaw, three chins, lizard eyes, and approximately one tooth in his head. He gnawed on a cigar as he grabbed room keys off a board on the wall and handed them to Duncan.

"Some of you with single-room assignments may have to double up while we're here," Duncan announced as he distributed keys. "But I hope you'll take it in stride. Who knows? Your accidental roommate could end up changing your life in some unexpected way. Every room has two double beds. I'll record who's in what room and will copy the list for Emily so we'll both know where to find you. Breakfast is served in the dining room between 7:00 and 9:00 A.M. And there's no need to look for a guest elevator because there isn't one. We're all going to have to use the stairs. Sorry for the inconvenience. But since we don't have luggage, at least no one has to haul an oversized pullman up four flights of stairs."

Good-natured laughter. Nods of assent. I couldn't believe how well everyone was taking the burned luggage thing.

The night clerk growled a string of Italian that caused Duncan to take a peek behind the front desk. "Correction. Someone is going to be getting some exercise. A pullman the size of a Ford Explorer recently arrived from the Florence airport. Emily? Where are you? Is this your missing bag?"

My eyes bulged. My heart leaped. "They found my suitcase?" I squealed, shouldering my way to the front of the crowd for a look-see. "But . . . but how did the airlines know I was going to be here?"

"I called Alitalia to report the change in venue," Duncan said, as I peered over the counter. Flush against the wall was my trusty pullman, its tapestried exterior dotted with a slew of orange stickers proclaiming it to be HEAVY. "That's it! I can't believe it! It's not in Kansas anymore!" I spun around and wrapped my arms around the person standing closest to me. "My stuff," I cried, bouncing up and down with Gillian Jones in her tragically crinkled silk pantsuit. "They found my stuff! This is so cool! I have my suitcase back!"

But Gillian wasn't smiling. And neither was anyone else. I froze midbounce.

Oops.

I escaped being assigned a roommate, so I wouldn't have to fight over which bed I wanted, both of which sagged in the middle. I didn't know what anyone else's room looked like, but mine was a pit. Soiled carpet. A solitary armchair with cigarette holes burned into the upholstery. Paint chipping off bare, grime-encrusted walls. No phone. No air-conditioning. No minibar with treats. The only goody for sale was a liter of bottled water that I could buy for twenty thousand lire. Ten dollars for water. Like that was going to happen. Boy, I could expect to catch an earful about this.

I ran to the bathroom and yanked open the folding vinyl door. EH! It was the size of a gym locker. There was no shower curtain. No mirrored medicine cabinet. Just a showerhead poked into the wall, an evil-looking drain in the middle of the floor, and a toilet and sink squashed against each other. Back home I *used* the bathroom; here, I'd be *wearing* it.

This wasn't good. This wasn't good at all. We had people the size of sumo wrestlers on the tour. What if they stepped inside the room to take a shower and got wedged between the walls? I raced for the medication sack inside my suitcase to see if I'd remembered to pack a large economy jar of petroleum jelly.

I heard a soft *tap tap tap* at the door. I froze. Oh, Lord, please make it a mindless complaint and not anyone who'll be using the words "Dick Teig," "shower," and "naked" in the same sentence. "Coming," I said, my heart in my mouth as I opened the door.

I expelled a relieved breath as I regarded the Severid twins standing arm in arm in the corridor. Oh, thank God. Britha and Barbro would never allow Dick Teig inside their room, especially if he were naked. They'd probably never seen a naked man in their lives. The twins were seventy-three years old, had never married, and still lived together in the same house they'd grown up in on the outskirts of Windsor City. They were purebred Norwegian with porcelain complexions, Wedgwood blue eyes, birdlike frames that made them look fragile as glass, and fluffy white hair that reminded me of the cotton candy we bought at the state fair. They were as identical as a couple of Keebler cookies, their only distinguishing feature being the different names pinned to their bib jumpers.

"We're sorry to bother you, Emily, dear," Britha apologized. Britha, who boasted of being the older sibling by ten minutes, had been head librarian at the local library for decades and still volunteered her services on a regular basis, maintaining the card catalogue and drilling other volunteers, like my mom, on the sanctity of the Dewey decimal system. "Would this be a good time for us to select a few articles of clothing?"

"Excuse me?"

"Your mother mentioned you'd brought way too many clothes with you, so you'd be happy to share."

I pondered that for a millisecond. "SHE SAID WHAT?"

Barbro's eyes widened with fright. "She said you'd packed so darn much stuff, there's no way you'd not have enough. But if that's not right, give us the scoop. We'll leave you here and fly the coop."

I stared at Barbro, stupefied. She'd been writing greeting card sentiments for so long that her brain no longer functioned normally. The upshot was, she couldn't just talk anymore. She had to talk in rhyme. It was really weird. "I'm sorry, ladies." I wrenched my gaze away from Barbro. "Would you run the part about my mother by me again?"

Britha happily obliged. "Margaret said you were so delighted to have your luggage back that she was sure you felt a moral obligation to distribute a few items of clothing to the poor unfortunates among us who lost everything in the fire." Her gaze drifted past me to the bed. "That's a lovely big suitcase, Emily. I bet it's new. We bought new suitcases for the trip, too. Of course, they're piles of ash now. Isn't there a Bible lesson in that, Barbro?"

Guilt smacked me hard in the face. Yes, my suitcase was the size of a big-screen TV. Yes, I'd packed my entire summer wardrobe, including a few fall and winter pieces that I knew would be indispensable should we run into a freak summer blizzard or a flood. But I hadn't packed frivolously! I'd only brought along outfits I was pretty sure I might wear. On the other hand, Britha and Barbro lived in bib jumpers, shells, and elastic-waisted polyester pants.

Neither one of them would be comfortable in my new one-shoulder sweaterdress with the leather shoulder strap, or my little stretch denim corset dress with the adjustable bra straps. *I* wasn't even comfortable in them, but they fit like latex and looked really hot, so I didn't mind that I couldn't breathe while I was wearing them.

I marked the expectant looks on the twins' faces and forced a half smile. There was only one thing to do. "You wouldn't know where my mother is by any chance, would you?" She got me into this mess. She could get me out.

"She's down in the lobby with those romance people," said Britha, nodding toward the enclosed staircase behind her. My room was at the top of the stairs, so all foot traffic from the ground floor would be passing by my door. Lucky me.

Barbro nodded. "I think their meeting's almost through, so stand right there and she'll see you."

I stared in awe. *How did she do that?* It was pretty clever, but it really set my teeth on edge.

"Look how pretty your room is," Britha said, jockeying with Barbro to eye the interior of my room. "We're hoping for a nice room like this at the next hotel, aren't we, Barbro? Is this what they call a deluxe suite?"

I opened my mouth to speak, but nothing came out. If this room looked good to them, what did theirs look like? Oh, God. I didn't want to know. "Is this your first trip abroad?" I inquired.

"It's our first trip anywhere," confessed Britha. "We're pretty much homebodies, aren't we, Barbro? Never been away from Windsor City in our lives, unless you count the time we attended the grand opening of the new Wal-Mart superstore outside of town."

"But once we went to Waterloo. Remember, Brit? You caught the flu."

Explosive clapping erupted from the downstairs lobby, nearly drowning out the sound of muffled *chirruping* coming from my room. "My phone," I announced, retreating back into my room. "Would you ladies excuse me for a moment?"

"Isn't that nice that you have a means of communication," Britha commented. "I don't believe we have a phone, do we, Barbro? Or a window. Or an armchair. Or a—"

I upended the contents of my shoulder bag into the chair and grabbed my cell phone. "Hello?"

"Emily, darling. Where are you? You said you'd call. What happened in Rome?"

"Um, the hotel burned down, and everyone's luggage got torched, so we're in Florence, settling into alternate digs." I smiled at the twins as they stood statue-still in the hallway, staring at me with hollow eyes. "We're all fine though, and the tour company plans to give people stipends so they can replace some of their belongings."

"I'm so sorry, darling. Did you lose everything? I regret not seeing you in the corset dress with the bra straps that you talked about." His voice dipped intimately. "I've been entertaining sinfully erotic thoughts about you in that dress."

My stomach did a little flip-flop as I watched the twins inch closer to my door, stalking my suitcase with their eyes. "Actually, I . . . uh, I didn't lose a thing." I regarded the eager looks on the women's faces. I regarded my obscenely overstuffed suitcase. I sighed as my conscience got the better of me. "Would you excuse me a moment?" I said to Etienne. "All right, ladies!" I waved my hand toward my suitcase. "I think there might be some slacks and jerseys in there that'll fit you."

They grinned in delight at each other before squeezing arm in arm through the door and approaching the bed.

"What was that about?" Etienne asked, when I returned to him.

"Girl talk." I watched one of the twins remove a few items from the top of my suitcase and place them carefully on the bed. Satisfied that they were as fastidious as I was, I turned my back on them for privacy and walked toward the bathroom.

"I'm impressed with your tour company, darling. It's usually impossible to find accommodation in Florence on such short notice. I wonder how they managed it."

I wasn't absolutely sure, but I guessed that someone had dialed 1-800-FLEABAG.

"Have the complaints been wearing you down?"

"Not yet. Everyone seems to be rolling with the punches pretty well." But I suspected all that would change when they flipped on the lights in their bathrooms.

I heard feet stampeding up the stairs and a loud chorus of voices as the romance contestants stomped onto the landing and paused outside my door to schmooze with each other. I guess this meant the meeting in the lobby had broken up. Unable to hear myself think, I stuck a finger in my ear to block the noise, then stepped into the bathroom and closed the folding door behind me. "Enough about me," I said to Etienne as I leaned claustrophobically against the sink. "What's happening on your end of the phone?"

He laughed seductively. "My luck is holding at the casino."

"Maybe you should try your luck in Iowa. We have casinos, you know."

His voice grew soft, husky. "Do they have *chemin de fer* tables?"

"Iowa has something better than *chemin de fer*." I frowned as the bathroom walls vibrated with the increasing noise from the hallway. Jeez, these women were louder than the New York delegation at the Democratic convention. "Iowa has . . . me," I said in a breathy whisper. "With or without my corset dress."

A pause. Heavy breathing. "*Dio Santo*, Emily. I wish you wouldn't say things like that when I'm standing out in public."

BOOM! The walls shook. The floor rocked. The sink wobbled. *What the—?* I shoved open the bathroom door and stopped dead in my tracks. Oh. My. God. No wonder the noise had grown so loud. The romance contestants weren't gathered in the hall anymore. They were in my room! I looked left and right. My mouth fell open.

THEY WERE GRABBING ALL MY CLOTHES!

"I've got an emergency here," I said to Etienne. "Gotta go."

"WHAT ARE YOU DOING?" I screamed as I rushed forward to enforce order. A silk cardigan sailed over my head. A pair of white capri pants flew in front of my nose. "Put that down. Give that back!" I snatched at the flashes of color that whizzed by. "YOU'RE NOT SUPPOSED TO BE IN HERE!"

"This is better than Filene's basement!" someone yelled above the fracas.

"STOP IT!" I let out an earsplitting whistle that could stop traffic on a dime, but it didn't stop these babes. They just kept squealing deliriously, overcome with the kind of frenzied adrenaline rush that happened to folks back home when Farm and Fleet announced their annual "Buy One, Get One Free" sale.

"I saw it first!" Brandy Ann hissed, tearing something out of Amanda's hands.

"It's not your color!" spat Amanda, grabbing it back.

"Hey, I want that!" whined an ash blonde, entering the fray.

Elbows flew. Hips bumped. Bodies tangled. "Give it up

before I flatten you!" cried Brandy Ann, sounding not at all refined.

"It has my name on it!" screamed Amanda.

"It's my ticket to fame!" snarled the blonde. "One look at me wearing this thing and Gabriel Fox will be eating out of my hand. Knock yourself out with your outlines, girls, but in this little number, I'll have the inside track without having to write one word. And you're not going to cheat me out of it! So . . . LET GO!"

"You guys are taking all the good stuff!" hissed a strawberry blonde, lunging at the trio. "That's just my size. Hands off!"

Growls. Grunts. I got sandwiched between two women and spun around. When I looked back toward the wrestling match, I saw a crumpled wad of denim fly into the air and land in the hands of . . .

Denim? "My corset dress!" I wailed, scrambling over backs and shoulders to reach it. "Don't you DARE take my dress!"

"You're going to rip it!" cried the strawberry blonde.

"Am not!" yelled the ash blonde. "It's that new denim. It stretches!"

"Get off me!" screamed Brandy Ann. "You . . . I . . . if you don't let this dress go, I swear I'll kill you!"

"Out of the way!" a burly woman barked at me, propelling me toward the outer fringes of the mob with a solitary bump of her hip. I recovered my balance before I slammed into the wall and inhaled an angry breath. Okay, that *did* it! There was no use talking to these dames. They were way beyond reason. But I knew one thing. They were getting out of my room, and they were getting out now!

I marched to the armchair where I'd dumped the contents of my shoulder bag and plucked my address book out of the clutter. I flipped to the back cover, spied the number I wanted, and punched it into my phone.

"Hello?"

"Hi, Duncan. This is Emily."

"What? Emily? Can you speak up? WHAT'S ALL THAT NOISE? WHERE ARE YOU? THE TRAIN STATION?"

"I'm in my room!" I yelled. "But I'm having a slight problem with crowd control, so here's what I need you to do!"

After delivering my message and signing off, I dropped my address book back into the chair and waited. One minute. Two minutes.

BRRRRRRRRRRRRRRRG! BRRRRRRRRRRRRRRRG! BRRRRRRRRRRRRRRRG!

"What's that?" someone shouted.

"Sounds like the fire alarm," I shouted over their heads.

I heard a collective gasp followed by a frantic, "Get out! Get out! The hotel's on fire!"

"You've gotta be kidding!" someone shrieked. "Not this one, too!"

Deafening screams. Major pushing and shoving. They shot out the door and pounded back down the stairs, leaving my room in utter disarray and my suitcase cleaned out of everything except shoes and underwear. Britha and Barbro clung to each other by the bed, looking severely shell-shocked. "If we need to vacate the building, would now be a good time to do it?" Britha asked.

I stared slack-jawed at my suitcase. I stared at Britha and Barbro. They looked so terrified, I ignored my own woes for the moment and hurried over to give them a reassuring hug. "It's not a real fire," I soothed. "It's just a drill. I can tell by the ring."

They sagged against each other with relief. "We're sorry about what just happened, Emily," Britha explained. "We didn't think to close the door, but we should have. When those romance gals saw us picking through your things, they thought it was a free-for-all. We didn't know how to stop them!" She paused, her expression changing suddenly from anguish to delight. "We did make our selections though. I've seen young people wearing clothes like this in the library, but I never thought we'd have a chance to wear them ourselves. Isn't that right, Barbro?"

Barbro nodded as Britha whipped out two pairs of cigarette pants and two bodysuits from behind her back. "This is so exciting. Look, Emily." She stretched my nude-colored bodysuit to and fro like a piece of softened taffy, then regarded me with the devil sparkling in her seventy-three-year-old eyes. "Spandex."

It was close to midnight when I finally hit the shower. To keep the toilet paper and towels dry, I piled them outside the bathroom door before I turned on the water. Surprisingly, the pressure was really good. Spray hit all four walls like a category three hurricane and started filling the sink. It made me think I could do handwash laundry while I showered . . . if I had any clothes left. *Why* had I let the twins keep my only remaining articles of clothing? I was such a pushover. But what else could I have done? When Britha held that bodysuit up to herself, she looked like a twenty-one-year-old about to order her first legal Bud Light. How could I have grabbed it away from her?

I observed the pool of water gathering at my feet. Hmm. Drain was a little slow.

I tried to rationalize the lunacy of my decision by reminding myself that the twins' father had been a Lutheran minister who'd probably frowned upon beer, bingo, patent leather, and any kind of stretch microfiber.

Introducing them to spandex could change their whole lives! I mean, look what it had done for the NFL.

I turned off the shower and slogged through two inches of water for my towel, hoping the backup didn't leak through to the ground floor. I stared at the clogged drain and wondered how to say "Drano" in Italian.

I heard an odd thump in the hallway as I was drying myself, but I wasn't about to check it out wrapped in a towel the size of a linen napkin. I cocked my head to listen more closely, but when I didn't hear any follow-up commotion, I chalked it up to typical hotel sounds, finished toweling dry, and climbed into bed.

I fell asleep the minute my head hit the pillow—awakened what seemed like hours later by a chorus of voices shouting in Italian just outside my door. I cracked an eye to squint at the ceiling, then reached over to hit the illumination bar on my travel alarm: 1:06. Okay, I knew Italians were night owls, but this was a public building, and some of us wanted to sleep!

I crawled out of bed, shrugged into my Laura Ashley dress, and staggered across the room, thinking fierce thoughts. I threw open the door. "Would you people *please*—"

The corridor was empty.

I looked left. I looked right. I stepped farther into the hallway and peered down the staircase. The voices I'd heard echoed up from the lobby. But they weren't the voices of rowdy Italian night owls. They were the voices of a half dozen uniformed police gathered around a woman whose lifeless body lay at the bottom of the stairs.

My eyes froze open in horror.

And she was wearing my new stretch denim corset dress with the bra straps!

CHAPTER 4

"Cassandra Trzebiatowski," Duncan reported in a gravelly voice. "Room 211." He stood outside my room, rumpled and barefoot—the same way he'd looked when I'd banged on his door an hour earlier.

"The police speculate she tripped over the runner at the top of the stairs and fell down the whole flight. Snapped her neck in two. Probably died instantly."

I remembered the thump I'd heard after my shower and silently berated myself for dismissing it. If she'd died instantly, I probably wouldn't have been able to help, but that didn't make me feel any better. Looking toward the staircase, I eyed the tattered piece of rubber matting that served as a runner. "Are they sure it was an accident?"

"Looks that way. She was wearing three-inch stiletto heels, one of which was sheared off from her shoe and wedged in the floor like an ice pick."

"So no one actually saw her fall?"

Duncan shook his head. "The desk clerk should have, but he was napping in a room off the lobby."

"While he was on duty?"

"This is Italy, Emily. There are no established rules. Only suggestions." He covered his mouth to hide a yawn, tears welling in his eyes with the exertion. "Sorry." He shook his head and threaded long fingers through his sun-streaked hair. "I'm used to operating on more sleep than this."

Guilt nibbled at my conscience. Unh-oh. "Maybe I shouldn't have bothered you."

"No! You did the right thing. You did great!" He gave my shoulder an unself-conscious squeeze of gratitude. "It's been a long day though. I'm getting a little punchy." He gave the top of his foot a vigorous rub with his bare toes, then fanned out all ten, staring down at them distractedly. "I left my shoes in the bathroom while I was taking my shower. Bad move. I don't think they'll ever dry out." He regarded my face then, his expression pained, his eyes like dark bruises. "Damn. I've never lost a guest before."

My heart went out to him. I knew from experience that the first one was always the worst . . . until you hit the second, third, and fourth. "You want to come inside for a few minutes and talk?" I opened my door wider for him. With a grateful nod he walked past me and angled himself into my tatty armchair, his powerful frame making the furniture look small and stunted.

"Five years on the job without a single death." He sighed miserably. "I had the best record in the company."

"Five years?" I seated myself on the edge of my bed, my voice filled with awe. I'd hardly been on the job five *hours* before I'd suffered my first casualty. I wondered if this was an indication that I should be rethinking my career choice.

"It's not that long actually. The odds are obscenely favorable in the tour industry. The chances of someone dying on your watch are astronomically low. Something like a trillion to one. Most guides go through entire careers without losing a single guest."

"Entire careers. Imagine that." I scratched my throat self-consciously. Maybe it was time to reroute the conversation before he thought to ask me about *my* record. "Did Cassandra have a roommate?"

Duncan nodded. "I accompanied the police when they told her about the accident, but she didn't seem too broken up about it. Strange reaction, but I guess it makes sense if you consider the women had probably never spoken to each other until I threw them together tonight. To be honest with you, the roommate seemed a hell of a lot more interested in working on her contest entry than in hearing about the details of the accident. She could hardly wait for us to leave."

"I have it on good authority that contests are a really big deal among aspiring romance novelists."

He flashed me a crooked smile. "Romance novels. My kid sister devoured them when we were growing up. Two a day when she could get her hands on them, which wasn't easy considering the nearest bookstores didn't always carry English translations."

I eyed him curiously. "Where exactly did you grow up?"

"Everywhere. My dad was in the foreign service, so we moved around a lot. It was his goal to ensure that our roots never grew too deeply in any one spot, and he succeeded admirably." He threw me a long look. "That must sound pretty dysfunctional to someone who was born and bred in Iowa."

Only one way he could have known that. "You read my travel information sheet."

"One of the perks of the job. Actually, I'm required to read all of them. And you know what always strikes me? How you can rarely guess from the look of a person what line of work they're in. Take the girl with the spiked hair and the screwdriver in her nose. Amanda Morning. She looks like she belongs in leather chaps on a Harley. Right?"

I nodded, though I suspected she'd need to have a helmet custom made to clear the metal in her nostrils.

"She teaches acrobatic ballet to five-year-olds."

"You're kidding."

He shook his head. "She probably wears a tutu and toe shoes to work. Cassandra Trzebiatowski? Classic beauty. Blond-haired. Blue-eyed. You saw the hot outfit she was wearing tonight. That clingy denim thing with the bra straps?"

I moaned. I knew that dress would have turned heads.

"Cassandra looked like the ballet dancer, but she was a tenth-grade physics teacher. And really focused. She wrote on her info sheet that she'd completed two romances and was beginning work on a third. A physics teacher. I never had physics teachers who looked like that when I was in school. Did you?"

"I had nuns." I watched him flex his shoulder and slide his hand beneath the placket of his shirt to massage an obvious ache—a casual gesture that struck me as oddly mesmerizing. I gave myself a mental slap. "Should you be telling me all this?"

"It's not confidential. The only confidential information on the Landmark travel form is the personal medical history, and you'll never pry those details out of me." He winked in a way that dimpled his cheek on one side.

"How do you remember everyone's name? I mean, I know name tags help, but it's only been two days, and you sound as if you have everyone's name memorized."

"Photographic memory. It was my biggest selling point when I applied for the job." He bobbed his head toward me. "What was yours?"

Mine? Hunh. No one had ever asked me that before. "I think it was that . . . I was available."

"Oh, come on." He laughed. "Someone hired you because you're good with people. You take initiative. You smile a lot."

He was obviously making a personal judgment here because I hadn't written any of that on my travel form.

"And you're kind enough to lend an ear when someone needs to talk." His eyes traveled to my mouth, where they lingered for a moment too long. "Thanks, Em." His voice was soft, his words slow. "I appreciate it."

He boosted himself to his feet. I rose at the same time, feeling a little emotionally awkward, and walked him to the door. "If your sister is such a romance fan, you should have Gillian and Marla sign their books for her," I said in full escort mode. "She'd probably be thrilled."

He paused on the threshold, his voice suddenly strained. "I wish I could. She was killed in an accident ten years ago. On her honeymoon. The biggest romantic adventure of her life gone miserably awry." He cleared the gravel from his throat. "Hey, get some sleep. I'll see you in the morning."

His sister had died? I closed the door behind him. *Good going, Emily. Way to rip open old wounds.* Oh, Lord.

I wandered around my room, craving sleep, but too wired to lie down. I thought about calling Etienne, but it was after two. I'd never call anyone at two in the morning unless it was an emergency, and this really wasn't an emergency. It was just one of those times in my life when I could use a little reassurance from someone who loved me.

Beating back my need for hand-holding, I rearranged my shoes along the wall, reordered the mess in my shoulder bag, then scanned the list Duncan had given me earlier to see what room Jackie had ended up in.

Ooh. Mom would love this guy. He'd taken time to alphabetize and cross-reference all the names. Let's see. *Thum* — 212. And directly beneath that, *Trzebiatowski*— 211. Hunh. Cassandra Trzebiatowski had been in the room across the hall from Jackie, but it was the name in brackets on the same line as *Trzebiatowski* that caused my heart to skip a beat.

Frounfelker.

Cassandra had been sharing a room with Brandy Ann Frounfelker?

I set the list down, reliving the scene that had played out earlier in my room. In my mind's eye I could see an ash blonde fighting over my denim dress and swearing that Gabriel Fox would be eating out of her hand when he saw her in it. I knew now the blonde had been Cassandra Trzebiatowski. I also recalled Brandy Ann Frounfelker in the middle of the fray, beating off the competition with her massive fists. And I knew that Duncan had been wrong about one thing.

Brandy Ann had indeed spoken to Cassandra this evening. In fact, I believe the exact phrasing had been, "If you don't let this dress go, I swear I'll kill you."

KNOCK KNOCK KNOCK!

I jackknifed upward out of a sound sleep. I squinted at my door. I checked my travel alarm: 5:43.

KNOCK KNOCK KNOCK!

Now what? I glared at the door and mumbled a groggy, "*Uff da.*"

"*Uff da*" is an expression of irritation and/or alarm used by many Iowans, especially those of Norwegian descent. It's kinda like the "F" word disguised in a rubber nose and glasses.

"Coming," I muttered. I struggled into my dress and

sleepwalked to the door. Dick Teig stood in the hallway looking like three hundred pounds of lime Jell-O in his too-small polo shirt embroidered with the words JOHN DEERE. He was as wide as he was tall, with a head as big as a medicine ball, but hey, at least he wasn't naked.

"What can I do for you, Dick?" I asked, unable to stifle a yawn.

"What time's breakfast? I didn't hear last night."

I slumped against the doorjamb. "Starts at seven. Ends at nine."

He checked his watch. By now it had to be at least 5:44. He looked relieved. "Good. We can still make it then."

I forced a smile. "Only if you don't dillydally."

"One more thing." He paused and took a deep, anguished breath, as if he hated to continue. "It's about Helen's . . . problem."

Helen had lost her eyebrows in a freak accident with a gas grill, so for years now, she'd had to pencil on fake ones, compliments of Revlon, L'Oréal, and Maybelline. His anguish could only mean one thing. "Unh-oh. Did her eyebrow pencil get incinerated in Rome?"

"It's her own fault. I told her she should carry a spare with her at all times. A woman's gotta take precautions when her brows keep sliding off her face. But what do I know? I'm only her husband. You have one she can borrow?"

"I don't use eyebrow pencil. But I have liquid eyeliner. Would that help?"

"Liquid, hunh? She said not to bring back anything that was water soluble."

I took a quick mental inventory of my cosmetic bag. "The only other thing I have is long-lasting lipstick. I can't guarantee its durability, but it comes in six luscious colors."

He slatted an eye at me. "She's tried lipstick before. It smudges. Then her eyebrows end up all over her cheeks. Folks begin to stare. It's not a pretty sight."

I had one last suggestion. "My friend Jackie might have an eyebrow pencil." She no longer had a dick, but she'd bought into something better. A great selection of expensive cosmetics!

Dick shook his head. "Helen's not the kind to borrow makeup from someone she don't know. You never mind about it then. She'll think of something."

I closed the door behind him, thinking I was about to fall asleep on my feet. *No more interruptions*, I implored as I stutter-stepped across the room. *I need my sleep!* I stepped into the bathroom.

BLUBblub*blub*.

Tepid water sloshed around my ankles and splattered the hem of my dress. I hung my head.

Damn.

By seven-thirty, guests were packed into the ground-floor dining room, seated at tables jammed together like stalls in a flea market. Voices echoed off the high ceiling as people sampled the hotel's Continental breakfast, but some people didn't look any too happy as they waved their hands at the small glasses of pink juice and plates of hard-crusted breakfast rolls before them.

"*Buon giorno*," I greeted the quintet dining at Dick Teig's table. I nodded to Dick and Grace Stolee and Lucille Rassmuson, my gaze skidding to full arrest at the sight of Helen Teig, who had resolved her "problem" with artfully applied slashes that looked to be compliments of a BIC pen. Medium point. Blue ink. *Oh, God.*

All five friends were wearing doughnut-sized campaign buttons emblazoned with a color photo of Dick Rassmuson,

Lucille's cigar-smoking husband who'd died unexpectedly a few months ago. The Dicks had been bosom buddies since childhood, so the loss of their brash-talking, practical-joking ringleader had left a huge hole in their tight-knit little group.

"What does 'bon jorno' mean?" asked Lucille, who was attired, for the second consecutive day, in a red wind suit that could have won her the role as a main entree in *Attack of the Killer Tomatoes*.

"It means hello," Dick Teig said flatly.

"No, no," Grace Stolee corrected. "The word for hello is '*pronto*.'"

"You're crazy," Helen accused. "Pronto means 'hurry up.' And I should know. I say it all the time, don't I, Dick?"

"The Italian word for hello is '*ciao*,'" Dick Stolee said from behind the lens of his camcorder. "Do something out of character for the camera, Emily."

Removing my eye makeup would have been pretty out of character, but it would have taken too long, so I gave him a little finger wave instead.

"Excuse me," Dick Teig said, addressing Dick Stolee's camcorder in an ever-increasing huff. "'Chow' means good-bye."

Helen thwacked her husband's arm. "It does not! It means food. Don't you ever hear me when I yell, 'Dick! Your chow's on the table! Get down here pronto!'"

Which just goes to show that a person can be bilingual and not even know it.

Lucille raised her voice to be heard above the din. "Well, I hope 'bon jorno' doesn't mean *bon appetit*, because that ain't gonna happen here." She whisked her breakfast roll off her plate. "Look at this thing, Emily." She whapped it against the rim of her plate, making a loud *chinking* sound. "They call this crust? It's an armadillo shell! And watch this." She dropped it onto the table and began hammering it with her fist. BAM! BAM! BAM! Plates leaped. Glasses wobbled. Juice sloshed.

Dick Stolee aimed his camcorder at his jiggling plate. "An early-morning earthquake in Florence."

"See what I mean?" Lucille ranted, holding the unblemished roll up for my inspection. "Somebody goofed and used cement instead of flour. No way am I biting into this thing. And my Dick wouldn't have eaten it either, would he?" she asked the table at large.

"Nope," Dick Teig agreed, patting the image on his button with genuine fondness. "He probably would have taken it home and used it as a doorstop."

Dick Stolee turned off his camcorder. "I think he would have climbed to the top of that domed church here and dropped it on someone's head. Might have fooled some unsuspecting tourist into thinking it was manna from heaven. He would have gotten a real charge out of that. What do you think, Grace?"

Grace Stolee, whose once ballet-thin shape had expanded to the size of a third world country, shook her head. "He'd had his teeth capped just before he died last year. Remember? So he never would have chanced breaking a tooth on one of these rolls and having to fork out more money for dental work. You know what a skinflint he was."

They heaved a collective sigh and nodded agreement.

"So what are we supposed to eat?" Lucille complained to me. "Where's the bacon and eggs and sausage and hash browns and pancakes and toast and jelly?"

"In Ireland," I said in a small voice. "But the good news is"—I flashed them a smile with my pearly whites—"Italian breakfasts won't kill you!"

"*Buon giorno*," Nana greeted the crowd as she shuffled up beside me.

Lucille regarded Nana with consternation. "Did we decide what that means?"

"I thought you said it meant *bon appetit,*" Grace fired back.

Nana stared at Helen, assessing her with her usual calm. "Jean Harlow used to have eyebrows just like them. But I think she used black ink."

"All I had on me was blue," Helen explained, "so it was either that, or Dick's red gel rollerball. I thought blue would look better with my skin tone."

Sure it would. If she was a Smurf.

"Just a minute," said Nana, rooting around in her pocketbook. "I got a Magic Marker. Will that help?" She squinted at the labeling as she held it up. "Nontoxic. Water resistant. Dries quickly. And lookit this! Permanent on most surfaces."

Helen leaned over and plucked the marker out of Nana's hand to inspect it. Behind me, I heard a bubble pop, which could only mean one thing.

I wheeled around to find Keely scanning the room for a place to sit. "You haven't seen Sylvia Root, have you?" she asked me. "I figure now's as good a time as any to make an impression on the ole literary agent. Maybe I can even convince her to drop her commission from 15 percent to 10."

I gawked at her, not because I was surprised at her gall, but because SHE WAS WEARING MY ROSEBUD SHEATH DRESS WITH THE RUFFLE AT THE HEM! "That's my dress!" I wailed. "It's brand-new. *I* haven't even worn it yet!"

She smoothed the slim skirt over her hips. "Tell you the truth, it's a little snug. Hope you don't mind. I let the seam out a little."

"YOU WHAT?"

"Yeah, I always carry a sewing kit in my pocketbook. Good thing, hunh? If it'd been in my suitcase, it would have gotten fried." She snapped her gum at me and scanned the room. "The bigwigs all sleep in this morning? They're supposed to make themselves available to us for consultations, or did they forget to read the small print?"

I narrowed my eyes at her. "Okay, here's the thing, Keely. I want my dress back."

"Yeah, yeah."

"Tonight."

"That might pose a problem."

"What kind of problem?"

She popped a bubble. "I'll have to go shopping to replace it with something else, and I need to put the finishing touches on my contest entry, so I don't know if I'll have time."

"Find the time."

"Yeah, yeah." She continued to survey the room. "I don't see too many of my fellow contestants here this morning. They're probably holed up in their rooms, working on their entries. A lot of good it'll do them. I have this contest all sewn up, so they're all just wasting their time." She shifted her position and glanced toward a point beyond me. "Well, well, well. Would you look at who just walked into the room? Philip Blackmore. Gee, can't have him eating breakfast all by himself, can I? Maybe he'd like to schmooze a little with the next best-selling author at Hightower Books. Ta ta." With a jarring crack of her gum, she headed off to intercept the publishing giant.

"I'm serious about my dress!" I called after her.

Her hand fluttered lazily in the air. "Yeah, yeah."

Was it my imagination, or had she just blown me off? Oh yeah, I'd handled that *really* well.

Nana shuffled around to face me and followed the direction of my gaze as I threw daggers at Keely's back. "Well, would you lookit that," she said, nodding toward the rosebud dress. "Her outfit's kinda like the one you bought for the trip. Same ruffled hem and everythin'."

"It's not 'kind of' like my outfit. It *is* my outfit!"

"No kiddin'? She find it in the same catalogue?"

"Not exactly. She found it in my suitcase." I latched on to Nana's arm and navigated her toward an empty table. "Let's sit. I have an earful for you."

When I finished informing Nana about my clothing crisis and Mom's unwitting part in it, she sat back in her chair and gave a little suck on her teeth. "I knew we shoulda done somethin' about your mother years ago, Emily, but your grampa was always hopeful she'd change." She shot a look heavenward. "Are you listenin', Sam? She changed all right. She got worse!" She exhaled a disgusted breath. "Okay, dear, short a killin' or maimin', you have any ideas what we should do about her? Now's a good time to plan 'cause she's back in the room, readin' the first contest entries that come in."

"Where's George?" I asked, aware of his absence for the first time.

She managed a hesitant smile. "He's makin' his way down to the dinin' room. And that's the other thing, Emily. We gotta figure out how to get her outta my room. If she hadn't went out with Alice and Osmond after the fire drill last night to buy some gelato, I never woulda had any time alone with George. By the way, I like it that this hotel has fire drills. They must have a real good safety record."

I let that pass. "You got together with George? Okay, 'fess up. Did you . . . *do* anything?"

She lowered her voice. "You bet. But we done it so fast,

I'm a little fuzzy on the details. Don't mention it to George, Emily, but we mighta left out a step or two."

"You can't recall which ones?"

She shrugged. "I betcha it was somethin' in the middle. But I don't understand how we coulda left anythin' out. We was followin' the directions in that book real good."

"Book?" My smile morphed into a frown. "What book?"

She peeked around her to see if anyone was watching, then quietly unzipped her pocketbook and slipped out a ragged paperback. I glimpsed the title.

"*The Barbarian's Bride?*" I eyed the blond hair, bare chest, and bulging biceps of the male cover model and realized that he looked a little like Duncan. "Where's the bride?"

"Inside the barbarian's lair, havin' a panic attack. The barbarian kidnapped her in chapter one, so he's struttin' around in his animal skins, makin' like he's gonna ravish her, which is really upsettin' 'cause she made a vow to her father on his deathbed that she wouldn't 'couple' with no one 'til her weddin' night. My guess is, she's Catholic."

I shook my head. "You better read fast before your book falls apart. Where'd you pick that thing up anyway? The senior center book sale?"

"I bought it new from that Michaels woman our first night in Rome."

"New?" I regarded the shabby cover, the dog-eared pages, the faded color. "You're kidding. It looks older than the Rosetta stone."

Nana touched the book's broken spine with affection. "It's on account a my hands. When I get to readin' them love scenes, it makes my palms all sweaty." She compressed her lips as she studied the book's cover. "George don't read much, Emily, but I'm not gonna let that come between us. He says he did read a best seller a few years back. Some book about the thrills a off-trail hikin'. All the famous climbers endorsed it, but George thought it was all hype and way too risky, so he didn't pay it no mind when he went to Yosemite."

"How is he able to climb mountains with only one leg?"

"Denial. I don't think he realizes he's only got the one." Nana stuffed the book back into her pocketbook and when she looked up again, broke out in a smile. "Well, would you lookit that. There's my sweetie pie now." She raised her arm to signal him.

I gazed toward the dining room entrance to find George taking small, robotic steps toward us. He was walking so stiffly and holding his head so erect that he looked as if he was wearing a straitjacket instead of the same tartan plaid shirt he'd been wearing yesterday. "Why is he walking like that?"

"Lower back pain."

I frowned. "He never mentioned back pain on his medical form. When did that start?"

"Last night. I was readin' the barbarian's first hot love scene out loud, and I asked if it was actually possible for a fella to twist hisself into the kinda contortion the author described."

"And?"

She winced guiltily. "It wasn't. He needs lots more practice."

"Good morning, everyone!" Duncan's voice suddenly filled the room. "Or should I say, *buon giorno*?" He strode into the dining room, positioning himself in a central location where he could be seen and heard by all of us, and rattled off a spate of Italian that was as incomprehensible to me as an aria sung by one of the three tenors, but just as captivating.

"For your benefit, allow me to translate," he continued.

"I have a few announcements for you this morning." As George eased gingerly into a chair beside Nana, Duncan raised a thick manila envelope above his head.

"This just arrived by messenger. Partial reimbursement for the loss of your belongings in Rome."

I cast a look about the room, noticing my red silk halter top on a perfect stranger, and my sleeveless button-front blouse on someone else. Was there *anyone* on this tour who hadn't ripped off a piece of my wardrobe?

"If you'll remain at your tables, I'll come around to distribute the funds. I have money for everyone except"—his eyes roved the room until they settled on me—"everyone except Emily, who's the only person on the tour lucky enough not to have had her clothes go up in flames."

My eyes grew wide. My mouth fell open. No money for me? But . . . but . . . he *had* to give me something! Okay, it was a minor technicality that I still had clothes, but the thing was, EVERYONE ELSE WAS WEARING THEM!

"This is a free day for you, so visit some of the open-air markets and replenish your travel supplies. Tomorrow we've decided to treat you to an unscheduled day trip to Pisa, with all entrance fees paid by us."

Oohs. Aahs. Titters. George stuck two fingers in his mouth to whistle, then froze up like a rusty pipe halfway through. I shot him a panicked look. "What's wrong?" I mouthed.

"Old rotator cuff injury." He hedged. "It flares up sometimes when I move the wrong way."

Right. Like when he tried to become a human pretzel. I massaged my temple. Oh, God. And this was only day two.

"The Leaning Tower won't be reopened until June of next year," Duncan went on, "but Pisa itself is a great place to spend the day. I'll assign a nine-fifteen departure time for tomorrow morning and to make sure you don't forget,

I'll post the time in the lobby as a reminder. Any questions?"

I saw a woman wave her hand in the air and when she stood up, I noticed something else. She was wearing my favorite lemon yellow sundress with the thin shoulder straps and fit-and-flare shape! AARGHHH!

"How are we supposed to find our way around Florence without getting lost?" the woman asked.

"I have city maps for each of you. I'll leave them at the front desk, so grab one before you head out."

I darted a look around the room—at all the strangers wearing my clothes—and started to hyperventilate. A sheen of perspiration bathed my throat. I became paralyzed by a single thought. *What if I never got my entire wardrobe back?* Oh, my God. I'd spent forever poring over Victoria's Secret, Spiegel, and Nordstrom catalogues to find just the right clothes for this trip. I wanted my stuff back! Now!

"My last item of business is information that I wish I didn't have to share with you," Duncan announced. "There was an accident on the stairs last night. Some of you might have been awakened by the commotion in the lobby. One of our tour guests tripped on the runner and fell down the entire flight of stairs. Unfortunately, she didn't survive the fall."

Gasps. Murmurs of shock. "Who was it?" Dick Teig called out.

"The guest's name was Cassandra Trzebiatowski. From Punxsutawney, Pennsylvania."

A perfect example of why including last name and place of residence on your standard three-by-four-inch name tag was often optional.

"We've notified her family, and they'll be flying someone over to handle all the necessary arrangements for the body. In the meantime I can't stress enough how important it is for you to watch your step on the stairs and to use the handrail. Let's try to avoid another tragedy while we're in Florence."

A hush fell over the room. I heard George whisper to Nana, "What's the body count now, Marion? Five or six? I've lost track."

I slumped forward, holding my head in my hands. Nana patted my back with a sympathetic hand.

"You didn't have nothin' to do with this, Emily, so try not to fret about it."

"I'm cursed. I really am. I'm right up there with the Red Sox and the Cubs."

Nana's hand worked faster. "Listen to me, dear. If you want drugs, I can help. There's no shame in takin' somethin' that'll help you cope." She rummaged in her pocketbook and slapped a small plastic tube onto the table. Anbesol. Extra strength.

"I don't have a toothache."

"Don't matter. This stuff will numb you up real good whatever your problem is."

I lowered my forehead to the table and groaned.

"Try to get a grip, dear. Remember what happens when you get stressed."

Remember? Good God, how could I forget? I got hives. But not just normal hives. I got . . . I shot straight up in my chair. Of course! Why hadn't I thought of it before? I grabbed Nana's face and kissed her. She was *such* a genius.

"Any other unfinished business you'd like to discuss before we break for the day?" Duncan asked.

I stabbed my hand in the air and, when Duncan acknowledged me, scooted my chair back and stood up. "Hi. I'm Emily. The person whose suitcase some of you helped empty last night."

Preening. Giggling. Wide smiles.

"I can see that many of you are wearing the clothes you borrowed from me, and I just wanted to say you look really great. I hope my wardrobe can add to your trip in some small way."

Cheers. Hoots. Scattered applause.

"You probably thought this was going to be a long speech, but that's all I really wanted to say." I waved to everyone in the room and started to sit down, only to pop back up and press my hand to my forehead to indicate my forgetfulness. "I'm sorry. There *is* one more thing I forgot to mention."

The applause died down. I smiled sweetly into the faces that peered up at me. "I have this embarrassing skin condition that's highly contagious, so if any of you start breaking out in a gross-looking, itchy red rash all over your body, don't get too upset. If you get treatment quickly enough, the damage to your liver will be only minor. And you'll be happy to know that the recommended treatment is known to have caused infertility in only five of twelve lab rats, which means, you can look great in Italy and *still* have children! Maybe. Isn't that great?"

I maintained my smile as half the room made a sudden stampede toward the door.

I might be from a little town in Iowa, but I hadn't just fallen off the turnip truck.

CHAPTER 5

I was loitering in the hotel lounge a short time later, impatiently waiting for Jackie, when I saw a familiar face grab a map off the front desk and blow past me like a Ferrari. "I'm sorry about your roommate," I called toward Brandy Ann as she headed for the door.

She ground to a quick stop and turned around, her eyes locating me amid the dozen guests who were huddled in tight knots, examining their city maps. She hazarded a tense smile and retraced her steps back to me.

"You heard, huh?" She ranged a look around the room. "I guess everyone has heard by now."

"Duncan told the group at breakfast."

She nodded. "I don't do breakfast. Too many carbs and refined sugars in breakfast food. A person would be better off opening a vein and injecting cyanide." She doubled her fist and gave her arm a quick pump, inflating her biceps like a rubber tire. My eyes rounded. My stomach muscles twitched. A person of normal intelligence would *not* want to get on Brandy Ann Frounfelker's bad side.

"Really bad luck on Cassandra's part," Brandy Ann admitted. "But she brought it on herself. I don't want to be judgmental, but anyone who owns shoes like that has to have a death wish. They might have looked great with the dress she snitched from you, but look where they got her."

"You didn't seem too happy last night that she grabbed my dress away from you."

"I wasn't. I even made some inane remark, threatening her. Did you hear me? Heat of the moment. But I got over it."

Before or after Cassandra fell down the stairs? I wondered.

"The thing is, I can't let all these petty distractions grab my attention. I need to stay focused on my outline and pages and submit the best entry I can."

Personally, I considered death more than a petty distraction. "Duncan told me Cassandra had completed two novels and was beginning work on a third. Sounds as if she really knew how to stay focused."

Brandy Ann barked out a sour laugh. "She paid Keely a ton of money to coach her through those first two books."

"Cassandra subscribed to Keely's Internet service?"

"Until recently, when Keely raised her rates. Then Cassandra apparently decided to go it alone. I read some of her work last night. It wasn't half-bad. She had talent. It's a shame she's dead. Like they said in that old movie, 'she mighta been a contenda.'"

"Brandy Ann!" Amanda trotted up beside us, her inch-long hair devoid of spikes, but her nose still armed to open aluminum cans. "I'm ready to make the move. It's really easy when you don't have luggage."

My gaze drifted from one to the other. "What move?"

Amanda ruffled her hair into disarray and tossed her head back with attitude. I cocked my head to regard the result. Oh, yeah. Big improvement. "We're going to share a room while we're here," she said. "We're really on the same wavelength, and we need lots of time together to help each other with contest stuff. We could even tie for first place."

"I thought Keely was going to help you."

The women sidled meaningful looks at each other. "We've decided we don't need her help," Brandy Ann announced in a voice that dripped honey.

"Yeah," Amanda agreed. "Keely is obnoxious. She thinks she knows it all. I don't want her help, and I don't want to room with her anymore. So I'm moving in with Brandy Ann. I wanted to make the switch last night, but Keely wouldn't—"

"Look, we have to go," Brandy Ann interrupted, pulling Amanda away from me. "We have things to do."

"What were you going to say?" I called at Amanda's back.

Amanda threw me an off-balance wave as Brandy Ann dragged her out the door. *Keely wouldn't what?* I wondered. Agree to change roommates? Hmm. That hadn't stopped Amanda and Brandy Ann from getting their way though, had it? Was it the mother of all coincidences that Brandy Ann's room had suddenly "opened up," or what?

No mistaking it. I was getting a bad feeling about this.

"You can come along with George and me once he shows up," I heard Nana say close behind me. "Most days, he don't even need no map."

I turned around to find her standing with Marla Michaels and Gillian Jones, whose five-foot-by-five-foot Florence map was already resembling a wind-battered kite, and they hadn't even stepped outside yet.

"We need to get . . . here," Gillian said, poking the map with her forefinger. "Duncan says that's where the clothing stores are."

"Maybe we should be creative about our clothes situation," Marla suggested as she smoothed her muumuu over her hips. "We could try lashing some leaves together. Remember? You did that so cleverly in your book about the spoiled dyslexic supermodel heroine." She touched Nana's shoulder, making her a captive audience. "What a story, Marion. The heroine was marooned on a desert island with a playboy rodeo cowboy who was trying to fly to Fiji to see the son he didn't realize he'd fathered by her blind sister. Uh! A real tearjerker. And I did *not* agree with the *Kirkus Reviews* critic who said it should have been entitled, *Dumb and Dumber*. How unkind."

Hunh. I wondered if Jack had read that one.

Gillian refolded the map into an origami lump that resembled Texas . . . minus the panhandle. "It's so nice of you to say that, Marla. The critic certainly ended up eating her words, didn't she? Who would have guessed that *A Cowboy in Paradise* would go back to press twenty-six times and sell over two million copies?"

"Imagine." Marla clasped her hands to indicate amazement. "I bet you have a good chance of matching my *Barbarian's Bride* sales. You only have a meager—what, two million to go? And I'm sure you'll succeed, especially when the *New York Times Book Review* describes your writing as 'vibrantly pitch-perfect.' "

"Don't forget 'deceptively accessible and luminous,' " Gillian added.

"Luminous. How could I have omitted luminous? Not to mention, 'a deft portrayal of the human condition.' " Marla placed her hand over her heart. "Well-deserved praise, which just goes to show that the Amazon.com reviewer who said your heroine was 'too stupid to live' was way off base."

Gillian's mouth lengthened into a stiff smile. "Do you

suppose she was the same woman who gave your *Barbarian's Bride* that blistering one-star review?"

Marla stopped breathing for an instant. Her eyes lasered on Gillian. "That's the trouble with Amazon. Too many uninformed people handing out opinions. Take *your* one-star review, for instance. The reviewer blasted you for allowing your cowpoke to boink a woman six thousand times and not get her pregnant. I thought the criticism was completely unfounded, and very mean-spirited."

Gillian heaved a breathy sigh and wadded her map into a new shape that looked suspiciously like a headless crane. Obviously no subliminal implications there.

"If the reviewer had bothered to read to the end," Gillian sputtered, "she would have understood that Spur had contracted a mysterious disease years earlier that had left him with a low sperm count. He couldn't *have* children. That's why he was so hot to find the son he *did* father."

Spur? The hero's name was Spur? I cringed. Who'd name a baby Spur?

Nana tapped Gillian on the arm. "Might not a been the mysterious disease what caused Spur's condition. Mighta been his underwear. If it's too tight, it can cause a fella's privates to heat up somethin' fierce and to kill off all the little buggers. I seen it on the Discovery Channel. You recollect whether your cowboy wore boxers or briefs?"

"I can answer that," Marla piped up. "Gillian is so inventive. Spur wore a palm leaf the size of an elephant ear. It was the only thing on the island big enough to cover his 'ten inches of flaming virility.' I thought it was quite masterful how he avoided setting fire to the whole island. Every time he whipped off his palm leaf, I wasn't sure if the heroine was about to get ravished or incinerated!"

Gillian crushed her city map into another shape. I pondered the result. *Euw!* Now that was uncalled for.

Gillian regarded Nana. "Marla is much too modest to tell you herself, Marion, but she's known as the queen of the sensuous love scene. Although . . . her continued use of the cliché 'throbbing manhood' has provided grist for many a romance chatroom. People have actually done surveys, and the consensus is, *it doesn't throb!*"

I clutched my throat, sucking in an astonished breath. It didn't throb?

"Throbbing is the industry standard," Marla said offhandedly. "It *always* throbs."

Gillian's smile hardened into ice. "It doesn't."

"And how would you know that?" Marla challenged.

The ice melted into a smirk. "Because I conducted the survey!"

I cleared my throat and raised a tentative finger in the air. "If you ladies don't mind my asking, if it doesn't throb, what does it do?"

"Maybe it quivers," Nana said thoughtfully. "You know, kind of like a handheld blender. I'm pretty sure your grampa's quivered."

"Where's Sylvia?" Marla bellowed. "Is Sylvia here?"

"I want Philip," Gillian demanded. "Would somebody *please* get Philip for me?"

I looked from one diva to the other. Oh yeah. These two were the best of friends.

"It says here that construction began on the cathedral in 1296 and continued for over a hundred years." Jackie was bent over at the waist, sucking in air as she read from her guidebook. "Then in 1420 . . . a guy named Brunelleschi started building the dome and completed the project sixteen years later." She glanced up at me, gasping. "He must

have been on the same time schedule . . . as the guys super-
vising Boston's Big Dig."

I massaged the stitch in my side and trained a look up
ahead at the multitude of stone steps that spiraled blindly
to the top of Florence's famed Duomo. "How many
steps . . . does it say we have to climb?"

She scanned the page. "Four hundred and sixty-three."

"How many do you think we've climbed so far?"

"A thousand. The number in the book must be a mis-
print."

We were pausing for breath on a flight of ancient stone
risers that formed a tomblike staircase between the inner
and outer shells of the dome. It was 8:55 now, and fairly
cool, but later in the day, I suspected this place would heat
up like a blast furnace. The passageway was cramped and
hardly wide enough for our shoulders. The air was stuffy,
the masonry walls cold and implacable, the ceiling a low-
arched patchwork of brick and mortar that hung claustrophobically close. A solitary fifteen-watt light, shielded
within a mesh cage high on the wall, was our only source
of illumination. It was kind of like wandering through a
Disney World version of the human ear canal.

Jackie straightened up slowly, retrieved her minirecorder,
and spoke haltingly into the unit. "If you want an aerial view
of Florence . . . forget the one from the top of the Duomo.
Do yourself a favor. Take the helicopter tour instead." She
shoved the recorder back into her bag. "I don't get it. How
come I'm feeling this climb more than you? Why am I so out
of breath?"

"Maybe you're pregnant."

She speared me with a narrow look. "I have no uterus.
Remember? It's not standard equipment for transsexuals
yet. But speaking of those who have, and those who have
not, how would you like to—"

"I am NOT going to act as a surrogate when you and Tom decide to have children, Jack! Forget it. End discussion."

"My, my. Aren't *we* testy this morning. Come on, Emily, you can tell me. What's wrong?" She looked me up and down. "Well, other than your wardrobe is history, and you've been shlepping around in the same dress for three days."

Since she'd slept through breakfast, I'd given her the lowdown on last night's disasters on the trek over, so she was up to speed with current events. "My wardrobe is not history. I'll get my things back. You'll see. I've set a plan in motion."

"Good. Let's talk about me then." She clasped her hands in a pleading gesture, hung her head, and in a pathetic voice cried, "I hate my roommate! Can I room with you instead?"

Unh-oh. "Who's your roommate?"

"Jeannette Bowles. A food critic from Burlington, Vermont. She writes a column critiquing all the ski resort restaurants in the New England area. I'd like to write a column critiquing her. Too pushy. Too self-absorbed. Too arrogant. While I was sleeping last night? She drank all the bottled water I'd gone out to buy earlier and left me with the twenty-thousand-lire stuff, which, by the way, tasted so terrible, I spat it out and dumped the rest down the sink. Stay away from that brand, Emily. Where does the hotel get that crap? The local sewage treatment plant? And then she skulked out this morning before I could confront her about it. Plus, with *all* her skill and expertise in the field of journalism, she *knows* she has this romance contest all sewn up and feels *dreadfully* sorry for all the other poor shmucks who are even bothering to enter. Blahblahblah. Yadayadayada. On, and on, and on. Don't leave me in the same room with her, Emily. I'm bigger than she is. It could get ugly."

I exhaled a long breath that echoed softly through the stairwell. "Is there anyone on this tour who isn't having roommate problems?"

Jackie looked gleeful. "Oh, goody. You mean, I'm not the only one stuck with a dud?"

"Amanda Morning thought she was stuck with a dud."

"Amanda. She's the one with the spiked hair and the vegetable peeler lodged in her nose, right? I met her the other night at the book signing. I hear she's writing a groundbreaking zombie romance. You know what they say. Write what you know."

I rolled my eyes. "Well, she was apparently wanting to ditch her assigned roommate and move in with Brandy Ann Frounfelker, the body builder, when lo and behold! Brandy Ann's roommate conveniently takes a header from the top of the stairs and Amanda gets her way."

Jackie's windpipe rattled with an odd choking sound as she proceeded to suck all the breathable oxygen out of the passageway. "Oh, my God! That's what's wrong with you! You think someone deliberately pushed that woman, don't you?"

"I didn't say that."

"But that's what you're thinking. Out with it, Emily. What do you know?"

I regarded her sternly. "Oh, God, I'm *so* glad you asked. Okay, here's the deal." I gave her the blow-by-blow version of what I'd learned about Amanda, Brandy Ann, Keely, and Cassandra, and when I finished, she nodded.

"You're right. Way too many coincidences. I think she did it."

"Me too!" I hesitated. "Which she?"

Jackie shrugged. "I don't know. One of them. You have the

roommate thing going with Amanda. She might have given Cassandra a shove to open up space for herself in Brandy Ann's room, but that seems pretty over-the-top to me."

Over-the-top to a normal person, maybe, but would it seem over-the-top to someone who wrote zombie romances?

"Brandy Ann has the obvious body strength to push someone down a flight of stairs. You said she read Cassandra's stuff, so she knew the kind of talent she was dealing with. Seems possible Brandy Ann might have been trying to eliminate her strongest competition, especially if she heard Cassandra threatening to influence Gabriel Fox by offering him sexual favors."

Sexual favors in *my* corset dress. The nerve!

"Keely has 'suspect' plastered all over her. She'd worked with Cassandra. She knew her writing style. If she was the one who did the pushing, it was obviously for one of two reasons: either she wanted to zap her closest competitor, or she was getting even with Cassandra for canceling her subscription to her critique service."

I stared at Jackie, stunned. "That's the most extraordinary example of deductive reasoning I've ever heard you construct, Jack. I'm impressed. Really."

She fixed me with a numb look, eyes glassy, jaw slack. "You're right. It was freaking brilliant. Holy shit! How'd that happen?"

I sighed my frustration. "The only problem is, no one is going to bother listening to us. The police are convinced it was an accident precipitated by faulty footwear. Case closed."

"But what if they're wrong?"

I cast around for solutions. "Cassandra was in the room directly across from yours. You didn't happen to hear anything suspicious in the hall last night, did you?"

"Didn't hear a thing until Jeannette came clomping into the room at some wee hour of the morning. I hit the sack early to escape being subjected to any more of her self-adulation, so she decided to go exploring. You know how it is with self-centered people. They can't possibly function without an audience."

I smiled. She knew about that firsthand. "What time was that?"

"Sometime before midnight. She probably wanted to scout out some local eatery so she could write a critical review of their three-cheese pizza. You *will* talk to Duncan about getting me out of that room, won't you?"

"Promise."

"So what do we do now?"

I gnawed on that for a long moment. "I can't let it go. Etienne would discourage me from meddling, but I'm not comfortable with the police's conclusion. There's something going on here that doesn't feel right to me, and my gut tells me it involves Brandy Ann, Keely, and Amanda, either together or separately. I don't trust them, Jack. I think they're up to no good, so we better keep our eyes on them."

Jackie clapped her hands before tugging on my arm beseechingly. "This is so cool! Surveillance. Eavesdropping. Dirty tricks. Can we wear disguises? Please, Emily? You know how good I am with makeup. I could dress up like a guy! Remember how great I walked when I was a guy? Maybe I could do that again!" She peered down at her feet. "You think anyone will notice that my shoes aren't exactly butch?"

I guess her burst of deductive reasoning had only been a passing thing.

"Wow." I wasn't as high above sea level as when I'd stood atop Mount Pilatus in Switzerland, but I was still high enough up to make the bottoms of my feet tingle. The gallery was octagonal in shape, about ten feet wide, paved with white marble, and surrounded by a railing that stood waist high and might have been made of chicken wire. It was kind of like standing on the top tier of a wedding cake and being protected by a border of decorative frosting. Three hundred and forty feet below me, Florence lay in miniature, a jumble of brown and gray buildings squished helter-skelter beneath red terra-cotta roofs—like a third-grade plaster of Paris experiment that someone had accidentally sat on. Flanking the perimeter of the city, a forest of spired trees and lush Tuscan greenery spread toward the surrounding hills and disappeared beneath a cloud of what looked like California smog. Beyond the smog, to the north and west, I imagined vineyards and villas, hill towns and sunflowers, olive groves and . . .

"And another thing," Jackie gasped into her tape recorder, "if you have old folks on your tour, don't drag them up here, or they'll all be collapsing from exhaustion and you'll have to have them airlifted down." She stood near me, backed against one of the ornate columned arches that winged outward from the cupola. "Say, Emily, I've been thinking. Should we have a secret code or a password or something?"

I focused on the panorama before me, a stiff wind forcing me to hold my camera steady. The roofs. The forest. A little smog for atmosphere. CLICK. "We're keeping track of suspicious people, Jack, not launching nuclear missiles." I refocused on the bell tower that rose candlestick straight to my left. CLICK. "We don't need secret codes."

A snort of disgust behind me. "No disguises. No secret codes. No passwords. If you don't mind my saying so, Emily, you run a pretty rinky-dink surveillance operation."

"I never would have come up here if I'd known this was going to happen," I heard a familiar voice complain from somewhere nearby. "Are you sure you don't need some help up, Barbro?"

My heart slammed against my rib cage with a sickening thud. Barbro? *My* Barbro? Oh, no. Had she fallen down? Broken her hip? Shattered a vertebra? Didn't she realize we were 340 feet up? Oh, God. With my heart in my mouth, I raced through four archways to the south side of the gallery. There, facedown on the terrace, lying in a splash of sunlight beside a plastic sack stamped with the words *Farmacia Comunale,* I found Barbro Severid. "Oh, my God!" *Don't be dead. Please, don't be dead.* Reverting to CPR mode, I dropped to my knees and flipped her over like a burger.

Click clack click clack click. "Would it have hurt for you to *mention* you were leaving?" Jackie scolded as she ran to join me.

Barbro's eyes were open, her pupils fixed. "You're going to be fine," I chattered over her as I tested for a pulse in her throat. My hands were sweaty. My fingers shook. "The climb must have been too much for her. I CAN'T FIND A PULSE!" I cried at Jack.

Barbro sat up suddenly. "Are you sure?"

"EHH!" I screamed.

She pressed her fingertips to the side of her throat and began to search herself. "Don't worry, dear. It must be here."

"My goodness," Britha cried as she shuffled into view. "What's all this commotion? What are you doing to my sister?"

"Emily can't find a pulse!" Jackie wailed. "Stand back. She's about to start CPR."

"Where'd it go?" Barbro sputtered, testing her throat.

"Don't know, don't know." Shrugging, she thrust her hand onto my lap. "I insist. Try my wrist."

"Hurry up, Emily," Jackie prodded. "She could be dead."

"SHE'S NOT DEAD! She's sitting up!"

"You can't go by that! It could be a delayed muscle reaction."

"Look, Barbro," Britha said, circling around me. She opened her palm for all of us to see. "I found it. It must have ricocheted off the bottom of the railing and landed behind that column over there. But it's broken." She held up a clip-on earring that was a whorl of multicolored blue beads. "Brand-new. Isn't that a shame?" She wiggled the metal clip in the air to show how it was dangling like a loose tooth. "I guess we'll just have to look for new ones."

I regarded Britha curiously. "You mean, she didn't collapse from exhaustion?"

"Barbro collapse? Goodness, no. She was helping me locate my earring. She's very eagle-eyed. And quite thorough." Britha touched her hand to her ear and massaged the naked lobe. "But I do feel undressed without my earring. We always wear earrings to finish off our outfits, don't we, Barbro?"

"We always do. That's true, that's true."

Jackie nudged my leg with her foot and when I peered up, she slanted an odd look at Barbro. I warned her off with my eyes. "Well," I addressed Barbro, slapping my thighs, "now that we know you're not dead, let's get you back on your feet."

When we had her upright again, Jackie handed Barbro her plastic *Farmacia Comunale* sack then stood back and gaped at the two women. "Wow, you two are twins! I never would have guessed."

I stared at Jackie, deadpan. "You never would have

guessed? They look exactly alike. How could you not have guessed?"

She dropped her chin and narrowed her eyes at me. "Excuse me? Don't twins usually dress alike? Please note. They're not dressed alike. It's very misleading."

Britha smiled at Jackie with indulgent eyes. "You're very . . . tall, aren't you, dear?"

Jackie looked from Britha, to Barbro, and back again. "You're like little cookie cutters of each other. That's so cool."

"*Uff da!*" I said, giving the twins the once-over. "I got so caught up with Barbro, I didn't even notice what you were wearing! Would you look at you? Turn around now. Let me see." I made a little twirling motion with my finger.

Grinning, the twins spun around slowly, modeling the spandex bodysuits and cigarette pants they'd borrowed from me yesterday. "This is the first time in our lives that we haven't dressed alike," Britha confided. "It takes some getting used to."

The clothes fit like sausage casings, which shouldn't have been flattering to seventy-three-year-old spinsters who'd never been reconstructed by a Beverly Hills plastic surgeon, but the twins were so slim and trim, they looked like prototypes for Medicare Barbie. "You two look great!" I gushed.

"All thanks to you, dear," Britha said, "although—" She locked arms with Barbro and exchanged an anxious look with her. "Please don't think us ungrateful, but we did have a tiny question about your . . . skin condition."

"Skin condition?" Jackie frowned at me. "You have a skin condition?"

I brushed off the question. "It's nothing. Really."

"Unh-oh." Jackie wagged her finger at me. "Are your hives back?"

"No, my hives aren't back."

"You said it was highly contagious," Britha added. "So we were wondering if there was a chance we might catch it."

Jackie skated back a step. "Athlete's foot? 'Fess up. It's athlete's foot, isn't it?"

I rolled my eyes.

"Psoriasis?"

Barbro clung to her sister's arm. "The symptoms do inspire dread. You go bald, insane, then you're dead."

"Holy crap!" screamed Jackie. "It's leprosy, isn't it! You have leprosy!"

"We're not so worried about growing insane and dying," Britha explained, "but we'd rather not go bald."

"How could you *do* this to me, Emily?" Jackie cried. "After all we've meant to each other." She scratched a sudden itch on one arm, then the other. "Is there a rash involved? Oh, my God! I've caught it! I'm going to die! And I haven't even figured out who I am as a woman yet!"

I smiled benignly at the twins. "Don't mind her. She's a little high-strung."

"She should ask her health-care professional about Paxil," Britha suggested. "Or is it Plavix?" She strained to think. "It's the one that in most cases doesn't cause erectile dysfunction, serious heart problems, or death."

"Okay," I said, hoping to restore order. "The truth is, I lied about my skin this morning. But I had an ulterior motive. I'm trying to get my clothes back."

Britha made a metronome of her finger. "You lied? Did you hear that, Barbro? She broke a Commandment."

"But I *do* have a skin condition! At least, I did last month. It's just not active right now. So you're not going to go bald and die anytime soon," I assured the twins. "Keep my clothes for as long as you need them. Just get them back to me before we leave, and whatever you do, don't tell anyone they're mine!"

"You made it all up?" Jackie accused, fire in her eyes. She gave it a moment's thought. "Euw, I like it. You are *so* clever, Emily." She embraced me in a bear hug that lifted me completely off the floor. "So," she said when she set me back on my feet, "I've seen enough. Can we leave?"

"Before you go—" Britha removed her camera from around her neck and held it out to me. "Would you mind taking a picture of us with the rooftops of Florence as a backdrop? No one back home will believe how far up we are. I bet we're even higher than Lars Bakke's grain elevator."

The standard height against which all things are measured in Nepal is Mt. Everest. In Chicago, it's the Sears Tower. In Windsor City, it's Lars Bakke's grain elevator.

"What'd you think of that climb?" Jackie asked them, as I took the camera. "A real ball-buster, wasn't it?"

Oh, yeah. "Ball-buster" was a great term to use in front of women whose father had been a Lutheran minister. I angled Jackie a disapproving look.

Britha tidied the seams on Barbro's bodysuit and picked off a speck of lint. "I thought we'd never make it to the top," she confessed. "Barbro was real fleet-footed, but I'm afraid I slowed us down something fierce. We could have been up here way sooner if I hadn't had to stop halfway up."

Jackie splayed her hand against her chest. "I'm so glad to hear you say that. I was beginning to think it was just me." She slanted a smug look back at me. "Wasn't it awful? The shortness of breath? The burning calves? The feeling that your heart is gonna burst out of your chest any moment?"

"I stopped to tie my shoe." She heaved a sigh. "But

you're right. It was awful. It must have thrown us off schedule by a good half minute." She balled her hands into anemic fists and gave them a disheartened look. "My fingers aren't as limber as they used to be, are they, Barbro? If I'd been smart, I would have bought the shoes with the Velcro closures."

"Do I have to do anything besides point and shoot?" I called out to Britha as I peeked through the lens of her superslick digital camera.

"That's all there is to it, dear. Oops. Just a minute." She reached up to remove her remaining earring. "Don't want to be lopsided."

Seeing this, Barbro reached up and with a satisfied smile, removed hers, too. Aw, that was so sweet! They didn't want to be seen dressed any differently than was absolutely necessary. Boy, twins really had some major bonding going on. "Okay," I instructed. "Big smiles." CLICK. "Good one." Now let me zoom in for a closeup." A strong gust of wind blew their hair back from their faces like little white haloes. CLICK.

"Thank you, Emily." As Britha retrieved her camera and looped the strap back over her head, the bottom of Barbro's plastic sack gave way, dumping the contents all over the gallery floor. Toothbrushes. Toothpowder. Bar soap. Dental floss. Sewing kit. Band-Aids. Rubbing alcohol. Skin cream. A jar of what looked like petroleum jelly. Aha! They must be getting ready to try out the shower.

"Replenishing all your supplies, I see." I scrambled to collect their articles.

"There's a very nice drugstore by the train station," Britha informed us. "It has everything, except sturdy sacks."

I stuffed all the items into a gallon-size Ziploc bag I'd tucked away in my shoulder bag for emergencies, then handed the bag to Barbro. "That should hold until you get back to the hotel."

"You've thought of everything," Britha complimented me. "You take good care of us, Emily, dear. Thank you again. We're going to take a few more pictures from up here, then we're going shopping. We're anxious to see how the prices in the open-air market compare with those at Wal-Mart."

"Do you need any help back down the stairs?" I inquired.

Barbro smiled sweetly. "You're nice to ask, but the advice I'd lend, is leave us here and help your friend."

Jackie's mouth twitched with annoyance as we circled back to the stairs. "What *is* it with that woman? Why does she talk like that?"

"Occupational hazard." I stopped to shoot a few more pictures. "She writes sentiments for greeting cards. I think she's been doing it for so many years that her brain is permanently geared that way."

"Well, she should get it *un*geared because it's *really* irritating." She peeked back toward where we left them. "They're kind of cute though, aren't they? Are they really as identical as they look?"

"Yup." I swung around and captured Jackie in the lens of my camera. "All except for one . . . elusive . . . characteristic."

"And what's that?" she asked, striking a pose for me.

"They won't tell anyone. Family secret. Smile." CLICK.

CHAPTER 6

"I still think you should have sprung for the leather coat," Jackie admonished four hours later, as we seated ourselves at the last open table in a crowded outdoor *ristorante*. "Five million lire was a steal."

We were in a triangle of space between ancient buildings that hunched claustrophobically together, all crooked angles and shuttered windows. Around us, leafy bushes in terra-cotta planters fenced us off from the intrusion of foot traffic. Above us, an umbrella the size of a parachute shielded us from the sun. In nearby alleys, speeding Vespas disturbed the Florentine siesta with their constant chain-saw buzz.

"Blow twenty-five hundred dollars on a coat?" I cried. "Are you nuts?" Much as I adored leather, I liked food on the table and a roof over my head better.

"Yeah, but it was full-length."

We stashed bags labeled *Intimissimi, Eredi Chiarini, Ferragamo,* and *Versace* near our feet for safety and grabbed the plastic-encased menu from the middle of the table. None of the bags were mine. I was just a pack mule.

"Pizza looks good," Jackie said, studying the menu. That was nice to know, especially since pizza was the only item *on* the menu. The choices were written in Italian; but I'd been in Italy for two days, so my translation skills were improving by the minute.

"Just for your information, Emily, *salsiccia* is sausage, *vongole* is clams, *cipolla* is onion, and *olive* is olive. So, do you know what kind of pizza you want?"

"Yup." I pointed a proud finger at my selection. "Hawaiian." When I looked up again, I found Philip Blackmore navigating his way through a maze of tables toward us, Sylvia Root, Gabriel Fox, and the two divas traipsing close behind.

"Excuse me, Emily," he interrupted politely, his right shoulder drooping from the weight of the huge bottle of water he was toting in a sturdy L.L.Bean harness. Guzzling designer water might be considered trendy these days, but not if you ended up looking like Quasimodo. I wondered if Philip Blackmore was familiar with the term "water fountain."

"I realize we haven't been formally introduced," he continued, "but would you mind if we joined you? Duncan recommended this cafe to us, and as you can see, all the tables are filled . . . except yours."

Our table was big as a wagon wheel and could easily accommodate eight. "Um, sure," I said. "Happy to have you join us." Did I have a choice? I scooted my chair closer to Jackie's. Marla stood back, drilling me with a wary look.

"Should you be out in public? Philip warned us that you're highly contagious."

"Well, I don't know about the rest of you," Sylvia griped, pulling out a chair and plopping herself into it, "but I'm starving." Then to me, "If you're contagious, do me a favor and don't breathe on me. Is this the menu?" Her jacket and pants puddled around her like hundred-year-old-wrinkles. Her hair was thin and manishly cut, her face bland and colorless. She lacked style, sex appeal, and soft edges, but she oozed the kind of self-confidence and control that made you think the only time Sylvia Root wouldn't have the upper hand would be if she were eating a plate of spaghetti in that jacket of hers.

Gillian Jones looked slightly unsettled as she hovered beside Marla. "Is your skin condition very painful?" she asked me delicately.

"Why don't you ask her if it throbs?" Marla said under her breath.

"I heard that," Philip Blackmore said. "And as I cautioned the two of you back at the hotel, we are not having this conversation."

"Are you people going to stand there jabbering, or are you going to sit down and order?" Sylvia demanded.

While making introductions all around, Philip directed Marla and Gillian to adjacent chairs, which I thought was pretty risky considering they might be given access to silverware later. Gabriel Fox slid into the chair beside me. "So what's the story with your skin condition, Emily? No need to be embarrassed. We're all friends here." His light brown hair was razor cut to within an inch of its life, his beard a precise quarter inch of growth, his fingernails buffed and polished. His mouth gleamed with what I would guess was ten thousand dollars' worth of veneers, but his smile couldn't do the teeth justice. He looked about as comfortable smiling as Dumbo had looked flying.

"No story," I answered, raising my hands in the air. "I have everything under control."

He gave me a slow look up and down. "Somehow, I

would have guessed that. So you can guarantee we won't be sorry we dined with you?"

"Not unless you choke on your food," said Sylvia. "And if that happens, you're on your own. I never learned the Heimlich maneuver."

"I know it!" Jackie volunteered. "I could save him."

"Don't waste your energy, honey." Sylvia dipped her head to eye Jackie over the top of her reading glasses. "It'd be a shame to break one of your pretty nails over him."

Gabriel grinned his amusement. "Sylvia's charm is her trademark. You should catch her on a bad day." He hugged his arms to himself and shivered. "Brrrrr!" Lowering his voice, he said in a more conspiratorial tone, "The problem is, she's been lusting after me for years and has no outlet for all her pent-up sexual frustration."

Philip Blackmore cracked his invisible whip. "That will be quite enough, Gabe."

"Is there anything on this menu besides pizza?" Sylvia griped. "I didn't come all the way to Italy to eat pizza."

"Why did you come to Italy?" Gabriel grazed his knuckles over his fine facial hairs, seeming to enjoy the abrasive rasp against his skin. "For the seafood? You should be in luck, Sylvia. I hear they run daily specials on barracuda."

Sylvia smiled at the comment before removing her reading glasses and skewering him with a cool, patronizing look. "I'm here for the same reason as everyone else. To gather whatever pearls of wisdom the good 'book doctor' will be kind enough to share with us. Because, as we all know, whenever Gabriel Fox speaks, the publishing industry listens, no matter what he says, or whom he destroys."

Was it my imagination, or was I detecting some major undercurrents here?

"Granted, he wields some power," Philip said, favoring Gabriel with an oddly guarded look. "But lest you forget, Sylvia, so do you."

"You're all kidding yourselves," Marla said, laughing. "The person with the real power is Oprah."

"She's right," Gillian agreed. "You become one of her book club selections and *pow!* You get it all. Mega print runs. Endless publicity. More money than you can spend in six lifetimes. Literary stardom." She straightened her spine and set her clasped hands firmly on the table. "I want to be an Oprah selection."

Gabriel Fox pounded the table with his fist in a howl of laughter. "Why don't you aim for something more realistic? Like ... like discovering a vaccine to prevent whooping cough?"

Jackie nudged my arm. "Didn't somebody already do that?"

"You have no chance of *ever* becoming an Oprah selection," he went on. "Oprah's books are deeply intelligent, complex, multilayered. They refract truth through layers of falsehood. They render prose with subtlety and grace. They're masterpieces of modern-day literature."

Marla looked confused. "I thought they were books about torment, depression, lost children, suicidal characters, and dysfunctional families, in which case, Gillian has a point. Her books would fit in just fine."

"So there!" said Gillian, her glee diminishing suddenly as she paused to reflect on Marla's words.

"Oprah is a cash cow," Sylvia announced flatly, "and if you were smart, Blackie, you'd be waving Gillian's and Marla's upcoming books in front of her nose so you'd have a chance of getting in on the action. So what if her taste doesn't run toward cowboys and barbarians. Her reading habits could change. Think of the quarterly profits. The cash bonuses at Christmas. It's all about the money, and you're blind if you say otherwise."

Philip Blackmore looked decidedly uncomfortable. Uncapping his bottle, he took a long swig of water. "I've always admired your bluntness, Sylvia, but this is neither the time nor the place for a financial analysis of the effect Oprah has had on publishing."

She cackled with laughter. "Woo the lady, Blackie. And if you won't do it for Gillian and Marla, do it for Gabe, who would sell his left nut to be known as the man who edited one of Oprah's anointed literary masters." She sidled a wry look at Gabriel before casting an impatient glance around her. "What do you have to do to get a waiter in this place?"

Considering the escalating tension at the table, I hoped everyone's utensils turned out to be plastic. "Wasn't that sad about the woman who fell last night?" I ventured, hoping to tap into some of their more sympathetic emotions.

"Speaking of that—" Gabriel leaned forward to address Philip. "I'm not judging her entry if she's dead."

"Are you sure you didn't give her a little shove yourself to ensure you wouldn't *have* to judge her entry?" Sylvia accused.

Gabriel's eyes became hostile slits. "Okay, babe, this time you've gone too far."

"Well, I think this whole tour was a bad idea," Gillian complained. "First, you expect me to give up all my secrets to the wannabes, telling them how to write a romance, then you concoct this idiotic contest, *guaranteeing* that one of them will be given a free ride. I'm glad the fire destroyed all my lecture materials. Do you know what I had to go through to get my first book published? How many years of rejection I went through? I tell you, Philip, not only is this contest grossly unfair, it's positively insulting."

"Ditto," said Marla in an unexpected show of unity.

It was nice to see them finally agree on something, but it caused me to wonder where they'd been last night while Cassandra was falling down the stairs.

"Is that the waiter?" Sylvia asked. "Hey, you!" she shouted. "Over here!"

Philip appeared suddenly tired beneath his killer tan. He leaned forward and steepled his fingers, looking as if he were gearing up to deliver a history lesson. "I don't need to tell you that publishing has changed dramatically in the last three decades. Back in the old days of the business, the whole industry was kinder and gentler. The slush pile was a potential gold mine. I started out as a reader in a small publishing house and moved on to a position as an assistant editor, but even then, I read every manuscript that came across my desk and wrote letters to everyone I rejected. I always tried to blunt the blow with a few personal words of encouragement."

Aw, that was so sweet.

"These days, editors have no time to give personal critiques, and the slush pile is, regrettably, a relic of the past. Literary agencies have become clearinghouses, and literary agents are performing the tasks that were once the sole responsibility of in-house editors. It seems everything has become a little cockeyed, and a great deal more impersonal. Ask Gabe. He'll tell you."

Gabriel looked as if he wished he were somewhere else. "Whatever."

I caught his eye. "Did you start out your career as a reader, too?"

He sighed restlessly. "I started out as a reviewer. A miserable choice of employment for a kid straight out of college who graduated Phi Beta Kappa from Bennington. I assigned stars to the schlock that came across my desk so readers could decide if they wanted to buy the latest action hero novel, sci-fi thriller, or pulp romance. The quality of the fiction was so pathetic, it gave me ulcers, so I moved on to a position where I could influence the quality of the books being published. I made Hightower's name synonymous with superior literary fiction."

"Oh, yes," Sylvia said, laughing, "you've improved the quality of literary fiction so much that it's completely incomprehensible to most humans—even the pseudointellectuals who *claim* to understand what these bozo writers are talking about. Wake up and smell the coffee, bud. Commercial fiction is where it's at these days, and Hightower is finally realizing what I've known for a long time: people want to read stories that have plots!"

Gabriel seemed deaf to her words. "My authors don't need to be fettered by plots. Their vocabulary alone elevates them to a class by themselves. Their sentence structure is superb. Their verb usage is a thing of beauty. They learn from me, Sylvia. They don't use just simple present or past tenses. They intermingle the imperfect and the pluperfect with equal skill. Once, one of my prodigies even used the rare but ever dynamic . . . superpluperfect."

Gillian stared at him, agog. "What the hell is he talking about? Imperfect? Superpluperfect? If he tries pulling that kind of crap on me, I'm telling you right now, Sylvia, I'll want another editor."

"Me too!" Marla chimed in. "Barbarians don't use verb tenses. They grunt."

"Ladies, ladies," Sylvia soothed. "You're making way too much of this. It's all quite easy to understand."

A smile snaked across Gabriel's lips. His eyes snapped arrogantly. "Why don't you explain it to them then, Sylvia? Save me the trouble."

"Gladly. I'll even give examples. Shall we start with the

present tense? That would be: The editor is an asshole. The perfect would be: The editor had become an asshole a long time ago. The imperfect would be: In fact, as a child, the editor would act like an asshole all the time. The superplu-perfect would be: If only we would have known the editor was such an asshole, we would have asked to be assigned to someone else. Get it?"

Wow! I'd been using the rare but dynamic superpluper-fect a whole lot and didn't even know it! But Gabriel wasn't looking any too happy about Sylvia's grammatical exper-tise. In fact, he was looking decidedly miffed.

Jackie's mouth dropped open. "That is *so* impressive. Were you an English teacher or something before you became an agent?"

I could swear I saw a flicker of unease cross Sylvia's face before she plastered a stiff smile on her mouth. "I attended Catholic schools for sixteen years. Does that explain any-thing?"

"But Jackie raises a good point," Philip interjected. "All the years I've known you, Sylvia, and we've never discussed our postcollege years. You didn't start out agenting right away, did you? What was your first job after you graduated college?"

"Look, look." Gillian waved her hand madly to catch our attention. "There's that woman with the funny eye-brows. Over there with that group of people standing in front of the tobacco store."

Funny eyebrows? I looked for Helen Teig among the half dozen or so people milling around the doorway, but failed to see her. Heck, those people weren't even tourists. They were natives. Look at them! Their tasteful, form-fitting slacks and tops. Their sumptuous colors. Their intricately tied scarves. Their hot sunglasses. They could all afford to shed a few pounds, but leave it to the Italians to accent their least flattering features with style and flare, not to hide them.

I nodded in their direction and commented to Gillian, "Those people aren't on our tour."

"Yes, they are. I can tell from their campaign buttons. They were all wearing them when they went out this morning. It looks like they're backing some old bald guy who smokes a cigar. I wonder what office he's running for. The woman with the Magic Marker eyebrows has hers pinned to her scarf. See?"

Campaign buttons? I darted another look at the group. Oh, my God! She was right. They weren't Italians. They were my Iowans dressed up like Italians! Eh! The two Dicks, Helen, Grace, and Lucille had traded in their farm caps and polyester wind suits for Ferragamo and Prada. They looked *nothing* like themselves anymore! *Uff da!* How would I ever find them in a crowd if they didn't stick out like sore thumbs? A ripple of panic fluttered along my breastbone. This was terrible!

"Sorry for interrupting," Gillian apologized, "but I had to point that woman out to you. Don't you think someone like that would make a great character in a book?"

"I couldn't agree more," Marla said agreeably.

Wow. These two had really turned a corner.

She touched Gillian's hand with genuine affection. "Those are the kind of brows that could definitely 'wing upward in heart-stopping shock' at the sight of ten inches of flaming virility."

Okay. So maybe I'd been a bit premature.

Gillian didn't miss a beat. "But you have to agree, Marla, dear, that she looks like the kind of woman who would be smart enough to know that no matter the size, it wouldn't throb."

Gabriel tented his hands over his face. "Kee-reist."

"Okay, Philip," Marla snarled, "I know what you said back at the hotel, but you need to settle this for us. When you're in the act, does it throb or not?"

Gabriel dropped his head to the table and huddled beneath his crossed forearms. "Kee-reist."

"Really, ladies," Blackmore said, chagrined. "I'm not in a position to—"

"I'm warning you!" Gillian raved. "You need to sign her up for a course on basic human anatomy. She just doesn't get it!"

"Come to think of it, it doesn't actually throb," Jackie said, angling her head in thought. "It kind of . . ." She flipped her hand back and forth, searching for the right word.

"Quivers?" I asked excitedly.

"Nope. It's more like . . ." She snapped her fingers with sudden inspiration. "Imagine you're a steam locomotive that's chugging uphill. Slowly at first, then a little faster, throttle wide open, whistle blowing, smokestack steaming, boiler blazing, faster, hotter, faster, hotter, until . . . BOOM!" She smacked her palm with her fist, knocking everyone back in their seats. "You hit the crest of the hill and explode like a volcano. BOOM. BOOM. KAPOW. WHOOSH." She nodded with satisfaction. "It's kinda like that."

Gabriel lifted his head, joining the others around the table who were gawking at her, mouths open, eyes wide. They looked really stunned, but I couldn't tell if they were reacting to the content of her presentation or the fact that she'd mixed her metaphors so badly.

"You know this . . . how?" asked Philip.

Jackie paused, her smile inching into a grimace. "Um . . . *Reader's Digest*?"

This elicited a bout of restrained laughter from everyone except Sylvia, who was slouched with relief, looking as if she'd just dodged a very large bullet.

"I don't think they bought the *Reader's Digest* thing," Jackie lamented an hour later. "I mean, I'm not trying to cover up my procedure, it's just a whole lot easier if people don't know. Then I'm spared having to answer all their dumb questions. I just think it works better if I keep a low profile, don't you?"

"Oh, yeah. You have low profile down to a science." We'd run into an open-air market on our way back to the hotel, so we were making our way down a narrow street that knifed between two cramped rows of merchant tents and stalls, bumping and grinding with men who had cell phones grafted to their ears and women sporting skintight pants, spike heels, skinny tops, bare midriffs, and overinflated bosoms. The Miracle Bra was obviously a big seller in Florence.

Chirrup chirrup. Chirrup chirrup.

I fished my phone out of my bag. "Hello?"

"Did you mean to cut me off last night?" Etienne asked with mild amusement.

"Hi, sweetie. I'm so sorry!" Jackie rolled her eyes and gathered all her packages out of my arms, then scissored two fingers at me to indicate she was going to wander around while I talked. I gave her a thumbs-up and cradled my phone more tightly against my ear. "I should have called you back, but I had all these . . . fires to put out."

"More fires?" A pause. "I don't mean to alarm you, Emily, but—"

"No, no. Not real fires. That's just an expression. Like 'kicking the bucket.'" I smiled with sudden inspiration. "Or 'jumping your bones.'"

Another pause. " 'Jumping your bones'? I've never heard that before. Tell me what it means."

"Unh-uh," I whispered seductively. "I'd rather show you."

"You . . . *KRRRRRRKKK* . . . me, darling."

"Your voice is breaking up. Hello?"

" . . . in Italy. Tell me quickly, are you enjoying the people in the tour group?"

"I'm running into some real characters." Some of whom I might trust more if I knew a little more about them. Which prompted a brilliant idea. "Etienne, would you be willing to do me a huge favor? We're conducting a contest, and we'd like to make sure all the contestants are playing by the same ground rules, so could you run a few background checks for us?"

"That's highly irregular, darling."

"Yeah, but we don't want anyone taking unfair advantage. It's really important. There's a substantial cash prize involved."

KRRRKKK. " . . . I'm getting into, but, I'm not sure how to refuse you."

"I knew I could count on you. Thank you *so* much. Do you have a pencil? Here are the names and this is what I need to know."

When I finished, he waited a beat, then sighed. "I'll see what I can do but—" *KRRRRRRKKKK. KRRRKK.*

"Etienne? Hello? Are you there?" I winced at the static and held the phone away from my ear, staring at it dismally. It wasn't my imagination. No matter what we tried to do, we were *constantly* being interrupted. *Aargh!* I was too rational to call it a curse, but "hex" was a definite possibility.

I stuffed the phone back into my shoulder bag and rotated in place, looking for Jackie, but instead spied Fred

Arp hanging out in front of a stall layered with pallets of leather briefcases, shoulder bags, handbags, clutch purses, and backpacks in every jellybean color except tutti-frutti. He was holding two handbags in the air while a fierce, beefy guy with wild hair and bristly eyebrows barked Italian at him from behind the counter. I shivered at the clerk. If he was green, he'd be mistaken for the Incredible Hulk.

"Hi, Fred," I said, coming up beside him. "Buying something for your wife?"

He jumped at the sound of my voice and shot me a frightened look from beneath the brim of his hat. "I don't have a wife."

"Girlfriend?"

He shook his head. "No girlfriend either." His cheeks flushed pink. "I've never really dated much."

No surprise there.

The clerk growled something unintelligible that caused Fred's nerves to fray even more. "I want to bring something home to my mother, but I don't know how practical a handbag is. She doesn't get out much anymore. And I'm not sure what this guy is trying to tell me, but he's getting spittle all over his merchandise."

"Maybe I can help." I made eye contact with the clerk and smiled. "Do you speak English?"

He made a broad gesture toward the street, then made a hook of his right index finger and stuck it between his teeth.

"Scandinavian languages?"

He bit down harder on his finger, which told me nothing other than he was probably current with his ten-year tetanus booster.

"*Uff da*," I tossed out, trying to dazzle him with my multi-lingual expertise.

He stared at me, looking a tad confused.

Okay. Maybe French. "*Sacre bleu,*" I said with authority.

He made a guttural sound in response.

Having exhausted my entire vocabulary of Norwegian and French, I resorted to my only remaining option. "You betcha," I said in flawless Minnesotan.

Another hand gesture. Several animal growls. I grabbed Fred by the arm and ushered him toward the adjoining stall. "How about a nice silk scarf?"

Fred's chest collapsed with disappointment. "But I wanted something made of leather. Never mind. I'll look someplace else."

"Are you all by yourself?" I made a visual scan, looking for other tour members.

"What's wrong with that? I do lots of things by myself. I don't need to be part of an entourage. I like my own company. Besides"—he straightened the tilt of his hat and assumed a stoic look—"no one invited me to join them."

I flinched at the hurt in his voice.

"Amanda and Brandy Ann hinted that we could hang out today, but they left without me this morning. Women shouldn't do that. They shouldn't say one thing, then do something else."

"I bet you anything they simply forgot," I said in a placating voice. "You know what women are like when they have serious shopping to do. Pouf! Everything goes out of their heads."

He regarded me in silence, jaw stiff, eyes unwavering.

Yup. This was going well. "Tell you what, Fred, you're welcome to hang out with me. I could help you find something for your mom and—"

"I don't want to spoil your afternoon. I'll be okay. Maybe I'll run into Keely. No one likes her either. Say, have you seen any pet stores around here? I want to find something to bring back to my cats."

"Like a little leather collar? That would be so cute! Maybe in a variety of rainbow colors. How many cats do you have?"

His face cracked with a smile as bright as a quarter moon. "Twenty-three."

Click clack click clack click clack. "Emily! You've gotta see this!" Jackie whipped off a quick, "Hi," to Fred before snagging my arm and leading me several stalls down to a green-and-white-striped tent hung with leather vests, belts, neckties, and some of the most adorable leather jackets I'd ever seen. "Oooh," I said, my gaze leaping from color to color. Root beer. Bubblegum. Tangerine. Grape. "How much?" I asked, pointing to a waist-length zippered number in bright raspberry.

The middle-aged salesclerk was tall and rangy with a cigarette dangling from his lips. His eyes were ink black. His skin as leathery as the jackets he sold. "Six hundred thousand lire."

Drop three zeros. Divide by two. "Three hundred American dollars?" I winced. It was cheaper than the twenty-five-hundred-dollar coat I'd seen earlier, but it still wasn't the bargain I wanted. "I'll have to think about it."

The clerk whipped it off its hanger so I could see it up close and personal. "Six hundred thousand lire, but for you"—he removed his cigarette and blew a mouthful of smoke in the air—"five hundred thousand lire."

"Four hundred thousand," said Jackie.

"No, no!" the man complained. "Two hundred American dollar? You ask me to give it away." He plugged his cigarette back into his mouth. "Two hundred and fifty American dollar."

"Too high," Jackie argued. "There's a man in a stall farther down who'll sell us the same thing for two hundred. Come on, Emily."

Oh, I got it. We were dickering! My only other dickering experience had been with my nephews over how much Nintendo time they'd earn if they refrained from lacing the dog's food with gummi worms.

"What man?" The clerk threw a contemptuous look down the street. "Antonio? *Testa di merda!* You no listen him. He a snake. His jackets"—he made a spitting motion—"no good. His leather . . . bad. You no do business with Antonio. You do business with Vincenzo!" He slapped himself on the chest. "All right. I sell you for four hundred thousand lire. What size you need, *signorina?*" He looked me up and down. "Small size."

Wow. Two hundred dollars. I could actually afford that, but I wondered . . . "A hundred and fifty dollars," I demanded.

"One-ninety."

"One-sixty."

"One hundred seventy American dollar. You take that or go buy from Tony the Snake."

"One-sixty-five," I countered.

"Sold," he said, looking proud to have cheated his reptilian competitor out of a sale. "You want this color, I no have in small, but I take you to my shop. Many more choices. Angelo!" Vincenzo yelled, summoning a younger man from the back of the tent. He spouted some instructions at the teenager in rapid Italian, then led Jackie and me through a narrow maze of booths onto a street called the Via Canto di Nelli and a shop named Giorgio.

Inside, the smell of leather hit me in the face, which wasn't surprising considering the place was practically wallpapered with leather goods. Vincenzo grabbed a hooked pole, lifted a raspberry-colored jacket off a twelve-foot-high rack, and motioned me into an anteroom with mirrors on all sides. He lit a fresh cigarette before removing the plastic covering from the jacket and holding it out for me. "This size forty-two. This be good for you."

Hardly able to contain my excitement, I dumped my shoulder bag at Jackie's feet. "Watch that like a hawk."

Scurrying back to Vincenzo, I slid my arms into the silky lining of a leather jacket that felt smooth as whipped butter. "Wow."

"You like?"

Chirrup chirrup. Chirrup chirrup.

"It's your phone, Emily. You want me to answer it?"

"Appreciate it," I said to Jackie, as Vincenzo did the honors of zipping up my jacket. He stood back to assess me, smoke swirling around his head.

"Very pretty. *Va bene.*"

I turned this way and that in the mirror. "The sleeves are a little long."

"I mark them. We shorten them in one hour. You come back and pick up."

"Really?" This was better than fast food at Blimpie's.

"Emily's phone. Jackie speaking." A pause. "Oh, hi, Etienne. Yeah, she's here, but she's tied up at the moment. Can I give her a message?"

"This the best leather in all Italy," Vincenzo attested as he pulled a butane lighter from his pants pocket. He flicked the striker wheel then waved the flame down the length of my arm.

"EH!" I snatched my arm away. "ARE YOU NUTS? What are you doing?"

"Bad leather burn," Vincenzo claimed, grabbing my arm back and reapplying the flame to my sleeve. "Good leather not burn. This good leather."

"Okay, I believe you!" I stared at the flame licking my

elbow and could feel my skin heating up in protest. "Hey, I can feel that. You can stop anytime."

"Etienne is sorry you were cut off," Jackie announced.

"The leather good everywhere," Vincenzo droned around his cigarette. He swung the lighter flame toward my shoulder.

"Enough with the lighter!" I said, shrinking away from the flame.

"Every panel good." I eyed Vincenzo in the mirror as he circled around to my back with the exposed flame. "Some people mix the bad leather with the good leather, but Giorgio only use—*Merda!*" Up flew his hands as his cigarette fell from his mouth. "*Oy!*" He caught it in midflight, bobbled it in his hand, then cursed loudly as he dropped it to the floor and stomped on it.

"What's that?" Jackie asked. "Can you speak up a little, Etienne? There's a lot of background noise where you are. One-armed bandits? Euw. That's not good. How much is that in American dollars?"

I felt a little palpitation in my chest. He'd lost money. I *knew* that would eventually happen. I just didn't want to know how much.

"*Scusi,*" said Vincenzo, airing out his hand.

"Did you burn yourself?" I asked.

"It's nothing," he said, massaging his palm. "I get chalk to mark your sleeves."

I preened before the mirror as he disappeared into a back room. The jacket didn't look terrific with my Laura Ashley dress, but with a pair of black leather pants, it would look sensational.

I wrinkled my nose. Phew! The air stank of Vincenzo's cigarette. Italian tobacco was powerful stuff. Little streamers of smoke still floated in the air above my head. They could use a better air-filtration system in this place.

Jackie's voice rose in volume. "I'm still having a hard time hearing. Hold on. Maybe if I walk out—" A pause. "Holy shit!"

I spun around to find her charging at me full throttle. "EHHH!" I screamed.

WUFF! She tackled me around the waist. BOOM! We crashed onto the floor. I bumped my head and cracked my elbows. Air escaped my lungs in a painful *whoosh*.

I beat at her with my fists, trying to fend her off. "WHAT ARE YOU DOING?" I shrieked. "ARE YOU CRAZY?"

"Your hair!" she yelled, slapping my head with her hands. "It's on fire!"

CHAPTER 7

"How bad does it look?" I fretted, as we dashed into the lobby of the Hotel Cosimo Firenze.

"You don't wanna know," Jackie replied. "And that awful garbage smell? It's not garbage. It's your hair."

Great. This was *just* great. I thought I'd had problem hair before. I couldn't imagine the styling challenge I faced with half of it missing!

"Vincenzo was crushed you didn't buy the jacket," Jackie anguished. "Losing that sale really hit him hard. I felt sorry for him."

"HE SET MY HAIR ON FIRE!"

"Still. You might be sorry later on. You don't find bargains like that every day. Hold up a minute." She unloaded her packages on the floor at the front desk and smiled at the unshaven desk clerk. "*Cuscino?*" she asked.

He regarded her through half-lidded eyes, then snaked his gaze toward me and sniffed the air unpleasantly. "*Si.*"

She made a gimme gesture with her hands. "*Per favore.*"

Looking put out, the clerk heaved himself off his stool

and shambled around the counter toward the lobby. "What's he getting?" I questioned.

"I asked him for a telephone book. We need to find a listing for hair designers and get you to a salon pronto."

I watched the clerk disappear down the hall and heard a creak of hinges as he opened a door. I eyed Jackie skeptically. "Shouldn't 'telephone book' have the word 'telephone' in it someplace?"

" 'Phonebook' is an idiom."

"So?"

"So Italian idioms don't sound anything like what they mean. Just relax. I have the situation under control."

No cause to worry there.

A moment later the desk clerk rounded the corner by the staircase and with a churlish look on his face handed Jackie a bed pillow.

I rolled my eyes. Obviously, not the right idiom. "Tell you what." I dug my key out of the pocket of my shoulder bag. "It looks like you might be a while down here, so I'm going up to my room, and when you're done, give me a holler. Okay?"

Jackie stared at the pillow. "But *cuscino* is the right word. I know it is."

I trudged up the stairs, brightening a little when I saw the heap of clothing piled in front of my door. All right! Did I know how to get results, or what? I unlocked the door and shoved it open an inch, then hunkered down and scooped my clothes off the floor. My black silk cardigan. My rosebud dress with the ruffled hem. My lemon yellow sundress with the thin shoulder straps. Capri pants. Blouses. Looked like a pretty good haul! Straightening up, I shoved the door wide with my hip and—

"Hi, Em."

"EHHH!" I spun around to find my mother propped up

on my bed, surrounded by orderly piles of paper, a modest stack in her lap. "Mom!" I screamed, my heart in my mouth. "What are doing in here?"

"You've been shopping," she announced, marking the clothes in my arms. "But it would have been nice if they'd given you sacks for your purchases. Looks like you bought quite a bit."

"*How* did you get in here? The door was locked!"

"The light's so bad in my room, Emily. I was about to go cross-eyed reading all these manuscripts. So I went down to the front desk to ask if I could borrow your key to see if the light in your room was any better, and no one was there, so I wiggled your key off its hook and let myself in. And I'm so glad I did. The light really *is* much better in here. I hope you don't mind."

"You wiggled my key off its hook?" I dumped my clothes onto the bed.

"It's not very hard. All the keys are hanging on the wall right there in the open by the front desk."

It certainly made me feel secure knowing that if the front desk was unmanned, our rooms would be accessible to anyone.

Mom wrinkled her nose. "My goodness. What's that awful smell?"

"Me," I said, dragging myself around to her side of the bed. I sat on the edge and twisted around so she could see the back of my head. "I had a run-in with a Zippo lighter. Other than smelling awful, does it look really bad?"

"Tilt your head back a little, Emily. That's good. Oh my!" I heard a little intake of breath. "Well, to tell you the truth, it burned in a real pretty pattern. Kind of like one of those English crop circles. And the ends of your hair have an attractive crinkle to them now. Much prettier than the split ends you sometimes get. And I bet if you pin your hair up in a French twist, no one will ever notice that semi-bald streak down the center of your head. It's nice the sides are still long. If you could only do something about the smell. Maybe room deodorizer would help."

I patted the back of my hair for the first time, my hand freezing in place when it grazed a patch of roughened bristles where corkscrew curls used to be. "Oh, God."

"It looks far better than the hairdo your grandmother came home with from Ireland."

Which wasn't saying much. Poor Nana still looked like a denuded rabbit, and she'd been cut and styled by a pro.

"How did this happen?" Mom asked, giving me a motherly pat on the back.

So I told her the whole story about the incident at the leather market and when I was done, she shook her head and offered me a grim smile. "You've started smoking, haven't you?"

"No! That's the truth! I even have a witness!"

"Accidents like that don't happen in real life, Emily."

"They do to me!"

"Really, hon, maybe you should put the escort business on hold and try something else. You were always good in English, and you have your grandmother's beautiful penmanship. Maybe you could write a novel. I'd have an easier time reading a manuscript handwritten by you than by the person I'm reading now. I think it must be a doctor. Tell me, does this sound right to you?" She pushed her glasses higher up on her nose and angled the paper in her lap toward the bedside light. " 'She gently caressed his cork with her lily white hard.' 'Hard' could be 'hand,' but I don't know where the cork comes in. They weren't even drinking wine."

Euw boy. I returned to the other bed and began sorting through my clothes. "Maybe she caressed his 'coat.' "

"Coat?" She chewed on that for a while. "Hunh. Coat might work, but this person really needs help with syntax."

"So how are the entries looking?" I asked as I noticed a huge coffee stain on my yellow sundress. Damn!

"These are the ones I've read," she said, sweeping her hand over the neat piles on the bed. "There are entry numbers instead of names on them, so I've arranged them alphabetically by title to keep them in order. And I have to give these people credit, Em. Some of them are really talented. And their stories are so original."

I inspected my rosebud sheath to find the zipper slide off the track and the tape pulled away from the fabric. Keely had obviously been in a huge hurry to get out of it, but how was I supposed to wear it with a broken zipper?

"There's one about a pirate who kidnaps a headstrong Irish girl off a sailing ship and takes her to his pirates' den in the Caribbean, where they eventually fall in love. And one about an Indian who kidnaps a headstrong Irish girl off a wagon train and takes her to his village on the plain, where they eventually fall in love. And one about a highwayman who kidnaps a headstrong Irish girl from her carriage on the moors and takes her to his cottage in Cornwall, where they eventually fall in love."

I examined tops, pants, cardigans, and dresses to find jam stains, split seams, cigarette holes, lipstick stains, missing buttons, and broken snaps. How could they have been so careless? I couldn't wear anything now! I dug through the pile again. Where was my one-shoulder sweaterdress with the leather shoulder strap?

"And this one's *really* original, Em. It's about a Montana cowboy who kidnaps a young woman from her best friend's wedding ceremony and takes her to his cabin in the Rockies! Isn't that different?"

I threw her a confused look as I tossed my stuff right

and left in search of my coral sweaterdress. "I don't think I get what's so different. Is this one where they don't fall in love at the end?"

"Of course they fall in love, Emily. But she's not a headstrong Irish girl. She's Lithuanian!"

No sweaterdress. Unh. I pouted in complete despair at the clothes on the bed.

"You could do something like this, Em." Mom waved a page at me. "I know you could. Have you ever dreamed of writing a book?"

I sank down on the bed. I dreamed about Etienne . . . and obscenely large body parts. "Can't say that I have."

She clutched the page to her chest, looking suddenly nostalgic. "I probably never told you this, but when I was younger, I dreamed of becoming a stewardess. There was nothing I wanted more than to fly the friendly skies in a stylish little uniform and matching cap."

Mom had wanted to be a flight attendant? Serving peanuts and beverages to people? Showing them how to fasten their seat belts? Instructing them what to do should the plane lose cabin pressure? Who knew? But her revelation gave me pause. I guess I'd never really looked at Mom as being anyone other than my mom. "So why didn't you follow your dream?"

I caught a twinkle in her eye behind her wire-rims. "Because I was kidnapped from St. Kate's College by a strapping man on a John Deere tractor and carried off to his grain farm in Iowa, where we fell in love."

Aw, life imitating art. That was so sweet! Despite my depression, I felt my mouth curve into a smile.

"You know who else wanted to fly the skies years ago?" Mom continued. "The Severid twins. Britha told me when we were shelving aviation books at the library one afternoon. That would have been the six hundred section, located in the northeast corner of the building by the restrooms."

"They wanted to travel the world?" I asked, testing the back of my head again in the hopes that my hair had miraculously grown back. "But they've hardly set foot outside Windsor City their entire lives."

Mom shrugged. "Britha said her father didn't want them parading around in those skimpy uniforms or demeaning themselves by serving demon liquor, so they never got to go. But Barbro did the next best thing. She wrote a book about the romantic adventures of a stewardess from a little town in the Midwest. She was even thinking of turning it into a continuing series. Can you picture Barbro writing a book like that?"

I'll say. Love and romance written by a woman who'd probably never dated a man in her life.

"What an imagination she must have, Emily. Think about it. She wrote that entire book without ever having set foot on an airplane!"

I stared at Mom for a long, numbing moment. Mmm, okay.

"Too bad it never got published, but writing it made Barbro realize she really liked tinkering with words, so her greeting card career grew out of the whole experience. She's made a wonderful contribution to the industry. Did you know she was the first person to pen the rhyme, 'Roses are red, violets are blue'? And once, when she had writer's block, she even came up with, 'Have a nice day.' I don't know how she does it."

Me either, but I wish she'd stop. I gave Mom a hard look. "Have you been outside the hotel today?"

"Not yet. With all this work who has time to sightsee?"

Iowans were so responsible. Even the ones like Mom, who'd been born and raised in Minnesota.

Knock knock knock.

Had to be Jackie. I crossed the room to let her in.

"I found the perfect salon," she announced, when I opened the door. "It's not too far from the Duomo and according to the ad, they specialize in damaged hair. It's called 'Donatella.' Sounds pretty upscale, hunh? Hey, you got some of your clothes back!" She wandered into the room. "Oh, hi, Mrs. Andrew. I didn't know you were in here."

Mom fixed Jackie with a vacuous stare. I'd explained about Jack's transformation into Jackie before the trip, but so far the only kind of communication she could manage with the female version of Jack was blank stares . . . and a brief comment on the plane about how pretty Jackie's outfit was. But this was fairly typical. Even at her most freaked out and confused, Mom was always complimentary. She lifted her hand toward Jackie in an awkward greeting. "Lovely outfit you're wearing."

"Not for long. I bought some new threads, and I'm going to jump into them right after we get Emily's hair fixed. Hey, Em, you mind if I leave my bags here and pick them up when we get back?"

"No problem." But there *was* a problem I still needed to address, and it suddenly became clear how I might resolve it—much to my dismay. But what the heck, I didn't have any big plans for the evening anyway. "Say, Mom, why don't you spend the night in here with me? We can have a sleepover."

"A sleepover? Why, Emily, that's so thoughtful of you. I haven't thought of sleepovers for years. Remember the ones you used to have when you were a girl?"

Jackie rolled her eyes. "I hope they were more fun than the one we had in Ireland."

Mom sighed with disappointment. "I'd love to, Emily,

but I really can't. I need to take care of your grandmother."

"Mom! She doesn't need taking care of! She has a white belt in Tae Kwon Do!"

"That doesn't matter. She's my mother, and I can't expect George to keep her company indefinitely. Especially with her hearing loss. He was a saint to take up the slack for me today, but enough is enough. George Farkas didn't come on this trip to babysit your grandmother."

I smiled. At least she got that part right. "Well, here's the thing, Mom. I need to spend the evening mending and treating the stains on that stack of clothes on the bed, and it would go a lot quicker if I had your help."

"Stains on your clothes? My goodness, Em, what did you do? Buy them at a resale shop? That's not like you at all."

I could go through the whole long explanation, but what was the point? Much as I'd like to blame someone for my clothes fiasco, I really couldn't fault Mom. As always, she'd only been trying to help.

"I'd be delighted to give you a hand, Em." Mom's face split into a smile as wide as an octave on a piano. "In fact, I'd be *thrilled* to help you. I even have a little sewing kit. But do you think George would feel I was taking advantage of him if I asked him to keep your grandmother company again this evening?"

Oh, yeah. Nana was going to owe me bigtime.

"Bless you, Emily. When I die, you're gettin' all my money," Nana vowed fifteen minutes later. "You've earned all eight million."

"I thought it was seven million."

"Bull market, dear. My investments are all on an earnin' streak."

We were standing at the northwest corner of the eight-

sided baptistry that fronted the Duomo, trying to hold our
own against the hordes of tourists who swarmed the
square. Jackie and I had wended our way down some side
streets and along the Borgo San Lorenzo to discover that it
was impossible to get lost in Florence by day, because if
you were headed anywhere near the Duomo, all you had to
do was look up, and there it was. We'd spotted Nana on the
fringe of the baptistry crowd, taking pictures of all the
activity, so we'd crossed the street to join her, which is
when I'd made her day with the news about my pre-
arranged sleepover with Mom.

"Don't know how you ever spotted me in this crowd,"
Nana said as she coddled a stack of Polaroids in her hand.

"Radar," I teased, and the fact that she was the only person in Florence wearing Minnesota Vikings wind pants
and a pink teddy bear top.

"Did you get some good shots of the baptistry, Mrs. S.?"
Jackie held her hand out to indicate she'd like to see the
photos. "The tour book said the building is at least seven-
teen hundred years old. Can you believe it? I mean, that's
older than the Empire State Building!"

I threw her a bewildered look. Thank God we'd never
had children.

Nana lifted her chin and sniffed. "Do you smell somethin', Emily?" Grabbing on to my arm, she checked the bottoms of her sneakers. "I hope I didn't step in nothin'. These
are the only shoes I got left."

Jackie shuffled through the photos. "I guess unbaptized
people weren't allowed to enter a church way back when,
so the congregation had to construct a whole other building for the sole purpose of baptizing babies so they could
enter the real church." She looked suddenly perplexed.
"You don't have any pictures of the baptistry here, Mrs. S."

"I know, dear," she said, rubbing her nose, "but I got

some dandy shots a the crowd. Only time Windsor City gets a turnout like this is for the Hog Days Festival and parade."

"Where's George?" I asked, scanning the crowd in search of his seed-corn hat.

She nodded toward the baptistry. "He's just north, takin' pictures a the door some fella spent twenty-somethin' years makin'. Too bad he couldn't a gone prefab. Woulda saved a whole bunch a time."

"Well, well, well. Would you look at this." Jackie handed me one of Nana's photos.

I perused the glossy photo, surprised to find three familiar faces staring back at me. But the picture could have been better. Brandy Ann's hair looked washed out in the sunlight, and Fred's safari hat cast a dark shadow over his face. The only thing that had photographed well was the bolt in Amanda's nose. Funny about Fred though. After his remarks in the open-air market, I didn't think he'd be cozying up to Brandy Ann and Amanda anytime soon. I held the photo up for Nana. She squinted at the image.

"That's the girl with the rugged sinuses," Nana said in a whisper. "Amanda. She was real good about lettin' me take her picture. They'll never believe this back at the Legion a Mary. I bet knowin' a girl with a can opener in her nose will be way better than knowin' a guy who used to live in a closet."

"How long ago did you shoot this?" I asked.

"Five, ten minutes."

"Can I see that again?" asked Jackie, removing the photo from my hand. She studied it briefly. "Aha! If you concentrate on the foreground, you can miss things in the background. You want to know what my roommate looks like, Emily? Here you go." She handed the photo back. "She's the busty blonde Gabriel Fox has his arm draped around in the far right corner there. Our Mr. Fox doesn't waste any time with the ladies."

"He hit on your roommate?" I checked out the blonde, my eyes focusing on the slightly grainy image. "SHE'S WEARING MY CORAL SWEATERDRESS WITH THE LEATHER SHOULDER STRAP!"

"Euw, that's yours?" Jackie took another peek. "Nice color. Where'd you get it? Catalogue? Is the scarf yours, too?"

"What scarf?"

She poked the photo with her fingernail. "Fox's arm isn't the only thing draped around Jeannette's neck. See? There's a scarf trailing down the front of her dress. Frankly, I don't think the neckline of the dress calls for a scarf. She might know a lot about food, but she obviously doesn't know diddly about accessorizing."

I went up on my tiptoes, searching the crowd. "I wonder which way everyone went?"

"Amanda and them was headin' for that famous museum over by that famous plaza with all them famous statues, but I told them how I'd just read this mornin' you might have to wait in a long line if you don't have no advance tickets. They decided to climb to the top a the Domo instead, though the man with the hat said he didn't much like heights."

I looked at Jackie. Jackie looked at me. "I guess maybe I should keep an eye on them," she said, handing all the photos back to Nana. "But I still think it would work better if I had a disguise. Oh, *God,* this is exciting." As she bounded through the crowd, she turned around and yelled back at me, "Meet you at the hairdresser's in a couple of hours or so!"

Nana waved her photos at Jackie in farewell, then to me, "She's very tall, isn't she, dear?"

I tugged on the cloth sack hanging from her arm. "Been shopping?"

"You bet." Eyes gleaming, she sidled a surreptitious look over each shoulder, then opened the sack just wide enough for me to spy a big wad of black leather.

"What is it?" I whispered. "Slingshot?" My nephews would love it. My sister-in-law would kill her.

"Undies," she said.

My eyebrows shot to the top of my head. "For you?"

"For George. I found 'em at the leather market. The fella in the stall tried to sell me a nice leather thong like the one your young man had on last month, but I knew George would balk at that."

"Too racy?"

"Too flimsy. George needs extra support." She pulled a pair of what looked like Bavarian lederhosen out of the sack. "So I got him boxers."

I squirmed my way through the foot traffic clogging the piazza, circled around the north side of the Duomo with its gleaming pink, white, and green marble, and found the hair salon located in a pristine limestone building with brown-shuttered windows, decorative stone medallions, and window boxes hanging from wrought-iron balcony grills. Before opening the polished wood door, I gazed upward at the monstrous Duomo, wondering why Fred would agree to climb to the top if he was afraid of heights. Talk about being a glutton for punishment. And why make the climb with Brandy Ann and Amanda if they'd hurt his feelings so badly?

Something had happened to get them together. Maybe they'd kissed and made up. But in light of my suspicions about Brandy Ann and Amanda, I hoped Jackie watched Fred closely. I'd hate for anything to happen to the poor little guy. He just seemed so . . . helpless. Or maybe a better word was, hopeless.

However, speaking of kissing . . .

I retrieved my phone, punched in a number, and waited.

"Miceli."

"I'm sorry we were cut off, too."

A pause. "Ahhh, Emily. I miss you."

"I think we need to remedy that. Where are you? The casino?"

"I'm at my great-aunt's. They've lit all ninety candles on her birthday cake and she's methodically blowing each one out, which could take a while. She's been a two-pack-a-day smoker for seventy-five years."

Gee, if the party was winding down— "I have an idea. When the party's over, you could hop a train and tell me how much you miss me in person."

"The next time I see you, darling, I'll be doing more to your person than just telling you I miss you."

Euw, I liked the sound of that. "Would tomorrow be too soon? I don't necessarily have to visit Pisa." I stared at my reflection in the window of the salon. "But I should warn you. The next time you see me, I might look a little . . . different."

Another pause. "Different can be good." He breathed heavily into the phone. "Different . . . how?"

Bless his little Swiss heart. He was trying so hard to be open-minded. "I'm hoping it'll be a pleasant surprise." To both of us.

"And I hope you don't mind, Emily, but I've assured the entire family that they'll have an opportunity to meet you very soon. They tell me I made the same promise before leaving for Ireland last month and that I vowed to return home with surprising news, but my mind is a little fuzzy on what the surprise was supposed to be. Did I give you any indication about a surprise?"

Okay, this was encouraging. "You did mention something about a *question* you wanted to ask me."

I heard a frustrated sigh from his end. "It's not much to go on, but I'm a police inspector. I've solved crimes with less information than that. Perhaps—Damn!" Shouting. Scuffling. Then in a rush of breath, "I need to go. My aunt was too slow. The tablecloth is on fire. Someone grab the water pitcher! Love you." Click.

"Hello, pretty."

With the phone still pressed to my ear, I turned around to find Duncan giving me an odd look. "What happened?" he asked, touching his hand to my hair.

I smiled self-consciously. "An encounter with a Zippo lighter. The lighter won."

"Ouch." He winced before mustering an optimistic grin. "But you've come to the right place. Donatella cuts my hair. She's a genius. You wouldn't believe what I looked like before she got her hands on me. Cowlicks. Split ends. Sun damage. People mistook me for Don King."

"You're just saying that," I accused, disbelieving that his stunning mane of hair could ever have been anything other than gorgeous.

"Scout's honor. No worries. She'll make you beautiful." His eyes did that lingering thing again. "Or should I say . . . more beautiful."

Unh-oh. Okay, moving right along— "Would you be able to switch Jackie Thum to another room?" I was all business again. "She seems to have a personality conflict with her present roommate."

"Jackie Thum." He pinched his eyes shut, plucking data from behind his lids. "Her roommate is Jeannette Bowles. Food critic. Burlington, Vermont. She's won a truckload of writing awards and listed every single one on her travel form—in the Medical History section. I guess you have space for that if you're healthy."

Another award winner? I bet Keely wouldn't be too happy if she found out about that.

"Since Jackie's part of your group, I could move her into your room."

I thought about Jackie. I thought about Mom. I thought about the two of them in the same room for eight hours or more. I broke out in a cold sweat. "Um . . ."

"Or I could put her in with Keely."

Gum snapping. Bubble blowing. Incessant chatter. Endless self-promotion. "That would work." Okay, so maybe I still had unresolved issues from when Jack walked out on me when we were married. I'll admit it. I'm human.

"Problem solved." Duncan opened the salon door and, with an encouraging arm around my shoulder, ushered me inside. "I have a couple of minutes, Em. Come on in. I'll introduce you."

Two and a half hours later, I exited the salon with hair that was shiny, sassy, and short. It framed my face. It hugged my neck. The style would look good wet, dry, or mussed, with or without gel, mousse, or pliable styling paste. She'd added color that enhanced the richness of my natural shade. I didn't feel like Emily Andrew, Iowa tour escort, anymore. I felt like Emily Andrew, Italian sexpot. Sultry. Steamy. Voluptuous. Broke.

It was damned expensive transforming into an Italian sexpot.

Click clack click clack click clack.

"Wow! Would you look at you?" Jackie shouted as she hurried in my direction.

I spun in place so she could get the whole 360-degree view.

"I love it. I absolutely love it. Turn around so I can see the back again. This is *so* you, Emily. It's perky. Stylish. Avant garde. I told you you needed to update the old frizzy curls. Don't you think it's you? Don't you love it?" She ruffled the top of my hair with her fingers. "Okay, Tom would insist that I ask. How much?"

"A million lire."

Her hand froze in midair. "Five hundred dollars? Girl, you got robbed."

"Yeah, but I don't smell like raw sewage anymore. What about Brandy Ann and those guys. Did you find them?"

"Did I ever. I spotted them in line at the side entrance of the church, so I played it real cool and spied on them from behind a parked car. And guess who else I spotted standing at the front of the line."

I shrugged.

"Gabriel Fox, my roommate, and our friend, Keely."

I frowned, suddenly bothered by Keely's proximity to the award-winning Jeannette Bowles. "Odd combination. But Keely is sucking up to everyone, so I shouldn't be surprised. So what happened at the top of the Duomo? Were there any words exchanged when Keely ran into Brandy Ann and Amanda? How was Fred holding up? Did he look like he was having a good time?"

"How would I know that?"

I waited a beat, steadying my gaze on her. "Didn't you follow them to the top?"

"Climb those stairs again?" She howled with laughter. "What are you? Crazy? Do you have any idea how hot that stairwell is right now? This late in the afternoon, everyone coming out of that place is gonna be dying from heat exhaustion."

I stared at her, deadpan. I wondered if this would be a good time to tell her who her new roommate was going to be. "Okay, Jack. Here's the thing. When you say you're going to tail someone? YOU ACTUALLY HAVE TO FOLLOW THEM!"

"Hey, I did my part! I stood over by that car in the hot sun, waiting for them to come down."

"And?"

She lifted her shoulders. "And people had to be crawling up and down those stairs because I never saw any of them come out." She curled her lip in distaste. "No offense, Emily, but this surveillance business isn't as exciting as I thought it would be. In fact, it's pretty boring. I'd much rather—"

"EEEEEEEHHHHHHHHHHHHH!"

A woman's scream. Loud. Shrill. Terrified.

"EEEEEEEHHHHHHHHHHHHH!"

"Where's it coming from?" Jackie cried.

I turned in a circle, listening. "I can't tell. It's bouncing all over the place." But the horror of the sound was undeniable, causing the down on my arms to stand on end. I saw a man race toward the back end of the Duomo, followed by another man, and another. Curiosity seekers hotfooted past us—a few stragglers that swelled into a sudden crowd. I looked at Jackie; Jackie looked me—the obvious remaining unspoken between us.

That scream could belong to anyone, including any of my group of Iowans.

We hurried down the sidewalk, following the crowd toward the east end of the church.

"EEEEEEEHHHHHHHHHHHHH!"

The crowd stampeded across the street and followed the fenced barrier around the back end of the Duomo. We ran past a massive hexagonal pod that bulged outward from the structure, and after rounding a second one, caught sight of a mound of colorful fabric abandoned on the pavement near the base of the church, in the narrow bay between the south and east pods.

Men stared upward, pointing to the top of the Duomo. Women cupped their hands over their mouths, eyes wide with shock. Mothers scooped up their children and hugged their small heads to their chests, shielding their eyes.

"Oh, my God!" Jackie gasped behind me.

I looked toward the abandoned fabric again, my legs growing suddenly wobbly. I was close enough now to see that the fabric wasn't a random assortment of cloth. It was a one-shouldered coral sweaterdress with a decorative leather shoulder strap, but it had looked better on Jeannette Bowles when she'd been alive.

"That's my roommate!" Jackie cried.

I stared at the dead body, my stomach juices turning sour.

I guessed Jackie wouldn't be moving in with Keely after all.

CHAPTER 8

"No one actually saw her fall," Duncan informed us the next morning on our way to Pisa. "Unfortunately, most of the people on the gallery were congregated around a man who'd collapsed from apparent heat exhaustion, so while they were administering to him, Ms. Bowles, regrettably, fell to her death."

"That could have been me," Jackie whispered beside me.

"Jeannette?"

She gave me a narrow look before covering up a yawn. "The guy suffering from heat exhaustion. Now, aren't you glad I had sense enough not to climb those stairs again?"

"Rough night?" I asked, when she yawned a second time.

"My sleep cycle is really messed up."

Mine was improving. Surprisingly, I'd slept pretty well after Mom had helped me mend my clothes last night, so I was feeling good today. I was feeling *especially* good that I was out of my Laura Ashley dress and into a pair of white capri pants with a black-cropped U-neck. Yes!

"The authorities are still investigating whether the death was accidental or deliberate," Duncan continued over the loudspeaker.

"Have they ruled out suicide?" someone asked.

"The police captain I spoke with informed me that it's rare for tourists to commit suicide while on holiday, especially if their plans involve leaping from a tall building. Historically speaking, people usually do that at home."

Unless they're from Iowa, where the local architecture pretty much eliminates that option completely.

"So what do the police think happened?" Dick Teig called out.

"They're not clear about what happened," Duncan replied. "And they're frustrated that by the time they arrived on the scene yesterday, people who might have been potential witnesses had already descended the stairs and exited the cathedral. They did round up some stragglers in the stairwell to question them, but from all accounts, no one saw much of anything."

"I'd like to say a few words if I may," Gabriel Fox said, rising from his seat in the front. He turned, facing the rear of the bus. "Jeannette and I had an opportunity to chat at length yesterday while we were in the queue at the cathedral."

Not to mention while he was wrapped around her outside the baptistry.

"For those of you who didn't know her, I would characterize her as a confident, well-spoken woman with an insatiable appetite for good food and an award-winning talent for writing about it. Her reviews appeared in the cuisine section of national newspapers and travel magazines, and if she said the lobster thermidor at the Mount Washington Hotel was unsurpassed for flavor and texture, you knew to order it. Her awards included"—he slid his hand into his pants pocket—"just a minute. She gave me a list. Let's see. The Julia Childs Food Review Award. *Yankee Magazine* Award for Culinary Excellence. The *Washington Post*'s Reviewers Choice Award. The Vermont Romance Writers Sexiest Cowboy Award."

She'd been writing about a cowboy? Hmm. I guess Gillian Jones couldn't expect to corner the cowboy market forever.

"The New England Romance Authors Spiciest Love Scene Award. The list goes on and on." Gabriel returned the paper to his pocket. "Her passion for critiquing food was surpassed only by her passion for hiking dangerous mountain trails, spelunking, and wanting to write the quintessential love story. Unfortunately, we'll never know how popular she might have become as a romance author. Her tragic death touches us all, so would you please join me in a moment of silence to commemorate the loss of fellow traveler and aspiring romance writer, Jeannette Bowles."

When the moment was up, Duncan nodded thanks to Gabriel before addressing us again. "Ms. Bowles was single and had no immediate family. We're having trouble locating her contact person, so we're in limbo until we can make the connection, which, in the long run, might not be a bad thing. The Florence police aren't likely to release her body until they determine a cause of death, and it could take them dozens of man-hours to look over all those videotapes."

"What videotapes?" Fred called out from the seat across the aisle.

"I suspect those of you who climbed to the top of the Duomo never noticed, but for insurance purposes, there are several security cameras mounted inconspicuously on the cupola. Even in Florence, Big Brother is watching. I imagine in a case like this, though, having a visual diary of the activity on the gallery will be even better than having an eyewitness."

"Everything that happened on the gallery is on tape?" Fred asked in a brittle voice.

"Just like downtown London," Duncan answered smoothly. "Or Disney World."

But Fred didn't seem to find that comforting. He looked suddenly agitated. And a little gray.

"I cautioned you yesterday about the stairs in the hotel," Duncan continued, "and in light of this second accident, I'm going to caution you again. Please. Everyone. Be mindful of every step you take, no matter where you are, or how safe you think it is. And be especially cautious in Pisa around the Leaning Tower because it's known as a haven for pickpockets and purse snatchers. To reiterate our schedule, when we arrive in Pisa, we'll be meeting a local guide, who'll conduct the tour of the buildings in the area. That should take a couple of hours. Afterward you'll be on your own to eat lunch and shop until we head back to Florence at four. I'll ask you all to be aware of the time and be as prompt as possible returning to the bus, which will pick us up where it drops us off, so make a note of where that is. Landmark is treating you all to dinner this evening at the elegant La Taverna del Bronzino, and our reservation is for seven-thirty sharp, so we don't want to be late."

Oohs. Aahs. Titters of excitement.

"Any questions?"

I had plenty, but they had nothing to do with our schedule.

A quick hour and a half later, I found myself in the city of Pisa, gaping at four marble buildings so brilliantly white, I feared staring at them in direct sunlight might cause permanent blindness. They sat perched on a long span of lawn as manicured as stadium grass, with the famed Leaning Tower spiraling upward to my far right, looking like a fancy grain silo knocked off kilter by a gale force wind. We were on a walkway that fronted a huge cathedral, huddled around an attractive middle-aged woman who spoke heavily accented English. "My name is Giovanna, and I be happy to be your guide today."

I stood on the outer fringe of the group, close enough to keep tabs on the handful of guests who'd had access to Jeannette right before she died, but far enough away so as not to be obvious. One accidental death on tour was suspicious enough, but two had raised enough red flags in my mind to cause major clutter. I'd been through this before. Twice. And I knew that anything mimicking an accident usually wasn't. If there was death involved, it was always deliberate. In my book, there *was* no such thing as an accident on tour.

"You suppose they have a restroom somewhere around here?" Jackie asked, dragging herself up behind me.

"You could wait for the question-and-answer period and ask the guide."

"Nah. That'd probably start a stampede." She shifted a cloth sack she was carrying from her hand to her shoulder.

"What's in the sack?" I asked.

She flashed me a coy smile. "Just stuff."

"I take you tru two buildings on duh Campo dei Miracoli—duh Field of Miracles—dis morning," Giovanna announced, indicating the expanse of lawn to our left. "Duh catedral behind me was begun in ten sixty-tree and fuses to-gayder Roman, Islamic, and Byzantine architecture. It is very particular. And like our fay-mous bell tower, it also tilts, but not so much. Duh building, it's so much bee-ger."

But for her *teensy* problem pronouncing "th," Giovanna showed great command of the English laguage.

"How come the buildings are lopsided?" Dick Teig threw out.

"The subsoil, it's made of sand. No good for building. And duh founday-tions are shallow. So duh buildings, dey lean. Duh bell tower was begun in eleven seventy-tree, and a hundreyd years later, even before duh tird story was complete, it began to tilt sideways. Duh architects and engineers warn us for six hundreyd fifty years dat duh tower will collapse, but duh tower, it still stands, and is very suggestive. You follow me now and I give you more history of duh Torre Pendente."

The tour group moved en masse down the pathway to the tower, guided by the upward thrust of Duncan's striped umbrella. Brandy Ann and Amanda were slightly ahead of me and when the crowd around them thinned, I scooted up beside them.

"Hi, guys. How's the writing going?" I figured that was a much more benign opening than, "How very curious that you were at the top of the Duomo yesterday when Jeannette Bowles fell to her death."

Brandy Ann glanced at me, her expression not exactly mirroring delight. "The writing's coming along. We helped each other tie up some loose ends yesterday, finished up our proposals last night, and dropped them into the box in the lobby this morning. So it's over except for the waiting."

I wondered if "tying up loose ends" could be a metaphor for "knocking off the competition." "You two are really fast. Sounds like rooming together worked out pretty well for you."

"Yeah," said Brandy Ann in a tight voice. "It was unfortunate about Cassandra, but what are you going to do? We had to make the most of it."

"We were lucky to get *any* writing done yesterday though," Amanda complained. "We were taking the stairs back down from the top of the Duomo yesterday afternoon when that Bowles woman fell, so we got stopped by the police for questioning when we reached the bottom. We both remembered seeing her on the gallery because she was with that snot, Keely, but neither one of us spoke to her. The police were insistent that we had to know more, though, so the questioning went on forever. I was afraid they were going to haul us to the police station for more interrogation, but they finally let us go."

"After taking our names, local address, and passport numbers," Brandy Ann added. "I mean, what was the point? We had to have been halfway down the stairs when she took her leap. How could we have affected anything? Telekinesis?"

"Hey!" Amanda snapped her fingers. "That might make a good story. The first parapsychological romance. Could be groundbreaking."

"Where was Fred?" I asked. "Didn't he climb to the top with you?"

"Fred is such a dweeb." Amanda gave her nose a dangerous rub. I held my breath, hoping she wouldn't need stitches afterward. "He has like . . . no self-esteem. We found him moping around the baptistry, so we asked him if he wanted to join us, and he thought that might be okay, but first, we had to apologize to him for taking off without him yesterday morning. The guy is such a loser. I can't believe he knows the first thing about writing a romance."

I shrugged. "I thought that's why he signed up for the trip. To learn from the experts."

"Well, he's not going to learn anything, is he?" said Brandy Ann. "Not with everyone's lecture notes going up in smoke. He was all over us for pointers yesterday, but it was way too hot on those stairs to talk shop."

"So where was he when Jeannette fell?" I asked.

Brandy Ann pumped her arm unconsciously, giving her biceps a practiced caress. "He wanted to stay a little longer up on the gallery, so Amanda and I headed down before him. Kind of surprised me that he wanted to stay longer. He has a thing about heights."

So Fred had stayed behind? Hmm.

Amanda stopped suddenly, looking me up and down. "There's something different about you today, but I can't figure out what."

Oh, boy. People were noticing! I primped my freshly shorn locks. "I got my hair cut."

She studied my shiny new coif. "Nah. That's not it."

"Have any of you seen restroom signs?" Jackie asked, pulling up behind us as we rounded a wing of the cathedral.

Up ahead, the umbrella stopped moving, and those of us at the rear of the pack slowed our pace, spreading out along the paved terrace at the front of the cathedral. Fifty feet in front of us stood the Leaning Tower, in all its crooked glory. "Duh tower took one hundreyd seventy-seven years to build," Giovanna shouted out to us. "In tirteen fifty, it leaned one-point-four meters off vertical. In nineteen ninety-tree, it was leaning *five*-point-four meters off vertical."

Wow. Five meters off vertical. I imagined the statistic would be even more impressive if I knew how long a meter was.

"If you need a restroom, I think it's over that way," Amanda whispered to Jackie, indicating a long butterscotch-colored building north of the cathedral. "Duncan pointed it out on our way in."

With a nod to me, Jackie pattered off, her latex-soled

sandals barely making a sound on the stone terrace. Poor Jackie. Her feet must be really sore to be wearing flats today, especially since heels would have looked much better with her new trumpet-skirted sundress. Or maybe it was a question of balance. Considering her insomnia last night, she might have fallen off her stilettos.

"Duh tower was closed to duh public in January of nineteen ninety," Giovanna continued. "But duh engineers work hard to correct duh tilt, so it will reopen agayn next year, in Deceymber, a full tirty-eight centimeters straighter."

I wondered how much that was. A couple of inches or something? I angled my head to the pitch of the tower, then slowly returned to vertical. I appreciated the problem that the tower might be in imminent danger of collapsing, but I wondered if anyone had stopped to consider the economic disaster that would occur if the engineers got too successful. I mean, who was going to slap down money to see the Lineal Tower of Pisa?

Chirrup chirrup. Chirrup chirrup.

Hurrying away from the group, I snatched my phone from my shoulder bag. "Hello?"

"*Buon giorno, mi amore,*" Etienne said in his beautiful French/German/Italian accent. Unh, I *loved* it when he whispered Italian to me. Made my toes curl like a fresh perm.

"A friend in the department owed me a favor, so I have the information you asked for."

"Great!" I scurried to the farthest end of the terrace to be out of hearing range of Giovanna's narration. "Okay, shoot."

"Brandy Ann Frounfelker. We found no listing for occupation other than bodybuilder. Monthy income is zero. I believe bodybuilders earn income by winning regional and national contests, and she hasn't won any recently. She seems to be living off five credit cards and pays the minimum balance each month out of savings. She's behind on rent, utilities, telephone, car payments, and gym membership, and is only a half step ahead of the bill collectors. No criminal background."

"Okay." Soft voice. Big muscles. No financial expertise.

"Amanda Morning. She works as a dance instructor and recently applied for a bank loan, but her income was too low to cover the size of the loan, so her application was rejected."

"What did she want the loan for?" I slanted a look to my left to find Giovanna cutting a path through the center of the group and making wide gestures toward the arched colonnades of the cathedral.

"She wanted to open a—" He paused as if double-checking his notes. "It says here a tattoo and body-piercing parlor. Can that be right?"

"Afraid so."

"Criminal record. Let's see. She received a ticket for jay-walking in California three years ago and never paid it. No other violations."

In the background I watched Giovanna motion the group to follow her toward the cathedral.

"And finally, Keely Mack."

I watched the activity on the terrace as people marched toward the entrance of the cathedral, but surprisingly, Nana and George lagged behind, asking one of the Severid twins to snap a picture of them against the backdrop of the tower. Aw, how cute. Boy, Nana was growing mellow! Any other time she'd be sprinting to the front of the line to be first inside. Then again, maybe it wasn't so much her growing mellow as it was George's inability to walk faster than a shuffle with his ailing back.

"Ms. Mack is the manager of a Mr. Bulky candy store," Etienne continued.

I guess that explained the endless supply of bubble gum. I saw Marla Michaels shoot a quick picture of the tower and suspected she must have been shopping at the street market because she was carrying a shoulder bag that I know I'd seen in one of the stalls yesterday. It was oversized, triangular, and made of delicious purple leather that I swore I could smell from here.

"She earns a decent wage, pays all her bills on time, owns her car outright, attends weekly church services, and she's never had so much as a parking ticket. She appears to be something of a paragon."

How come it was always the obnoxious ones who were the bastions of virtue?

"She even operates an online critique service that supposedly helps would-be romance writers perfect their first chapter. Did you know she's won every regional first chapter contest in the nation?"

I rolled my eyes.

"It's a fee-for-service operation, and it looks as though she's raised her prices recently to keep pace with declining subscriptions. I'm no prognosticator, but I suspect if she doesn't find some way to boost her client base, she'll have to close up shop. Perhaps if she had more impressive literary credentials."

Credentials like having a published novel under her belt? *Uff da!* It looked to me as if *everyone* was suspect. Including someone whose safari hat was nowhere in sight and a man who had the potential of making Casanova look like a wallflower. "Could I ask another favor?"

"Anything, *bella*."

I felt a little fluttery sensation arrow downward from my navel. I gave him two more names. "Find out whatever you can about them. Dig as deeply as you can."

A hesitation. "It sounds as if you're involved in more

than a contest, Emily. Is there something you're not telling me?"

Was this a good time to change the subject, or what? "Are you still at your great-aunt's?"

"I had to move to my cousin's apartment actually. Too much smoke damage at my aunt Philomena's."

"Smoke damage? Oh, my God! The birthday cake. The burning tablecloth. What happened?"

"One of the relatives grabbed what she thought was apple juice to extinguish the flames. Unfortunately, it turned out to be brandy."

I saw movement from the tail of my eye and pivoted my head to find a handful of people still milling about the terrace, snapping shots of the tower and each other from every angle. And wasn't that handy. One of them just happened to be Keely.

"Etienne, would you excuse me? I see something that needs my attention. I'll get back to you later. Okay?"

"Of course, darling." And then in a throaty, seductive undertone, "*Ti vorrei mangiare per colazione. Ti voglio. Ti amo.*" Click.

"Etienne? Wait! WHAT DOES THAT MEAN?" I was pretty sure *ti amo* meant "I love you," but I had no idea what the other words meant. Nuts! Maybe Jackie would know.

I stashed my phone, dug out my camera, and scrambled across the terrace to find the group lined up at the door of the cathedral and passing through quickly. I caught Keely's attention and waved my camera at her. "You want me to take your picture?"

"I'd rather you just keep your distance," she said, backing away from me.

"It's the skin thing, isn't it? Hey, I'm on a new medication. It's under control."

"Yeah, well, I was itching a lot last night, and if it turns out to be fatal, I'm suing!"

I smiled serenely and nodded at her tight slacks and skimpy top. "Looks like you spent some time shopping yesterday."

She glanced down at her outfit and popped a huge pink bubble that she sucked back into her mouth. "Duh? I had to go shopping after what you pulled on me yesterday." She scratched her shoulder and worked her way across her collarbone to her throat.

"Looks as if a lot of people went shopping," I said, indicating the stragglers in their new togs filing through the cathedral door. "But I guess Jeannette Bowles never found the time."

"Jeez. Jeannette. Too bad about her accident. She was hanging around Gabriel so much yesterday, I thought I'd never get him alone, and then . . . *splat.* Gross way to die."

"I heard the three of you climbed the Duomo together."

She worked her gum as if it were a wad of chewing tobacco. "Yeah, we were both following him around yesterday, but she cornered him at the baptistry, so when I saw them get in line at the cathedral, I hopped right in there behind them. Did she ever hog the conversation though. Yak yak yak about her food columns and stupid awards. Talk about being a shameless self-promoter."

"Sounded to me as if she'd won as many awards as you."

"My awards actually *mean* something in the romance world. So she gets a food critics' award. Who cares what she thinks of the foot-long hot dogs on Mount Washington? What does that have to do with romance?"

Nope. I wasn't going there. "She'd won a few romance awards. Seemed to me she was providing you with some pretty stiff competition."

"No way. She was way out of her league. I'm a veteran at this."

"Were you on the gallery when she fell?"

Keely slitted her eyes at me. "Who are you? The police? Jeez, you ask more questions than they did. No, I wasn't on the gallery when she fell. I got sick of listening to her brag about herself, so I split. But I split too late to avoid the police. I guess they hadn't identified the body yet, so they wanted to know if I was missing a companion. But even when I told them no, they still needed a bunch of information from me. What a pain."

"So the last time you saw Jeannette, she was on the gallery with Gabriel?"

"She was telling him how wonderful her writing was. It was nauseating." She blew another bubble. "I probably could have been more helpful if the police had told me that the woman who jumped was wearing a peach sweater-dress, but they said she was wearing orange."

"It was coral."

"Unh-uh. Peach."

"It was coral! I should know. It was my dress!"

"No kidding?" She scratched the back of her neck. "Well, I'm not surprised the police said orange. Men never get their shades right. They think almond is beige. Rust is red. Good thing electrical wiring comes in primary colors. That's probably added decades to the life expectancy of male electricians." She sighed. "That was some hot dress though. Gabriel even mentioned how great it looked on her . . . when he could get a word in edgewise."

"And she never mentioned it was *my* dress?"

Keely's eyes shifted nervously. She lifted one shoulder in a half shrug. "Well, she might have said something about the dress being yours, but I was pretty much tuning her out."

"So she told you the dress was mine, and you never bothered to tell her about my contagious skin condition?"

"Hey, you said it was under control!"

"It is! But you didn't know that yesterday! Why didn't you warn her?"

She stared me in the eye, her gum fattening her cheek like a giant matzo ball. "You unpublished people don't have a clue about the business. It's cutthroat. Dog eat dog. If Jeannette got a rash and was too miserable to finish her proposal, that's one less person I'd have to compete with. Get it?"

"But you have a business where you help people with their writing! How can you help them with one hand and stab them in the back with the other?"

Keely smiled. "M-O-N-E-Y! Prepublished writers will pay *anything* to have someone help them get into print. I'm not stupid. I know how to make a buck off the system."

"How much did you make off Cassandra when you critiqued her writing?"

Keely gave her elbow a vigorous scratch before eyeing me curiously. She snapped her gum with a loud, juicy crack. "How did you know about Cassandra? My client list is confidential."

I shot her a steely look. "I have my sources. Tour escorts have access to a great deal of information."

Keely fanned her fingers through her hair. "Well, you know something? I don't like it that you know so much. And I *really* don't like it that you're sniffing around me like you think I had something to do with the deaths of those two women. So how about you go do what escorts are supposed to do and leave me alone."

"No problem." I'd let her know I had my eye on her. I guess that's all I could do at the moment. "Are you going into the cathedral?"

She waved off the suggestion. "I've seen churches before. I don't see what the big deal is." She capped off her statement by working her gum to the front of her mouth and beginning to blow.

Okay. I didn't need any instant replays. I headed across the terrace, but had only taken a half dozen steps when I heard an angry, "UHH!" behind me. Pausing, I glanced over my shoulder to find Keely grabbing a fistful of her long red hair and whining pathetically as she regarded the bubble-gum-coated strands. "UHH!" she grunted again, stomping her foot.

I guess her bubble had burst. Literally. Always disappointing when that happens. I brandished my camera in the air at her. "You want me to get a picture of that?" I asked helpfully.

I guessed her scowl meant no.

The morning was so wonderfully warm and sunny, I couldn't face the coolness of a dark cathedral right away, so I followed the path around the outside of the structure, realizing for the first time that the cathedral was built in the shape of a Roman cross, with a huge dome popping up from the transept. Another dome. God, I hoped no one tried to climb it. I stopped to snap some pictures of the intricate geometric patterns and spiky niches carved into the cathedral's facade and realized these were the same arches and columns and curlicues used in the design of the bell tower and the circular building west of the cathedral. I loved all the replication in the building designs. It was so well coordinated. Kind of like having your belt, shoes, and pocketbook all match.

I rounded the corner at the rear of the church, mulling over my conversation with Etienne and thinking about patterns, because I saw the makings of a definite pattern hidden within the information he'd given me. And it all boiled down to one thing.

"Emily!" I glanced straight ahead to see Fred barreling toward me in an outright panic. Sweat beaded his brow. Alarm strained his voice. "Where *is* everyone? Do you know? They've disappeared. How could they disappear on me like that?"

I recalled my episode at St. Peter's and smiled. Déjà vu all over again. I pointed to the cathedral. "They're getting the grand tour. Take a deep breath and calm down. No one left you behind."

"Geesch, I went to the men's room and when I got out, I couldn't find the group anyplace." He mopped his forehead with his sleeve, looking slightly less frantic now. "Gave me a scare."

His hat was hanging by its chin strap around his neck, which looked kind of dangerous to me. If he accidentally caught it in one of these five-hundred-pound cathedral doors, he'd choke to death. "How come you're not hanging with Brandy Ann and Amanda today?"

His eyeballs quivered in their sockets. He fiddled with his chin strap. "You know how it goes. Three's a crowd."

Now this was interesting. He'd turned pale at the mention of security cameras on top of the Duomo and was looking *really* uncomfortable at the mention of Brandy Ann and Amanda. Hmmm. "I'm going to pop into the cathedral to catch what I can of the tour. You want to join me?"

He hesitated. "You go on without me. As long as I know where everyone is, I'd just as soon wait out here. I don't want to bother anyone."

I guess this is what could be referred to as withdrawing back into your shell. But what had prompted it? "Hey, Fred, did the police stop you for questioning yesterday?"

He inched back a step. "Why do you want to know?"

"Just wondering. They apparently questioned a lot of people. Were you able to help them at all?"

"I didn't see anything! How many times do I have to repeat myself? I saw nothing. Now leave me alone, would you?" Looking fitful and anxious, he headed off in the opposite direction.

I had such a knack for getting people to open up to me.

The center door of the cathedral swung open, and in the next moment I saw familiar faces start to exit the building. Quick tour. I shot a couple of photos of the mosaics over the doorways and the four tiers of arched colonnades that climbed to the roofline, then found Nana in the crowd, talking to the twins.

"Was that the abridged tour?" I asked them.

"Well, would you lookit you?" Nana chirped, circling around me to get the full view of my hair. "I seen you when you got on the bus, but I couldn't believe my eyes. I like it, dear. I really do." She patted the ragged strands and intermittent bald spots on her own head of professionally cut hair. "Kinda reminds me a my own hair . . . now that I got the good cut."

I hung my head. Oh, God.

Britha, still attired in my cigarette pants and body suit, nodded toward the cathedral. "We would have had a longer tour, but there was a funeral going on, so we just got the highlights. The fancy pulpit. The big mosaic in the apse. The crooked chandelier."

Barbro chimed in. "And an altar on two angels' backs. Tell it all, Brit. Don't be lax."

"You follow me now," we heard Giovanna call out. "I show you someting around duh corner of duh catedral."

"Where'd you leave George?" I asked, as we moved en masse with the group.

"Him and Osmond needed to use the potty, so they had to duck out early." Nana looked up at the church, beaming with excitement. "Your mother's gonna be sorry she missed seein' all this, Emily. There's no way you coulda talked her into comin', hunh?"

"Nope. A whole bunch of new entries were in the box this morning, so she decided she needed to stay behind to read them so she could pass them on to Gabriel and Sylvia later this evening. I guess they speed-read, so they don't need as much time as Mom. Good thing they're going to announce the winner tomorrow night. If they extended the contest any longer, Mom's photo album of Italy would consist of interior shots of hotel rooms."

"That reminds me." Nana tapped Britha's shoulder. "Can I show Emily?"

Britha handed over her camera to Nana, who pressed a couple of buttons and flashed me a picture of her and George standing in front of the tower. "Isn't this somethin'? That's exactly what the picture's gonna look like and after it's downloaded, they can erase it and use the film over again. It's digital. You think I could use somethin' like this, Emily?"

We came to a halt at some nondescript point along the side of the cathedral and gathered around Giovanna, who stood next to the building with her hand on the facade. "I give you all a chance to see, but what I show you is duh liyttle holes in the stone here. You all step close now so you can see."

"I thought you said digital cameras were too expensive," I whispered as I took the camera from Nana.

"They are," she whispered back. "But this one's got all sorts a fancy gizmos on it. I can't help it. I love them gizmos."

I glanced at the photo displayed on the viewer. Aw. The

Leaning Tower of Pisa with a miniature Nana and George standing in front of it.

"Press that button to see the next one," she instructed me.

I pressed the button to find a close-up of a smiling Nana and George in front of some crooked colonnades.

I looked more carefully.

EHH!

Giovanna ran her finger down the cathedral wall. "If you try to count duh liyttle holes, you won't be able to, because duh number never comes out duh same way twice. It's because of duh day-vil."

I angled the camera toward Nana. "What happened to George? WHERE'S HIS FRONT TOOTH?"

"Duh day-vil plays with duh liyttle holes," Giovanna continued. "He changes duh number and moves dem around. You can try to count, but duh day-vil, he won't let you."

"What's a day-vil?" asked Nana.

"Devil," I fired back. "Where's George's tooth?"

"He's keepin' it in the front pocket a his trousers. But it's not a real tooth, dear. It's only a cap."

"Why isn't it in his mouth?"

"It got knocked out," she said sheepishly. "Accidentally."

Oh, Lord. "You want to tell me how?"

"It was on account a my knee."

I leveled quizzical eyes on her. "Your knee?"

She motioned me close and whispered in my ear, "I got to play the barbarian last night . . . but I got carried away some. I think it was the leather boxers that done it."

Oh, God. Good thing leather hadn't been popular in Brainerd. Grampa Sippel might have had to file for permanent disability at a very young age.

"Duh cloister behind you is Pisa's main ceymetery," Giovanna remarked, indicating the massive rectangular building north of the cathedral. "It was built between duh tirteent and fifteent ceynturies and eart' from duh Holy Land was brought back to bury duh bodies of prominent people."

Nana tugged on my arm. "What's eart'?"

"I think she means earth."

"Maybe she should try sayin' soil."

While Giovanna continued to talk, I punched the button on Britha's camera to catch a peek of what other pictures the twins had taken. Euw. Very nice artsy composition. A statue of a naked man with a beard, bulging muscles, and an extremely large . . . Yup. I punched the button again. A statue of a beardless naked man with big hands, big feet, and a *really* big . . . Unh. Next photo. A statue of *two* naked men with beards, killer physiques, and appendages the size of— I studied the display more carefully. Wow. I wondered if either of these guys was related to Etienne.

"I take you now to duh baptistry," Giovanna announced, working her way back to the head of the group.

I kept punching the display button. Oh, look at that. A picture of the Stolees, Teigs, and Lucille in front of the hotel in all their Florentine finery. Alice and Osmond at an outdoor café, showing off their camcorders. Duncan standing outside the Duomo. The rooftops of Florence. The picture I'd taken of the twins on the gallery. Boy, it had come out really well. And the close-up. Even better. You could see every feature on their faces with perfect clarity. This camera was really good . . . and I nearly dropped it when someone whacked me in the arm with a handbag an instant later.

"Eh!" I bobbled the camera, catching it in the crook of my arm at the last minute.

"Oh, I'm sorry!" Gillian Jones apologized, thwacking

me again when I turned around. Looking abashed, she clamped her hands around her shoulder bag like a pet owner controlling a frisky pup. "I'm sorry, Emily. I bought this new, and it's quite a bit bigger than my usual pocketbook, so I'm a little out of control. But I couldn't resist. It's one of a kind. Isn't it beautiful?"

I eyed the bag. Triangular. Purple leather. Euw boy. It was beautiful all right. It was also exactly like the one Marla Michaels was carrying. I guess the divas hadn't yet run into each other this morning. "Yeah, that's a great-looking bag," I agreed.

"Damson leather," said Gillian. "It's so scrumptious. You can't find leather like this back in the States."

Nope. Not unless you were living in the same town as Marla Michaels.

"And I found the most gorgeous leather jacket in a little shop by the San Lorenzo street market. For a hundred and fifty dollars! What a steal. They had to shorten the sleeves, but they did it in an hour. Can you imagine?"

I regarded her hair, thinking it looked the same as it had yesterday. She must have discovered a shop where they'd eliminated the blowtorch demonstration.

"Duh baptistry was completed in twelve eighty-four and is duh largest in all Italy," Giovanna called out, before we started our march across the field. "Duh circular shape was inspired by duh Church of duh Holy Sepulchre in Jerusalem and dee acoustics are beytter dan some of duh finest opera houses in Europe. It is very particular and very suggestive. You follow me. Duncan will give you your teekets at dee entrance."

As the group surged forward, I handed Britha's camera back to her. "You've taken some nice shots there."

"Thank you, Emily. You can't find good nudity like that back home."

"There's George," said Nana, waving to him and Osmond as they strode back from the restroom amid a scattering of other people. George waved back and flashed a wide grin that highlighted the newly acquired space between his teeth. I winced. Oh, God. How many days left on this tour?

I slowed my pace, allowing the group to pass me so I could hang out at the back and keep a better eye on things. Of course, the chances of something happening when the group was all bunched up like this were probably slight, but being isolated was better than getting clobbered by Gillian's damson shoulder bag again. *Damson.* I guess purple wasn't descriptive enough. Boy, you could sure tell she was a writer.

"Psssst."

I glanced sideways to find a tall, ponytailed man in an untucked oxford shirt, slouch cap, and sunglasses beckoning to me with a curling motion of his right index finger. *Curling motion. Right index finger.* Oh geesch. Did that mean he wanted to boff me? I quickened my pace and kept walking.

"PSSSST!"

From the corner of my eye I could see the man making a furious motion with his entire hand. Unh-oh. He'd progressed from a single finger to the whole hand. I wondered if that was the gesture for group sex. God, these Italians were kinky. I angled my face away from him and broke out in a shuffling run to catch up with the group.

"Emily! Will you get *over* here?"

The voice stopped me in midshuffle. I turned around to regard the man in the slouch cap. "Jackie?"

"What? You don't understand hand gestures anymore?" She ate up the distance between us in a few long strides.

I gaped at her. Him. "We're in Italy. I thought you were motioning that you wanted to have sex with me."

She flexed her fingers and raised them to eye level. "Mmm, I think you use the fingers on your left hand to indicate you want to have sex. You want me to check my nonverbal Italian book?"

I looked him . . . her . . . him . . . up and down. "Why are you dressed like that?"

She whipped off her sunglasses to reveal a face devoid of makeup. "I'm undercover," she said in a low voice. "I think I can keep better tabs on our suspects if I'm in disguise. And besides, costumes are more fun. It's like being onstage." She struck a pose. "What do you think? Good disguise? You think anyone will catch on?"

"Oh, yeah. Great disguise." She'd gone from six-foot transsexual to six-foot transvestite. The only ones unable to catch on would be infants and blind people. "The sandals are a nice touch. Very . . . flat."

She tapped a finger to her temple. "That took a lot of planning. I even had to remember to remove my nail polish because, let me tell you, if you're a guy with painted toenails? You draw a *lot* of attention. So tell me. Who do you want me to tail?"

We lagged behind the group as I repeated Etienne's earlier phone conversation. "So that's the scoop," I said when I finished. "And I'm finding it very telling that Brandy Ann and Amanda both have the same failing in common."

"Euw. Did they let you read their contest stuff? Let me guess. They split their infinitives? Use double negatives?"

"Jack! We're looking for a motive for murder!"

She waited a beat. "Too much passive voice?"

"Money problems, Jack! They have serious money problems and need that ten-thousand-dollar cash advance. Keely could use the money, too, but she's banking more on the prestige that being a published author will give her. Even if she never published another thing, the words 'published author' in her bio would help her online consulting service take off like gangbusters. It all boils down to greed. Plain, simple greed."

Jackie sighed. "So who do you want me to follow? And you better tell me quick so I can catch up. Everyone just filed into that circular building over there. What is that anyway? Another baptistry?"

"The largest one in Italy. With the best acoustics in the world."

In the next moment I heard double screams so loud and bloodcurdling that they electrified every hair at the back of my neck. The sounds rang out . . . ricocheted . . . vibrated . . . then blended into a chorus of notes that lingered in the air, leaving an almost musical contrail behind.

Wow. I'd never heard such incredibly symphonic screams before.

We riveted our attention on the baptistry. Jackie stared down at me in exasperation. "Let me guess. Seeing that our whole group is inside there, I suppose you're gonna want to check it out. Right?"

CHAPTER 9

We raced down the path, bounded up the three stone steps of the baptistry, and flew through a door that was only slightly less tall than the space shuttle. *"Biglietti?"* a uniformed ticket-taker inquired as we entered the short foyer. *"BIGLIETTI! BIGLIETTI!"* she screamed after us as we tore past.

The interior of the building was a vast empty space encased in stone. I saw no frescoes, no statues, no chairs, no nothing. What I did see were people frozen in place, staring in shocked silence at the two women who were standing by the spa-sized baptismal font in the center of the room, swinging their damson leather shoulder bags at each other.

"You bitch!" screamed Marla. "I should have known you'd buy something just like mine! You can't *stand* not to copy me! First, it's my books. Now it's my shoulder bag!" WHAM! She connected with Gillian's thigh.

Looked like the divas had finally run into each other.

"Copy you? COPY YOU!" THWWWWACK! Gillian

delivered a blow to Marla's shoulder, driving her back. "The only similarity between your books and mine are the punctuation marks!"

"You used my first love scene in *Barbarian's Bride* almost word for word in your stupid cowboy island book!"

I sincerely hoped the cowboy had been more fortunate than George and escaped the encounter with his front teeth intact.

"You're accusing me of plagiarism?" Gillian shrieked. "Honey, if I'm going to commit plagiarism, I can do a whole hell of a lot better than stealing scenes from some unpolished, unprofessional, unimaginative hack like you!"

"I have half a mind to sue your *ass* off!" Marla raged, her voice mimicking the tonal brilliance of a really good sound system.

"That's exactly why you can't write!" Gillian's voice echoed in surround sound. "You only *have* half a mind!"

SWOOSH swoosh swoosh! They swung their pocketbooks over their heads. WHUMP! The bags thumped together in midair like boxing gloves.

"Ladies." Elbowing his way through the crush of paralyzed onlookers, Duncan reached the center of the room and inserted his commanding presence between the divas and their dueling shoulder bags. "Enough."

The women dangled their bags by their shoulder straps, looking as if they were contemplating sneak attacks. Oh, God.

"Protect your boys, son!" Dick Teig warned. "You might want to have children someday."

"Copycat!" yelled Marla.

"Drudge!" Gillian spat.

"Lickspittle!"

"Muckmouth!"

As the screaming continued, I listened to the demeaning barrage of insults reverberating off these sacred walls, feeling shock and awe at what I was hearing from the world's two most famous romance divas.

Boy, Giovanna was right. The acoustics in this place *were* incredible. They sounded even better on the inside than they did from the outside!

Forty-five minutes later, with the divas banished to opposite ends of the group, Duncan's manhood intact, and Giovanna's tour ended, I sat cross-legged on the grass outside the baptistry, wishing I knew yoga and trying to regroup.

"Mind if I join you?" Gabriel Fox sauntered in my direction and when I gave him a nod, he stretched out on the lawn in front of me. "After what you've witnessed these last two days, you mustn't think much of the people who work in publishing. But I'd like you to know, we're not all like that."

"Like what?"

"Like Marla Michaels and Gillian Jones. We're not all raving lunatics. Most of us actually enjoy working with each other the majority of time, but competition seems to bring out the worst in some people."

"I noticed."

"In Gillian's and Marla's case, it's because of the Irmas."

"Excuse me?"

"The Irma Award. The highest honor you can receive in the romance industry. They both have nine at the moment, and they're vying to be the first to reach ten, at which point they'll be retired from competition and be inducted into the Romance Hall of Fame. But look at what they've become. The stress is eating them up. And this tour has pushed them over the edge. Philip was crazy to expect them to give up their writing secrets to the masses. You heard them yesterday. They don't want new authors to come along and knock them off their million-dollar pedestals. Each wants to be top dog forever."

I smoothed my hand over the grass, looking him square in the eye. "They must be relieved they don't have to worry about Cassandra and Jeannette then."

"We never should have begun this contest. But Philip—" Gabriel wagged his hand in frustration. "You can't talk to Philip sometimes. Everything has to go his way, or no way at all."

"You were one of the last people to see Jeannette alive," I prodded. "Do you have any idea what happened?"

"I'll tell you exactly what happened. It became open season on Gabriel Fox! I haven't been able to take a breath these last two days without some contest hopeful getting in my face. 'Pick me. Pick me!' They've even followed me into the restroom, for Christ's sake."

I wondered if he realized that was no big deal since most of the restrooms around here were unisex.

"Jeannette practically attacked me in the *piazza* yesterday, and when I excused myself to do some sightseeing, she decided to tag along with me. I thought I might shake her by threatening to climb to the top of the Duomo—I mean, that dress of hers was so tight, I didn't think there was any way she could climb stairs, but wouldn't you know? She was a hiker. She could have made that climb in a straitjacket and leg irons. And to add to the occasion, some mouthy redhead joined us. The two of them talked at me so much, I think I've gone deaf in both ears."

"From your little speech on the bus this morning, it sounded to me as if you were quite taken with Jeannette."

"Hell. Give me credit for having some scruples. The woman died. I'm not about to announce she was a bootlicker. No matter what she was, I still have to do the good PR."

"So where were you when she died?"

He eyed me critically. "You ask that question as if you suspect I might have killed her. Just to ease your mind, I was nowhere around the woman when she died, and I told the same thing to the police. I wandered away while she and the redhead were locked in some kind of discussion about first-chapter endings, and I headed for the stairs at a run."

I guess that clinched it. *Everyone* had been descending the stairs when Jeannette died. How convenient.

No, wait a minute. I suddenly remembered. Everyone except Fred. I still didn't know where Fred had been . . . or what he'd seen.

"I might be a literary snob," Gabriel confessed, "but I'm not a killer. Frankly, I think it might have been suicide. She'd been involved in some kind of lawsuit years ago, and from what she hinted, the result hadn't gone well for her."

"Did she say what kind of lawsuit?"

"Believe it or not, that was the one thing about herself that she didn't elaborate on. Lucky me." He boosted himself to his feet and brushed off his khakis. "Don't look too hard for your phantom killer, Emily. I don't think you'll find one. On the other hand, should *I* show up dead, be sure and check out Sylvia's alibi."

I squinted up at him, blocking out the sun with my hand. "She doesn't like you much, does she?"

"Major understatement. She hates the ground I walk on."

"Why's that?"

"I'd like to say because I'm literary, and she's commercial, but I think it goes deeper than that. Sylvia Root has been uncivil to me since the first time we met. And to be perfectly honest with you, I have no idea why. But I never let it ruin my day. I can handle the Sylvias of the world."

I bet he could.

Jackie showed up five minutes later, awaiting last-minute instructions, which I was happy to supply. "Something's been up with Fred ever since he learned about the security cameras at the top of the Duomo. Something not quite right. So maybe you can follow him around and see if he does anything out of character."

"You mean, like walk with erect posture and look people in the eye? You suppose I should just ask him?"

I stared at her, deadpan. "You're not supposed to *talk* to him, Jack. You're supposed to *watch* him. He's not supposed to see you. No talking, just watching. Got it?"

She removed her tape recorder from the pocket of her shirt and said into the mike, "If you want to have fun on your holiday tour, AVOID THE ONE ESCORTED BY EMILY!"

I flashed her my most winning smile. "If you say one more word into that freaking tape recorder, I'll snap it in half."

Arching her eyebrows in a fit of pique, she shoved the gadget back into her pocket. "Have you by any chance been diagnosed with PMS recently?"

I continued with the plan. "I'll follow Brandy Ann, Amanda, and Keely. If I'm lucky, they might hit some of the same stores."

"What if they don't like to shop?"

A woman not like to shop? "You're kidding, right? Okay, you take off, and I'll meet you back at the bus at four." As she struck out along the path, I recalled Etienne's last enigmatic words to me. "Hey, wait a minute! Do you have any idea what *voray mange calzione* means?"

"I don't know French!" she called, backpedaling.

"It's not French! It's Italian!"

She erupted in hysterical laughter. "Sure it is! Jeez, you need language lessons. Okay, I think it means . . ." She paused in thought. "Someone wants to eat your shorts! Or maybe your socks."

My socks? I hadn't brought any socks with me. But I certainly didn't want to discourage his attempts at foreplay.

I wondered how he'd feel about panty hose.

I loved tailing people.

I loved it because it was so easy. Especially when I was tailing women who indeed liked visiting all the local shops.

I followed Brandy Ann and Amanda down a wide street called the Via Santa Maria, and while they popped into linen shops, alabaster and marble shops, stationery shops, jewelry shops, clothing shops, shoe shops, and leather shops, I watched them from a safe distance on the opposite side of the street. They developed a pattern of spending an average of thirty minutes in each store, then moving on to the next one, except for the jewelry store, where they spent an hour and a half. I figured Amanda was probably looking for attractive new jewelry for her nostrils. Maybe a miniature Tower of Pisa. Or a small cathedral.

I bought gelato at every ice-cream place I passed and stood nibbling on it as I watched my marks. I decided my favorite flavor was *frutti di bosco,* and maybe not so much for the flavor as for the color, which was a deep raspberry/boysenberry pink. I remembered having an Easter dress that color once, when I was five.

I spotted other members of the tour in my travels. Philip and Marla looked to be having a heart-to-heart over glasses of wine at an outdoor café. I saw Keely peeking into the storefront window of a hair salon and checking her watch before heading through the door. I guess I wouldn't have to worry about what she was doing for the rest of the afternoon. I noticed Sylvia Root and Gillian buying fruit from an outdoor vendor and wondered if Gillian's was for eating or chucking at Marla.

I saw several blondes wearing Landmark Destination name tags and stopped to exchange friendly chitchat with them, but not once during the entire morning or afternoon did I catch sight of Nana, or George, or the twins, or any of my Windsor City group. Odd that I wouldn't run into at least one of them. Oh, geesch. Could they have gone back to wait for the bus?

I shook my head. More than likely that's where they were. They were skipping the historic self-guided tour of Pisa in favor of being on time for the bus. I rolled my eyes. I had to hand it to them. At least they were consistent.

By 3:30 I was hot, tired, and with all the gelato I'd consumed, really thirsty, so I stopped at a restaurant with outdoor seating and a partial view of the Leaning Tower and ordered a tall glass of lemonade. My table was covered in white linen with a pottery bowl full of oranges and lemons as a centerpiece rather than your standard bottle of Chianti with a candle stuck in the neck. I inched off my one-band slides and flexed my toes while I waited for my order, disappointed that neither Brandy Ann nor Amanda had done anything criminal all day long, which made me wonder if the only time they reverted to criminal behavior was when there was a flight of stairs handy. I leaned in my chair to regard the sliver of tower visible in the distance and wondered how many stairs one had to climb to reach the top. A frosty sensation razored down my spine. Good thing it was closed to the public until next year.

My lemonade arrived in an exquisitely tooled highball glass with a slice of lemon gracing the rim. I chugged a mouthful before setting it back on the table with a frown. Nice glass. Warm liquid. No ice. Yup. The Italians really knew how to quench your thirst.

I scratched the soles of my feet with my bare toes, wondering what would happen if Jackie came up short with Fred. We couldn't keep following everyone around. At some point people would notice, especially if Jackie got increasingly more creative with her disguises.

There were just too many questionable motives floating around among the Passion and Pasta crew for everyone to be as innocent as they'd led me to believe. Money. Fame. Ego. Validation. But I couldn't figure out the logistics. Brandy Ann had both the opportunity and brawn to push Cassandra down the hotel stairs, but how could she have been involved with Jeannette's death if she wasn't on the gallery when the woman fell?

Amanda had opportunity to push Cassandra, too, but the same problem existed. She couldn't be responsible for Jeannette's death if she'd left the gallery before Jeannette fell.

Unless, of course, the videotapes proved otherwise.

I took a long draft of my iceless lemonade. Then there was Keely, who knew the caliber of Cassandra's writing, who was probably miffed that Cassandra had ended her *Romance Solutions* subscription, who might have been jealous of Jeannette's awards and threatened by her talent, and who wanted to be published more than she wanted to live. But Keely supposedly left the gallery before Jeannette plunged to her death, too. Or had she?

I shot up straight in my chair. *Uff da!* Had Fred seen Keely do something unspeakable on the gallery? Or Brandy Ann? Or Amanda? Or . . . or Gabriel? Is that why he was acting even more squirrelly than normal today? Why he seemed so frightened to be alone? Was he afraid Jeannette's killer might try to shut him up?

But if that was the case, then what was the deal with his anxiety about the videotapes? If they actually showed someone pushing Jeannette off the gallery, then—

A sudden, unlikely thought struck me. Oh, my God. What if the videotapes showed Fred pushing Jeannette? But that was absurd! Fred wouldn't hurt a fly. Physically, he seemed too small to muscle someone over the railing. Mentally, he seemed too timid. Then there was the question of motive, but I wouldn't be given any insight into that until Etienne got back to me. *Why* was this getting so complicated? I took another swig of my lemonade to help myself think.

"Is this seat taken?"

Startled, I glanced up to find Duncan standing beside my table, appearing the polar opposite of me—fresh, crisp, and every bit as commanding as he'd been in the showdown at the baptistry. "Oh, hi! Sure." I indicated the chair kitty-corner to me. "It has your name on it. But if you're thirsty, I don't recommend the lemonade, unless you have a thing for lukewarm beverages."

He sat down, a broad smile dimpling his cheeks as he waved his hand toward my glass. "Italy has it all. Lavish cathedrals. Garish fountains. Leviathan sculptures. Gorgeous women. The only thing it lacks is . . . ice." A soft, kindling light brightened the dark brown of his eyes. "And speaking of gorgeous women, I didn't want you to think I hadn't noticed."

He lifted his very large, very bronzed hand to my head and gave my short curls a gentle tousle. "Donatella did well by you. I think you look"—his eyes trailed lazily from my hair to my mouth—"spectacular."

OH, GOD! This couldn't be sexual attraction I was feeling. *Please* tell me it wasn't sexual attraction! I couldn't be attracted to Duncan. I was already taken!

"I'm glad you like it." I gulped down the rest of my lemonade in one long swallow.

"I like it very much," he said in a voice that would have melted ice if there'd been any around. "I'm curious, Emily." He lifted my left hand and brushed his thumb across my bare ring finger. "No wedding ring? How does a knockout like you avoid the inevitable trip to the altar?"

"I was married once," I confessed, "but it didn't work out."

"You married the wrong man."

"Um, you could say that."

"What about now? Are you seeing anyone?"

I nodded enthusiastically. "A Swiss police inspector. He lives in Lucerne, but he's on leave of absence at the moment." I tapped my fingertips to my head. "Migraines. He was injured last month, so he's . . . recuperating."

"A serious injury?"

"Head wound."

"Obviously not in the line of duty though."

"He was on holiday." I eyed him curiously. "How did you know that?"

"It's hard to be felled by a criminal element where no criminal element exists. Didn't your inspector tell you? There's no crime in Switzerland."

"That's not true! There was a crime when *I* was there." Unfortunately, we'd brought the criminal over with us, but why split hairs?

He smiled at me with his glaringly white teeth. "Do you see each other often?"

"Not often enough. Long-distance relationships are a problem that way."

"You could try applying for a job at Landmark. I happen to know there's a position opening up in Milan. Six-month minimum stay in the country. Competitive salary. Trains run frequently between Milan and Lucerne. You'd see your inspector more often, and if things didn't work out with him"—with the lightest touch of his fingertip, he sketched a pattern on the back of my hand—"I'll be moving to Milan in a few weeks, so I could offer you my services at . . . filling the void."

I could feel my mouth work, but nothing was coming out. He wanted to fill the void? He'd spoken to me a handful of times, and he wanted to fill the void? Had something happened between the two of us in the last couple of days that I'd completely missed?

Duncan's lips curved into a boyish grin. "I wouldn't mind meeting your inspector, Emily." He threw the words out like a challenge before leaning back comfortably in his chair. "Is he planning a visit while you're in the country? I always like to size up the competition."

"Competition? What are you competing for?"

"I thought that was obvious." He drilled me with a look that sizzled like a lightning strike. "You."

"ME? I'm not part of any competition. I'm taken!"

"No ring on your finger yet. You're not off-limits until it's official."

"Yes, I am!"

"No, you're not. I'm not usually this forward, but what

can I say? You're beautiful. Friendly. You're always smiling. You don't smoke. Do you know how refreshing it is to
see a woman who doesn't smoke over here? Old people
love you. You have a good heart. My family would think
you're wonderful." He lowered his eyes. "You have great
legs."

"My legs are taken."

"I should probably warn you. The men in my family
make up their minds rather quickly about the women they
intend to marry. My mother and father dated exactly two
days before he popped the question, and they were married in a week. My grandfather was even faster. He carted
my gramma off to the preacher on their first date. Lazarus
men know their minds when it comes to women."

I stared at him openmouthed for nearly ten seconds
before I uttered the only thing I could possibly say at a
time like this. "Have you run into any of my people today?
The guy with the prosthetic leg who's walking like a slug?
The woman with Magic Marker for eyebrows? I haven't
seen any of them since we left the baptistry and frankly,
I'm a little worried."

His gaze was unwavering. "Is that how Midwesterners
politely change the subject?"

I perked up. "Speaking of changing the subject, do you
happen to know what the phrase *voray mange calzione*
means?"

"Excuse me?"

I braced my forearm on the table and regarded him
gravely. "Do you think there's a chance it doesn't mean 'eat
my socks'? Could it possibly be an idiom?"

"Say it again. Slowly."

So I did, and when I finished, I watched his mouth
become a provocative curve. "If I fill in the blanks and use
a little literary license, I come up with, 'I want to eat you

for breakfast.' " His eyes grew warm, sooty. "I love the idea. Are you free tomorrow morning?"

"Thief! Stop! He has my pocketbook! Stop him!"

A sudden blur on the periphery of my vision became a young man pelting down the street with a purple shoulder bag stashed under his arm. Marla Michaels stood alone on the pavement, screaming and pointing at the retreating thief. "Somebody stop him! That pocketbook's brand-new! There's only one other like it in the world!"

"Oh, my God!" I leaped out of my chair. "A purse snatcher!" I eyed the barrier of potted plants around the restaurant. I eyed the disappearing thief. I eyed my one-band slides with the three-inch wedge heels. There was only one thing to do.

I turned to Duncan. "Should someone run after him?"

"No need," he said, rising calmly to his feet. Keeping a bead on the thief, he plucked an orange from the fruit bowl, took calculated aim, and hurled the thing through the air at twice the speed of sound. Or light. Whichever was faster.

The orange hit dead on. CLONK! Right in the back of the head. The thief's neck snapped forward. His legs buckled. He tripped on the pavement and skidded onto his stomach in a tangle of arms and legs. Marla's shoulder bag sluiced from beneath his arm into the path of a nun who scooped it off the street and held it protectively while the thief picked himself off the ground and hightailed it toward the tower.

I regarded Duncan in awe. "How did you do that?"

He gave a modest shrug. "I played a little football in high school. That's when we were stationed in D.C."

"Quarterback?"

"Only for two years."

With an arm like that, he should be playing in the NFL.

I wondered why he wasn't. "Did you play in college, too?"

"Unfortunately, the place I attended didn't have a football team."

What a waste. His father had probably been assigned to some tiny African nation, and he'd been forced to spend his college years in some vocational-technical school in the jungle. Imagine. He could be earning millions now, if only he'd attended the right school. My heart went out to him as I peered up at his handsome face. "Do you mind my asking? Where exactly did you attend college?"

"It was a university actually," he said matter-of-factly. "Oxford."

When I arrived at the bus pickup point at 3:50, I was happy to find the Windsor City gang all present and accounted for, exchanging lively conversation amongst themselves and shooting last-minute photos of the African street vendors who were hawking everything from pocketbooks, to carved animals, to umbrellas. Nana hurried up to me, tugging George behind her.

"I'm glad you're here, Emily. I was gettin' awful worried you might miss the bus."

I gave them a stern look. "I thought it was really odd I didn't run into any of you guys in town this afternoon. Please tell me you haven't been standing here all day waiting for the bus."

George grinned like a jack-o'-lantern. "We all *tha*yed together and had a real ec*th*yting afternoon."

I wiped spittle from my face.

"*Thorry,*" he apologized.

Nana handed me a tissue. "It's been like this all afternoon, dear. We're all soaked."

I held the tissue at the ready. "You all stuck together?" That was a first. "What did you do?"

"We was countin' them holes in the cathedral," said Nana. "You know. The ones the day-vil keeps changin'."

I stared at her, nonplussed. "You spent the afternoon . . . counting holes?"

"They're really not holes. They're more like dots, with attitude."

"I came up with a hundred and *th*venty," George hissed proudly.

Nana nodded. "Then Dick Stolee counted and he come up with a hundred and sixty-eight. Then Lucille counted and got a hundred sixty-four." She lowered her voice a decibel. "We didn't take Lucille's tally too seriously seein's how she's scheduled for cataract surgery when we get back. That day-vil, Emily, we kept 'im real busy today."

Euw boy. "After all that work, did you ever come up with a final number?"

"You bet." Nana smiled. "Osmond kept track a each tally. Alice called out the numbers. Dick Stolee done the videotapin'. We all took our turn countin', and the final estimate was—"

"*Th*umwhere between a hundred forty-four and a hundred eighty dots."

Yup. They'd sure nailed that down. "So you didn't do any sightseeing around Pisa?"

"We was too busy for sightseein', dear. And we was right there near the public potty, so it was real convenient. Especially for the fellas."

George nodded agreement.

"Dick's gonna make copies of the video and hand 'em out so's we can relive the experience. Isn't that nice a him? And he got some real good footage of the stream a people walking back and forth from the potty." She lowered her voice again. "He even filmed a big argument between that lady book agent and the bearded man who's the big shot editor."

"Argument?" Okay, now she had my attention.

Nana looked both ways before continuing. "They was really goin' at each other, Emily. Dick was standin' too far away to pick up the sound, but I heard Sylvia yell at the editor fella that he'd ruined enough careers to last 'im a lifetime, and if he thought he was gonna ruin anyone else's, it'd be over her dead body."

"No kidding?" Oh, geesch. Why did people say that? Wasn't anyone superstitious anymore?

"So he says, 'That can be arranged.' "

"Oh, my God. He said that?"

George removed his seed-corn cap and scratched his head. "It wa*th* either that, or, 'You're *tho* deranged.' I thawt he thed deranged."

Nana shrugged. "George might be right, dear. Tell you the truth, I couldn't hear too good at that point because it was Barbro's turn to count and she started in with, 'One, two, buckle my shoe. Three, four, shut the door.' She come up with some dandy rhymes once she got into the hundreds."

Unh-oh. Had Sylvia's dislike of Gabriel hit the breaking point? Great. That's what this tour needed. More ill will between the guests.

"And I seen Jackie pass by on her way to the potty," Nana continued, "but she looked real different. Tell me, dear"—she bowed her head close to mine—"why was she dressed like that?"

I touched my forefinger to my lips for secrecy. "She's undercover."

Nana made a quiet O of her mouth and nodded understanding. She lowered her voice even more. "As what?"

The roar of an engine vibrated the pavement, and

diesel fumes filled the air as our bus pulled up to the sidewalk. Bodies moved. Feet shuffled. And Nana and George hobbled off to beat the crowd. By the time the door *whooshed* open, the guests were lined up like beasts ready to board the biblical ark. I made a quick visual check.

I saw a lot of now familiar blond heads. Brandy Ann and Amanda were halfway back in the pack, weighed down by dozens of packages. Gillian Jones was standing beside Philip Blackmore, who was downing his water like a thirsty desert dweller. I hoped he realized there were no comfort facilities on the bus. Keely stood sandwiched between some guests I hadn't met, her red hair considerably shorter, but not half as stylish as mine. Sylvia Root and Marla Michaels stood side by side, examining the outside of Marla's shoulder bag. It would be a shame if her bag had gotten scuffed up in the purse-snatching attempt, but on the bright side, maybe the new markings would elevate it to one-of-a-kind status again.

I began counting heads starting from the back, where I found Fred looking nervous and agitated and checking behind him every five seconds. Curiosity getting the better of me, I sauntered over and took up a position behind him. "Did you enjoy Pisa?" I asked brightly.

He startled, then almost looked relieved to find me behind him. He trained a long, searching look over my shoulder. "You can have Pisa. I never want to come back here. Ever."

"Why?"

"Because some pervert was following me around all day, is why! Probably wanted to pick my pocket, or steal my hat. Some weird cross-dresser with really big feet and a sinister face. Cripes, it was terrifying. I just want to get back on the bus where I'll be safe."

I knew I could count on Jack. He had really perfected the art of blending unobtrusively into the crowd.

"I'm here! I'm here!" I heard a voice yell far behind me. "Hold the bus!"

I turned around. *Speak of the day-vil.* Jackie was pounding the pavement toward us, hair streaming, arms pumping, trumpet skirt flying. Look at that. She was back to being a girl again. I excused myself from Fred and walked a few steps to meet her out of earshot of the group. When she caught up, she lunged for my arm and doubled over at the waist, sucking in air.

"I thought you were going to . . . leave without me."

"I don't think tour companies like to do that. Too much liability involved." I slapped her on the back to assist her breathing. "What held you up?"

She waved her arm in the direction of the public restrooms. "Zipper got stuck. Then I couldn't find my . . . eyeliner. And I put on the . . . wrong color lipstick, so I had to . . . reapply. But those unisex restrooms . . . are great. You go in a guy . . . come out a girl . . . and no one notices."

She inched upward slowly, holding her side. "And to think I used to run . . . track in high school." Spying Fred at the end of the line, she turned her back toward him and made a head gesture for me to step closer. "I stayed with him all day, Emily, except for the last two hours when he kinda gave me the slip. Into museums. Out of museums. Down by the river. Through the botanical gardens. And get this. He never saw me. Not even once."

I smiled indulgently. "Imagine that. And did you find anything out?"

"Yeah, surveillance work is as boring as it was yesterday. I don't want to do it anymore."

"Being undercover didn't help?"

She shook her head. "They make it look exciting in the

movies, but it's all a crock. You're at the complete mercy of the person you're tailing. Like, get this. Fred didn't stop to have anything to eat today. Can you believe it? I'm starving! I'm surprised I haven't passed out from calorie deprivation." She glanced over her shoulder to watch the people filing onto the bus. "You have better luck with your three?"

"They shopped a lot. Pretty standard stuff. Nothing to report." I sighed. Had we wasted an entire day playing Dick Tracey when we might have been doing something constructive like grave rubbings at the Campo Santo, or counting holes in the cathedral wall? Damn.

We boarded the bus and chatted up several people as we took our seats. At 4:05 Duncan navigated the aisle, took a final head count, and stopped to converse with several guests at the front of the bus. At 4:10 he and the driver stepped outside, and while the driver lit up a cigarette, Duncan kicked tires. At 4:15 we were still there.

Jackie peered out the window. "What's the holdup? Mechanical problem? Jeez, we need to get going. If I don't get something to eat soon, I'll have to eat my shoe, and I'm not particularly fond of latex. Too chewy."

I could feel an undercurrent of panic sweep through the bus. "We're going to be late for dinner," I heard Alice Tjarks announce somewhere behind me.

"We're fifteen minutes late," Dick Stolee said to the group.

"*Th*venteen by my watch," George countered.

I could feel their collective blood pressure rising with the stress.

"Sixteen minutes now," said Dick.

"Twenty!" said Britha Severid, who obviously hadn't adjusted her watch properly for the time change.

Okay, time to find out what was going on. I walked the length of the bus and exited by the front steps. Duncan stood talking on his cell phone, glancing back toward the Field of Miracles. I waited for him to sign off before popping the million-dollar question. "My natives are getting restless. What's up with the delay? Mechanical problem?"

He flashed me a tenuous smile. "Guest relations problem."

"Anything I can help with? Guest relations are my specialty." At least, they were when the guests were still breathing.

"Unfortunately, I may have to take you up on your offer. It seems Gabriel Fox has gone missing."

Chapter 10

W HAT?"

"Mr. Fox is missing. Sylvia Root spoke to him outside the Campo Santo a couple of hours ago, but none of his colleagues have seen him since then."

My heart thumped an odd rhythm in my chest. "Do guests go missing very often?"

"Happens all the time." He flashed me a half smile and winked. "Happened to you on our first outing."

Oh, sure. He *had* to bring that up.

"Guests get separated from the group. Lose track of time. Don't notice their watches have stopped. Get too far off the beaten path and end up walking in circles. I've seen it all."

"So what do we do?"

"We wait for him."

"You didn't wait for me!"

"You're considered a tour employee. Employees are supposed to be more resourceful than your average traveler."

"But . . . but . . . what if I hadn't been resourceful?"

Laughter rumbled in his throat. "Yeah, right." He checked his watch impatiently. "We do have one extenuating circumstance in this case though. If we wait here much longer, it'll affect our travel time back to Florence, which means we might miss our dinner reservations. And if that happens, it won't be pretty."

I'll say. Especially if we had to watch Jackie eat her shoes.

"Landmark prepaid for fifty-three fixed price meals, so they will *not* be happy if they have to eat that bill."

"So . . . we leave him?" My guess was, Gabriel Fox was every bit as resourceful as I was.

"Not company policy, but I just checked with the head office, and they suggested a compromise. If someone stays behind to escort Mr. Fox back to Florence when he shows up, the company can avoid litigation for abandonment, mental distress, and pain and suffering."

"Escort Mr. Fox back to Florence . . . how?"

"By train. The station's a short taxi ride from here, just south of the river. And travel time to Florence is less than an hour. If he shows up within the next thirty minutes, we'd even make it back in time for dinner. So is your offer of help still good?"

"Ummmm . . . yeah," I hedged, not knowing what I was letting myself in for.

"Great, I'll even give you an option. You can either stay here at the pickup point to wait for Fox, or you can accompany the guests back to Florence. If you opt to head back with the group, remember that dinner reservations are at seven-thirty sharp and people need to dress, so try to impress that upon them on the trip back. No sweat suits. No running shoes. Plan to leave the hotel at six forty-five to allow time to navigate through traffic and it's quite a little hike down some narrow alleys to get to the restaurant, so you'll need time for that, too. The paving stones in those alleys are pretty uneven, so keep a watch that no one trips. Take your cell phone in case you need to call for emergency assistance. English isn't spoken at the restaurant, but that shouldn't be a problem for you. Smile a lot and use hand gestures. Should be a piece of cake. So what'll it be? Stay here and wait for Fox or take charge of the group?"

He was kidding, right?

I squinted at my Florence street map beneath a street-light on the Via Nazionale and realized I needed to make a right turn to get back to the Hotel Cosimo Firenze. It was after midnight, and if Gabriel Fox's watch had stopped, he never noticed, because he'd never shown up.

My imagination had kicked into overdrive as I'd waited for him at the pickup point. What could have caused him to miss the bus? Disorientation? Injury? Foul play? Was his disappearance somehow connected with the deaths of Cassandra and Jeannette? Was it odd that people had lost track of him at about the same time that Jackie had lost track of Fred? Or had his argument with Sylvia led to his disappearance? His words to me outside the baptistry played in my head: *Should I show up dead, be sure and check out Sylvia's alibi.*

Oh, God. I hated having an active imagination.

While I'd camped out in Pisa, I'd phoned the local hospital and police office to inform them of my problem and to give them a description of Gabriel in case he ended up at either place. My next phone call was to Etienne, to inquire if he'd been able to dig up anything on the names I'd given him.

"Your Fred Arp doesn't own a credit card, drives a sixteen-year-old Buick, and has a checking account that shows an incredible number of debits each month for cat food and kitty litter. He visits his mother at an assisted living facility five times a week, and for the past twenty-six years, has been employed as organist for the Unitarian Universalist Society in Cleveland. He's not hooked up to cable television, and he doesn't own a computer. The man appears wholly above reproach, except for the high levels of exhaust emissions he discharges by driving such an old car. I haven't received any information on the other name yet. I'll call you when I do."

There remained nothing for me to do then but wait. And the longer I waited, the more I began to question my theory that Gabriel had been the victim of some travesty.

Something didn't feel quite right about the whole situation. Gabriel Fox was a savvy New Yorker. Detail-oriented. Sophisticated and cunning. I'd lived in New York. I knew that savvy New Yorkers didn't lose track of time, even if their watches stopped. They were cognizant of schedules, and pickup points, and consequences, and I doubted they ever went missing . . . unless they wanted to.

And it was that thought that changed everything.

I berated myself all the way back to Florence for being so blind. He *wanted* people to see him arguing with Sylvia. He *wanted* people to think there was bad blood between them. And he'd played me like a harp about that one. If he disappeared, he wanted a cloud of suspicion hanging over Sylvia's head, not only because it might taint her career and make her life miserable, but because it would divert attention away from the real reason he'd disappeared.

I turned right on the Via Guelfa and quickened my pace.

I knew my instincts about Fred had been right. He was too shy and introverted to be involved in any kind of wrongdoing. The only thing Fred was guilty of was observing something at the top of the Duomo yesterday that had put the fear of God in him, and I'd finally figured out what.

He'd seen Gabriel Fox push Jeannette Bowles over the gallery rail. I didn't understand what had driven Gabriel to murder, but I could certainly understand why he went missing. Once Duncan mentioned the existence of the videotapes this morning, it was a moot point. Gabriel Fox needed to vanish before the videotapes proved him guilty of a heinous crime.

The clues had been there, but they'd been couched in so many untruths that I hadn't picked up on them. When he'd decided to climb to the top of the Duomo, I bet he'd encouraged Jeannette to join him. And I bet he'd doubled back after Keely had left the gallery to do his deed. It was pure bad luck on Jeannette's part that a commotion had given him the opportunity. But he was clever. Who knew? Maybe he'd *caused* the commotion! And then his eulogy on the bus, talking as though he'd been Jeannette's friend rather than her murderer. Too bad there'd been no security camera in the stairwell of our hotel. Dollars to doughnuts, it would have caught Gabriel shoving Cassandra to her death, too. But the question still remained. Why?

No matter where Gabriel Fox was, Sylvia Root was in Florence, and she and I were going to have a long talk in the morning. She knew more about Gabriel Fox than she was letting on, and I wanted to know what.

I turned the corner to the Via Santa Reparata, my stomach growling even louder than the scooters whizzing by in the street. I guess this was what happened when you survived on gelato and warm lemonade all day. At the far end of the block, I noticed a trio of blue cars parked cockeyed on the sidewalk and narrowed my eyes to make out the writing on the doors. P-O-L-I-Z-I-A. *Police?* What would the police be doing—

Unh-oh. With dread churning my stomach, I hurried

down the sidewalk and banged through the front door of
the hotel.

A half dozen policemen in crisp blue uniforms, white
belts, and stylish berets wheeled around to face me when
I charged into the lobby. They began shouting at me in
strident Italian and shooing me away, but not before I
caught a glimpse of the body lying at the bottom of the
staircase.

I covered my mouth with my hands. *Oh, my God.* This
was insane. This couldn't be happening again! The staircase. The dead body. The head twisted at an unnatural
angle. It was just like before!

Well . . . almost just like before. The only difference was,
Sylvia Root wasn't wearing any of my clothes.

"The police are treating Ms. Root's death as an accident," Duncan announced to us at breakfast the next
morning, "but they'd still like to reserve the right to question each of you before we leave for Montecatini tomorrow
morning."

"Why do they need to question us if they're deeming
Sylvia's death an accident?" Philip Blackmore asked.

"Because this is the second time in three days that
someone has fallen down these stairs," said Duncan. "I
don't think they're comfortable with the coincidence."

Coincidence? There was a serial murderer on the loose!
And it was futile to question the hotel guests. The killer
had already checked out. I'd told the investigating officers
as much last night.

"I believe the man you want is Gabriel Fox," I'd told
them in the wee hours of the morning. "I'd like to tell you
where to find him, but he conveniently disappeared in Pisa
so he could beat the rap for Jeannette Bowles's death. She's
the woman who was pushed off the Duomo yesterday. And

if you ever get around to looking at the videotapes, you'll see I'm right."

Officer Agripino Piccione lowered a bushy eyebrow at me. "What you mean, 'beat the rap'?"

A fellow officer whispered in his ear, which caused Officer Piccione's consternation to dissolve into a snaggle-toothed grin. "Ah. *Si*. One of you American idioms."

I rolled my eyes with frustration. "He killed Jeannette Bowles. He probably killed the other tour member you found here two nights ago, Cassandra Trzebiatowski, and if you want my opinion, he killed Sylvia Root, too."

Officer Piccione wasn't amused. "You say he disappear in Pisa. If he in Pisa, how he push dis woman down duh stairs?"

"There are trains, you know! He could have taken the train back this afternoon and been here waiting for her all along. The man is a book editor. He's probably read every Agatha Christie novel ever published. Things like this happen in Agatha Christie novels all the time! Haven't you ever seen Hercule Poirot on A & E?" I regarded the blank expression on Piccione's face. "Assuming you can pick up A & E over here."

"So you tink you Hercule Poirot?" Piccione questioned.

"No, of course not." For one thing, I had much less hair on my upper lip than he had. "But I'm telling you, while you're here scratching notes, Fox is being clever like one and getting away. I mean, he could be in Timbuktu by now! Don't you think you should issue an all points bulletin for him?" I regarded the blank expression on Piccione's face. "Assuming you have all points bulletins over here."

"Clever as Fox," Piccione repeated. "Another American idiom?"

"An adage, actually. A proverb. Kind of like, smart as a

whip?" I narrowed my gaze. "Dumb as a post?" I could tell by the look in his eye that adages were way over his head.

"You have reason why Fox want all dese women dead?" he asked.

Wasn't that the way? I practically give him his killer on a silver platter, and he has to have a motive. "Okay, here's the thing. I haven't quite figured out his motive. But whatever it is, I'm sure it'll make sense. At least, to him."

Duncan's voice drew me back to the present. "I can't begin to express my regret over what happened to Ms. Root. These accidents are so out of the ordinary, I don't know what to think. It's almost as if we're jinxed."

The Stolees and Teigs pivoted around in their chairs to train accusing eyes at me. "What?" I mouthed at them. Lucille Rassmuson raised her hand.

"Are you going to cancel the rest of the tour if more dead bodies show up?"

Duncan looked taken aback. Lucille's sensitivity always seemed to take people aback. "Did you . . . want me to cancel the tour?"

"How about we continue the tour, but you get the hotel to fix the damned runner on the stairs?" Dick Teig suggested. "Seems that might eliminate the problem entirely. Hell, I'll fix the damn thing myself if you get me some rubber matting and a hammer."

"I'll help," I heard Dick Stolee call out.

"Me too!" yelled Osmond Chesvig.

Aw, that was sweet. Iowans were so practical.

"I'll speak to the management," Duncan said, stunned. "In the meantime, please avoid the stairs. We've been given permission to use the freight elevator, which is around the corner to the left, for the rest of our stay, so I'd advise you to take advantage of the offer. And a reminder, this is our last full day in Florence, so plan to do the things you haven't done yet. Visit the Uffizi to see Botticelli's *The Birth of Venus*, the Galleria dell'Accademia to see Michelangelo's *David*, the Ponte Vecchio to check out the jewelry shops, or scout out that last-minute bargain at the leather market."

I wondered if I should try my luck at Giorgio's again and get that leather jacket.

I traced my twenty-nine-year-old eyebrow with an affectionate fingertip.

Nah.

"The results of your writing contest will be announced at eight o'clock tonight in the lobby, so those of you who've entered, please take note," Duncan advised. "This is your night. And now I believe Mr. Blackmore would like the floor." He nodded to Philip, who rose from his seat to address us.

"I can't tell you how devastated I am by Sylvia's death. Sylvia and I went back a long way, and even though I know she was often referred to as 'the barracuda,' I can say without equivocation that Sylvia Root was one of the most honest, most knowledgeable, most sensitive people in the industry, and I, for one, will miss her greatly. She had no family other than her Doberman, but I feel that all of us have become her family on this trip, so in light of that, I'm going to ask that we have a short memorial service for her tomorrow morning in one of the chapels of the Duomo. And if any of you had a care for Sylvia, I'd hope you'd see fit to attend. I'll give you more details this evening."

"What about Gabriel Fox?" Keely piped up. "How come he wasn't on the bus coming back from Pisa yesterday? Where was he last night at dinner? What's happened to him?"

Philip looked genuinely concerned. "It's a mystery at the moment where Gabriel is, but I have every reason to believe he'll rejoin us shortly. Knowing Gabriel's reputation with the ladies, I expect he may have found a lovely signorina in Pisa who made him an offer he couldn't refuse."

That elicited a few chuckles and seemed to lighten the dark mood that had settled over us, but I, for one, knew better. If Gabriel Fox was anywhere, it was on a plane, heading out of the country. The one benefit was, with Gabriel gone, at least we didn't have to worry about more people dying.

I hoped.

Chairs creaked and flatware rattled as we rose to our feet en masse. Mom gave me a troubled look as she joined the mob headed for the freight elevator. "And then there was one," she said grimly.

"Excuse me?"

"Haven't you noticed? I'm the only judge left. Sylvia's dead. Gabriel's missing. I don't mind telling you, Emily, it makes me feel a little peculiar. I'm the one who's going to have to decide someone's future, but I don't know if I'm qualified!"

I stared at her wide-eyed. She was the only judge left? Why did that make my legs feel suddenly gimpy? "I . . . I hadn't thought about that."

"I slipped notes under both Sylvia's and Gabriel's doors yesterday, saying I'd hand the manuscripts over to them midevening. I wrote down my room number and everything."

"Your room number, or my room number?"

"My room number. I figured I'd be through in your room by then. But neither one of them stopped by. Now I know why. What a shame about the Root woman. I'm going to say a novena for her tonight."

"Did you not go out to dinner with the group last night?"

"Your gramma told me about the plans when she got back from Pisa, but I was at a real critical point in my decision making, so I thought it was more important to finish up what I was doing than to eat. But I didn't go hungry. I found a little package of airplane pretzels at the bottom of my fanny pack, so I was just fine. They were really tasty, too. Mustard flavor."

Mom was the only judge left. Mom was the only judge left. Why did that seem so ominous? And looking at it from that perspective, I realized why.

What if the killer's real marks were the judges rather than the contestants? Without judges, there would be no contest. No winner. No prize. Was someone so opposed to this contest that he or she would resort to murder to stop it?

Oh. My. God. Could I have been wrong about Gabriel? Could he be as much a victim as the women who'd died? WHY WAS THIS WHOLE THING SO FREAKING CONVOLUTED?

Well, one thing was for sure, if Mom was the only judge left, I was going to make darn sure she stayed alive. I'd probably shoot myself later for what I was about to suggest, but the ugly truth was, if anything happened to even one little hair on her head, I wouldn't be able to live with myself. "Okay, Mom, you need to start enjoying your vacation, so I tell you what. Go back to your room and grab what you need, then meet me at the lobby door in fifteen minutes. You're going to see the sights of Florence with me today."

"That's sweet of you, Emily, but I think I'd better spend the day with your grandmother. She feels much safer when she's under my supervision."

"She has her own friends, Mom. George, and Alice, and the twins. She likes her independence. Let her do her own thing, and you can spend some quality time"—I forced the words out—"with me." There. I said it. Desperate times really did call for desperate measures.

"But what about her hearing loss?" Mom objected, as I scooted her toward the line snaking toward the freight elevator. "She needs me to interpret for her!"

I waved her forward. "I think she's been taking a new course at the senior center! Lip reading! Check your watch now! Fifteen minutes."

I felt like a human dynamo. Processing information. Analyzing results. Implementing strategy. I felt empowered, invincible, a little whacked-out. Oh, God. Maybe I wasn't a human dynamo. Maybe I was just a misguided tour escort suffering a really big nervous breakdown.

I checked my arms for hives.

Keely bumped into me head-on when I turned around. "Sorry," she apologized, her voice a sob, her eyes glistening with unshed tears.

"No problem." I took a step back, watching her pump air into a bubble that wilted suddenly like flaccid pasta. Either the gum was old, or something was bothering her. "Hey, are you all right?"

"No! This trip is turning into the biggest bomb. I sucked up to Sylvia Root, and she's dead. Do you know how depressing that is? She told me if I won this contest, she'd represent me. Can you believe it? Keely Mack represented by Sylvia Root. Now I have to start from scratch again! Do you know how long the process of finding an agent takes? Freaking forever! I sucked up to Gabriel Fox, and he's AWOL. A lot of help I'm going to get from him. I want to win this contest, dammit! But there's no one of any importance left to suck up to!"

I could take issue with that on my mother's behalf, but it was Keely. Why bother? "You could suck up to Philip Blackmore."

"Yeah, right. Mr. Personable. He might sound friendly and everything, but you can forget about having a private conversation with him. He doesn't have time for anyone except his elite little group."

"Then maybe you should think about trying to get published the old-fashioned way."

"How's that? Pretend I'm a West Coast literary agent looking to place one of my aspiring writers—me—with a prestigious New York agency before I retire?"

"I was thinking more like—finishing your manuscript."

She curled her lip at me in disgust. "You nonwriters are so out of it."

"Nice hair!" I called after her as she headed for the elevator.

She flicked her hand in the air. "Yeah, yeah."

But she'd left me with an intriguing little tidbit. Sylvia and Gabriel had been of more use to her alive than dead. I made a mental note of that and dropped her a notch in my list of possible suspects.

I found Nana sipping tea at a table by herself as I wended my way back through the room. I pulled out a chair and sat down next to her, noticing that the little white tufts of hair on the top of her head were so tortured and scraggly, she looked like she'd been run over by a power mower. "What are you doing all by yourself this morning?" I asked, trying not to stare.

"George and Osmond are outside takin' pictures a trash cans. I guess Osmond's family ran Windsor City Rubbish and Waste before they sold the business. Isn't that somethin'?"

"So what's on your agenda today?"

She gave me a hangdog look. "I'm havin' a real bad hair day today, dear, so you'll forgive me if I'm a mite grumpy."

"Your hair?" I gave her the once-over, suppressing a wince. "What's wrong with your hair?"

"Your mother's wrong with my hair. She left the toilet paper hangin' in the bathroom when she took her shower last night and soaked the whole roll clean through. I tried pullin' it apart to help it dry, but it was that cheap one-ply stuff. Shredded like confetti. So I had to sleep bareheaded. Lookit me! This is what happens when you don't have no cushion for your curls. I coulda used Kleenex, I suppose, but I woulda had to tape too many tissues together to get a continuous wrap. And that woulda been a problem because I didn't have no Scotch tape. The closest thing I come to tape was Post-it notes."

"Your hair doesn't look that bad, Nana," I lied, fluffing it here and there.

"You're a wonderful granddaughter, dear, but a bad liar. I look like I been through a car wash without the car."

I patted her hand. "Well, I have some news that's going to cheer you up."

"You're sendin' your mother home on the next plane?"

"Almost. I'm going to keep her under my wing today, so you and George can have the day, and your room, all to yourselves."

"No kiddin'?"

"No kidding."

She eyed me seriously. "You sure you wanna do this, Emily? It's your mother, remember. You might not be able to last the whole day."

"I'll be okay. I'm tough. But, I have a really big favor to ask. Could you do some research on the Web for me? I'd like to know what kind of link Sylvia Root had with Gabriel Fox other than the obvious agent/editor relationship. She was involved in another line of work before she began agenting. I'd like to know what it was. You might be able to find magazine articles. Interviews. Industry profiles. Anything would be helpful."

"That shouldn't be a problem, dear. I seen a bunch a cybercafés around. George will remember where they was."

"And I don't know how relevant this is, but Gabriel mentioned that Jeannette Bowles was involved in a lawsuit some years ago that hadn't gone well. Could you look into that? It might have nothing to do with the deaths, but I'm curious."

"How soon you need the information?"

"As soon as possible?"

She pushed away from the table and stood up. "Hunh. I'm feelin' less grumpy already. I'll get right on it. The quicker we get done"—she gave her eyebrows a little waggle—"the sooner we get to come back to the room." She bowed her head close to mine. "George says he's got a surprise for me."

Oh, God. I placed my hand on her shoulder. "Go easy on him today, okay? Replacement caps aren't cheap, and Medicare doesn't cover dental."

"You bet."

Chirrup chirrup. Chirrup chirrup. Chirrup chirrup.

I pulled my phone from the overflowing disorder in my shoulder bag and pressed it to my ear. "Hello?"

"*Ti amo, bella.*"

Warmth rippled through my body. "I love you, too," I said breathlessly.

"I have bad news for you, darling. My contact in the department has been called away. Family emergency. So I won't be able to supply you with any more information until I return to Switzerland. I'm sorry."

Good thing I'd put Nana on Gabriel's scent. It always paid to have a reliable backup. "That's no problem. I'll manage. But thanks for all your help. I do believe you've earned a reward for your efforts." I spied Duncan in the hall talking to the front desk clerk. "I take requests."

"An evening alone with you, *bella*. Champagne. Satin sheets. Candlelight. Massage oil." His voice dipped lower. "My tongue. Your flesh."

HOOCHIMAMA! "My calendar is open."

"So was mine until . . . early this morning. I might as well tell you, Emily. I was going to take the train to Montecatini to surprise you, but the department called about an hour ago to ask my assistance on a jewelry heist that took place last night at the local Bucherer store."

I remembered Bucherer. Last October I'd bought a watch there that had kept perfect time for all of one hour. "You have to go back to Lucerne?"

"On the evening train. I'm sorry, darling. I was hoping that seeing you again might jog my memory with regard to what I should have done in Ireland, but—"

"But you're on leave! Can't someone else handle the jewel heist?"

"It's my specialty, Emily. They need me. I've completed my duty to my family. I've had my fill of the casino. I haven't suffered a headache in almost two weeks." He paused. "I suspect it may be time for me to get back to work."

I realized I would have felt less disappointment if I'd never learned he was planning to surprise me. Damn. I heaved a sigh. "I miss you so much."

"I'm sorry, darling. It won't always be like this. I promise you."

But his words felt hollow to me at that moment. I needed more than words. I needed *him*.

Surly and frustrated, I shoved my phone back into my bag and headed for the lobby stairs. Duncan was just finishing up his conversation with the desk clerk and flagged me down as I approached him in the hall. "Can you spare me a minute before you head off?"

I stopped and forced a smile to my lips. "A minute is about all I have."

"About yesterday, Emily, I apologize if I—"

"No, no, *I'm* the one who should apologize—insisting that the police drag you out of bed to deal with Sylvia. If it's not them, it's me, right? You probably haven't had a decent night's sleep since we've been here."

He favored me with a smile that fit easily on his face. "You can drag me out of bed anytime."

Oh, no. I wasn't going there.

"Tell me, Em, how do you remain so calm and collected in the presence of a fresh corpse? Most people completely wig out. What's your secret?"

"Practice."

"I'm sorry?"

I shook my head. "I need to meet my mom, Duncan, so I really have to—"

Pulling me close by my shoulder strap, he bent down and kissed my mouth lightly, quickly, like a thief. "I was referring to yesterday afternoon," he whispered against my lips. "At the café in Pisa. I'm sorry if I seemed too brash, but I need to be honest with you." And then he kissed me again, deeply, urgently, like a man who knew exactly what he wanted. "I meant every word."

CHAPTER 11

"What's wrong with you?" Jackie asked outside my room minutes later.

I exhaled a long, exasperated breath. "I'm swearing off men."

She gave me a narrow look before throwing her arms around me and crushing me to her chest. "You're switching teams? That is *so* brave. So modern. So . . ." She stumbled backward and gaped at me, her eyes looking as if they might fly out of her head. "You don't have your sights set on *me*, do you? Oh, jeez, Emily, I'm really flattered, but, I'm a happily married woman!"

Speechless, I regarded her a full ten seconds before thrusting my room key in the lock and opening the door. "I have *not* switched teams! I like the team I'm on. I'm just . . . unhappy about the lineup. Too many minor league players wanting to come to the plate."

"Nice analogy," she conceded, following behind me into the room. "And you never even played baseball."

"Can we forget men for the moment and talk about

something serious? I think my mom may be in danger."

"Unh-oh. I saw Mrs. S. at breakfast and she told me about the toilet paper fiasco. Has she threatened to kill your mom? Trust me, once a jury gets a look at your grandmother's hair, they'll let her off the hook. It's a clear case of justifiable homicide."

"Listen to me, Jack! Of the three people appointed to judge this romance contest, one is dead, one is missing, and one is left. My mom. DO YOU KNOW WHAT THAT MEANS?"

She regarded me smugly. "Of course, I know what that means. They're going to need replacement judges."

"It means someone might be planning to kill my mother!"

Jackie executed a major eye roll. "Didn't I just say that? Your *grandmother* wants to kill her, Emily! Do you ever listen to anything I say? This is just like being married to you!"

I sank into the armchair and scrubbed my face with my hands. "I thought I had it all worked out. I thought Gabriel killed Sylvia because of the animosity that existed between them. Some kind of vendetta or something."

Jackie sucked in her breath. "Vendetta? You think Gabriel is *mafioso*? But he doesn't look Italian. I would have guessed WASP. Or Canadian."

"I thought he went missing because the videotapes would prove he pushed Jeannette to her death."

Another inhalation of breath. "He had a vendetta against Jeannette, too?"

"I . . . I don't know."

"You think he killed Cassandra?"

"He might have . . . but I haven't figured out why."

"What happened to murder due to plain, simple greed? Are you letting all the wannabes off the hook?"

"I'm not sure. I haven't figured that out either."

Jackie flopped onto the bed. "You want to tell me again what part of this you've worked out?"

"Hey! This whole thing has gotten very complicated. If someone wants to sabotage the contest by knocking off the judges, why begin by killing two of the contestants? Why not just stick to the judges?"

Jackie shrugged. "Maybe Cassandra and Jeannette were smoke screens. The killer wanted to cover up the real murder, so he started by pulling off a couple of fake ones."

"They weren't fake, Jack. Two women died!"

"But someone made them look like accidents, so they could have been fake!"

Groaning, I threw my head back and stared at the yellowed paint on the ceiling. "None of this makes sense. The killer should be targeting either the contestants or the judges. Not both."

"Maybe the killer doesn't have the same classification skills you have. Maybe he's just lumping everyone together in a general pool and picking them off like fish in a barrel."

Eh! I hoped that wasn't the case. But I knew one thing for sure. Whether Gabriel Fox turned out to be perpetrator or victim, I suspected he was the key to this whole mystery, and I wasn't going to rest easily until someone found him.

"So what's today's strategy?"

"Today, we're searching for Gabriel Fox. Dead or alive."

Jackie clapped her hands. "A manhunt! A manhunt's gotta be more exciting than surveillance work. Right?"

"And a little guard duty."

"Euw, more diversity. I like it. Who are we guarding?"

"Mom."

"Oh, no!" She catapulted herself to her feet. "You can forget that. No way I'm spending the day with your mother. In case you're unaware, Emily, SHE DOESN'T LIKE ME."

"She does so."

"Does not. Haven't you ever noticed the way she looks at me—like I'm a hologram she can't quite get into focus. And the only thing she ever says to me is, 'What a lovely outfit you're wearing.' She doesn't like me, and don't you dare suggest she does. It's taken a while, but I've become very sensitive to the vibes other people send my way. WHY DO YOU THINK I'VE HAD ALL THIS DAMN HORMONE THERAPY?"

I heaved myself out of the armchair and stashed some extra film in my shoulder bag. "Mom likes you, Jack. She likes everyone. Plus, she forgives easily, is always kind, and never holds a grudge. Nana thinks she's an alien."

Jackie folded her arms stubbornly across her chest. "She doesn't like me."

"She does so! Come on. Give her a chance. If you hang out with her a little, I bet you'll see loads of improvement with her conversation. She's really quite chatty at home."

"No." Jackie shook her head defiantly. "No, no, no."

"I bet that would be a lovely outfit on you," Mom commented to Jackie as we stood outside a clothing store not far from the Piazza della Repubblica. Jackie bared her teeth, crossed her eyes, and slashed a finger across her throat at me. I was so proud of her. She and Mom were really starting to bond.

We'd wowed Mom with a visit to the Duomo earlier, then crossed the street to tour the Museo dell'Opera dell Duomo, where we saw Lorenzo Ghiberti's original baptistry door panels under glass, another Michelangelo *Pietà* that was assumed to be a self-portrait of the sculptor himself, and a dimly lit room that housed the sacred relics of prominent saints in ornately designed reliquaries. Mom really liked that room. She used up a whole roll of film trying to get a good shot of St. Joseph's finger. She thought the pictures would make a good show-and-tell presentation at one of Nana's Legion of Mary meetings.

"A million lire," Mom said as she studied the dress on the headless mannequin in the store window. "How much is that in real money?"

"Five hundred dollars," I said as I trained a casual look over my shoulder, on guard for anyone who might bear a likeness to Gabriel Fox. I tried to imagine what he'd look like in a hat. With sunglasses. Without his beard. But the only people who looked familiar to me were the Severid twins, who were waving at me from the other side of the street. I shouldn't have been surprised they were still wearing my cigarette pants and bodysuits. One thing I'd learned on this trip: spandex wielded incredible power over dyed-in-the-wool Lutherans.

"We have a favor to ask," Britha announced as they joined us. "Would you mind telling us where you had your hair done, Emily? Barbro and I have decided we need a new look, don't we, Barbro? We were thinking about something a little more flashy. Something that suits our new outfits a little better."

Barbro picked it up from there. "Something bold and brash—a style that roars. A cut that looks the same as yours!"

The same as mine? It wasn't enough they were wearing my clothes? Now, they wanted my hair? I liked to think of myself as a nice person, but come on! Britha's request was a blatant violation of the unspoken code that a female should *never* copy a friend's car, clothing, or hair. Of course, the twins had done nothing *but* copy each other all their lives, so maybe that explained their ignorance of the code.

"Um . . ." I smiled. I hedged. I—

"I know the name of the salon," Mom said helpfully. "It's called Donatella and it's located by that lovely cathedral. Would you like me to help you find it?"

I shot Mom an evil look.

"I'll show you where it is!" Jackie offered. "In fact, I can take you right to the front door!"

My mouth fell open so far, my chin hit my knees.

"No, no. We don't want to take you away from what you're doing," Britha demurred. "If you just point us in the right direction, I'm sure we'll be able to find it. We're from Iowa, you know."

"*Pleeeeease,*" Jackie begged. "Please let me help you." She extended an arm to each of them. "I absolutely insist. Maybe I'll get a shampoo and style myself."

I threw Jackie a murderous look and mouthed the word "traitor." She favored me with a delirious smile that bespoke the thrill of escape.

"Would you mind if we made one small detour before the hairdresser though?" Britha asked Jackie. "We passed a little jewelry shop down one of these side streets that had some lovely earrings in the window. Clip-ons. Clip-ons are so hard to find these days. Would you mind stopping? We'd be quick."

"Maybe you should think about getting your ears pierced," Jackie suggested as she pointed them toward the dome of the cathedral. "You'd have a much wider selection of earrings to choose from. I could do it for you! All we'd need is a sterile needle, gold studs, an ice cube, and some disinfectant."

I shook my head as Jackie herded Britha and Barbro across the street. She really shouldn't get their hopes up about the ear piercing. The twins might already have a sewing needle and disinfectant, but this was Italy. They could forget about the ice cube.

"They're going to have such a nice time," Mom commented as she watched the trio disappear into the crowd. "You seem to know your way around the city so well, Emily, maybe we should offer to meet up with the twins later this afternoon so you can show them around, too."

"Maybe we'll run into them someplace."

"But if we don't make arrangements now, how will we find them?"

I sighed in defeat. "Shouldn't be too hard. We look for the only two septuagenarians in Florence running around with my hair."

We strolled along some of the main streets of Florence—Mom, oohing and aahing over the shoes and handbags in the stores—me, darting my eyes back and forth so often that I was making myself dizzy. When we turned the corner onto one particularly narrow lane, we caught sight of tables and chairs set up café style on the sidewalk, and clusters of people standing in small conversational groups on both sides of the street, waving wineglasses in their hands.

"Oh look," Mom said, as we passed a shallow niche in a building that was replete with a counter, a tiered backdrop of bottled wine, and stemware in every available space. "It's like the salad bar at Fareway, only with wine. Look at all those lovely bottles, Emily." A hint of excitement crept into her voice. "How do you suppose they're arranged?"

I hurried her along before she could offer to alphabetize them.

"Emily! Margaret!" a man's voice beckoned. "Over here!"

I nearly got whiplash trying to find the owner of the voice amid the clutch of midday tipplers, but the tanned arm rising over the dark heads in the crowd looked familiar, so we headed in that direction.

"I'm glad I spotted you," Philip Blackmore said in welcome, his hand wrapped around the stem of a full glass of red wine. "We were just about to offer a toast to Sylvia. Join us, would you?"

Marla Michaels and Gillian Jones stood on either side of him, looking uncomfortable and subdued as they balanced their drinks in their hands. Duncan completed the quartet, giving me a quiet nod that spoke volumes.

"Two glasses of Merlot for the ladies," Philip instructed, handing Duncan a fistful of lire. While Duncan dutifully bought our drinks, Philip girded an arm around Mom's shoulders, embracing her like a proud father. "I'm in your debt for all the work you've done to make our contest a success, Margaret. With our unfortunate turn of events, if not for you, we'd have no contest at all."

Color scorched Mom's cheeks. "It was nothing."

"I love you Midwesterners. You're so damned humble. How does it make you feel to know your decision will change someone's life tonight?"

"A little nervous actually."

She was nervous. I was a wreck. Maybe I should consider a drug stronger than wine.

Duncan returned with our drinks and lingered casually beside me. Philip elevated his glass reverently. "To Sylvia," he toasted.

"To Sylvia," we repeated, raising our glasses and clinking them in midair.

"She was incomparable," he declared, his voice gravelly with nostalgia. "The industry will shine far less brightly because of her absence."

While Gillian and Marla fought off tears, Philip Blackmore knocked back his entire glass of wine in one long gulp. "I think I'll have another," he said, spinning around and heading back toward the bar, his harness of bottled water swinging from his shoulder like a scuba tank.

"I can't believe she's gone." Gillian dashed tears from her cheeks. "Over the last few months she'd become one of my dearest friends. She was warm, witty, honest. She negotiated the most lucrative contract of my career. Three books. Twenty-city author tour. Four million dollars."

"Four million dollars!" Marla's glass slipped from her hand and shattered at her feet, spraying wine over her flowered muumuu like a deadly red pesticide. "Hightower offered you an advance of four million? They only offered me three. The shysters!"

Gillian took a long sip of wine before arching one superior eyebrow. "I guess that proves which one of us is more highly regarded in the writing world."

Marla shook wine from her hemline as she stepped away from the broken glass on the sidewalk. "The only thing it proves is that Sylvia didn't do enough by me to earn her f-ing 10 percent!"

Gillian inhaled a sharp breath. "Sylvia only charged you 10? She charged me 15! She was screwing me out of another 5 percent? The shyster!"

Mom looked happily from one diva to the other. "Maybe if you did the math, it'd work out that advance-wise and percentage-wise, you were both earning the same thing."

That was *so* like something Nana would say. I guess there was no denying genetics.

Gillian looked at Marla. Marla looked at Gillian. They both looked at Duncan. "Do you have a calculator?" they asked in unison.

He held his hands up defensively. "The only thing I have on me is my phone."

"I propose another toast," Philip bellowed as he returned with another full glass of wine. "This one is for Margaret." He raised his glass. "May your decision provide us with the next rising star in the romance world."

"I'll drink to that," I said, touching my glass to his. Marla and Gillian glared as he downed his second glass of wine.

"So how many millions are you going to pay the next rising star?" Marla sniped at him, angry fists poised on her hips. "More than four? Sylvia told me *I* was your highest-paid author. Funny how she forgot to mention that the *cowboy queen* was getting more!"

"I want my money back!" Gillian demanded. "Sylvia's dead. That 15 percent belongs to *me* . . . and I want it right now!"

Philip eyed each woman blandly before shoving his empty glass at Duncan. "Be a good chap and refill that for me, would you?"

Hmm. I wondered if Hightower had ever published a book on the dangers of binge drinking.

"Are we going to toast Mr. Fox?" Mom asked him.

"Hell, no!" Blackmore's face was so red by now that he looked like a Valentine balloon. "The little bastard. He had responsibilities on this trip and what's he done? He's run away."

Time to play a little devil's advocate. "How do you know?" I leaped in. "I mean, aren't you in the least bit alarmed that something terrible might have happened to him?"

"If he's not here, something terrible *better* have happened to him! He better be dead! But I won't hold my breath. He's done his disappearing act to get even with me, but the son of a bitch has forgotten it doesn't pay to piss off the guy who signs your paycheck. So he'd better use this time away from the tour to begin looking for another job, because as of now, he's fired!"

Gillian and Marla sucked in their collective breaths. "Can you do that?" they cried in one voice.

When push came to shove, I guess having a literary snob for an editor was better than having no editor at all.

"I can do whatever I damned well please," Philip corrected. "Ah, Duncan, good man." He snatched the glass from Duncan's hand and without bothering to offer another toast, guzzled the contents like an empty gas tank at the pump.

"But you said Gabriel was our ticket to respectability!" Marla whined.

"You said he was going to give romance a good name!" Gillian added.

Philip remained stone-faced. "There are other editors in New York. People who, unlike Gabriel Fox, know how to be team players. Now that he's out of the way, I'll find you the best, ladies. You'll see."

Was that a slip of the tongue? Mere speculation? Or did he know for sure that Gabriel Fox was "out of the way"?

Philip regarded his empty glass, seeming to ponder how it had gotten that way. "I need another drink," he said, but as he turned, Duncan stayed him with a hand.

"Why don't we grab something to eat first," Duncan said with quiet authority. "You mentioned you'd like to dine by the river. I know the perfect place. Great food. A spectacular wine list. Much better than anything you'll find at a wine bar."

It took a moment for Duncan's words to bore into Philip's skull, but when they did, Philip deposited his empty glass in Duncan's hand and nodded agreement. "A fine idea. I could use something to eat. What do you think, ladies? Shall we dine by the Arno today on Hightower's dime? I'll write it off as a 'memorial to Sylvia' on my expense account."

"You're not addressing my concerns, Philip," Marla blasted.

"You're ignoring mine as well!" Gillian spat.

"And I shall continue to do so for the remainder of the tour. If you have a problem with that, ladies, I suggest you buy your own damned lunch. Emily, Margaret, I hope you'll agree to join us. Maybe you can show Marla and Gillian how a typical adult conducts a conversation without all the bickering."

"We'd love to!" Mom agreed. "Wouldn't we, Emily?"

"You bet." Whether Gabriel Fox was dead or alive, I figured there had to be safety in numbers, even if Gillian and Marla did end up killing each other.

Duncan led the way back through the streets of Florence toward the Arno, with the dome of the cathedral constantly to our left. Outside the baptistry, Philip stopped for a slug of water and immediately spat it out. Unh-oh. Must be the expensive hotel water that Jackie had said tasted like liquid sewage. But instead of discarding the bottle, he gritted his teeth and chugged half the contents. Ick. Some people were obviously too proud to admit they'd just blown twenty-thousand lire.

We marched in the hot sun down streets lined with designer clothing stores and expensive salons, and when Marla made a detour into a gelato shop, Philip whipped out his bottle again and drained it.

"Just like I always told your brother," Mom said in a hushed voice as she watched him throw the bottle away. "Excessive drinking not only gives you a raging headache; it makes you thirsty. Then you end up going potty all night."

You could tell Mom was originally from Minnesota.

Her proficient use of the word "potty" in both its noun and verb forms was a dead giveaway.

While Marla slurped her gelato, we arrived at the insanely crowded Piazza della Signoria where we stopped to shoot pictures of an impressively naked Neptune rising from a really big fountain and an equally naked David without the fountain. As Duncan motioned us toward the arcaded walkway flanking the Uffizi, Philip lost his footing and went sprawling onto the pavement in a graceless heap. "I'm all right. I'm all right," he assured us, as Duncan helped him to his feet. But he didn't look all right. The sweat from his body was soaking through his shirt, and his eyes had that vacuous look that sometimes appeared in Mom's when she was talking to Jackie.

"You want to rest?" Duncan asked him.

"Tripped is all," he growled, pressing a hand to his stomach. "My shoelace. Get me to the restaurant. I'll be fine."

The liquor was obviously starting to impair his thinking. His shoes didn't have lacings. He was wearing loafers.

We dodged around people queued up in long lines for the museum and fought off young East Indian men hawking artwork and questionable articles of clothing. "You buy this, Madame," one man urged Mom, shoving a fishnet shirt in her face. "It look very nice on you. I have large size."

Mom offered the man a courteous smile and stopped to hold the thing up to her. "What do you think, Emily?"

I eyed it critically. "I think it would look great . . . at the end of a pole." I craned my neck to keep track of the rest of the group. "Come on, Mom, we're losing everyone."

We pushed, and shoved and beat off more men selling postcards and gaudy scarves. By the time we reached the end of the arcade and stepped into the sunlight, we'd lost sight of the entire group, except for Philip, who was staggering across the street, unmindful of the scooters that *vroomed* past like angry gnats.

"What's he doing?" asked Mom.

I cringed as a Vespa squealed to a stop just shy of plowing into him. The helmeted driver flipped him an obscene gesture and gunned around him, leaving him to fend off a half dozen more.

"Watch out, Philip!" I yelled, but he seemed not to hear me as he stumbled toward the opposite sidewalk and collapsed onto the low stone balustrade that overlooked the river. "Don't move!" I screamed at him. "I'm coming!" Then to Mom, "Stay right here and wait for the others, okay? I don't want to lose you, too."

I stepped into the street, leaping backward as a scooter nearly clipped me. I darted an anxious look at Philip. He was crumpled on the balustrade, his arms and legs dangling lifelessly. Oh, God.

I charged into the street again, stiffening as a pack of Vespas wishboned around me, their helmeted drivers shaking their fists at me amid the deafening buzz of their motors. I glanced back at Philip.

I did a double take.

He was gone.

What?

I looked right. I looked left. WHERE WAS HE?

I heard a sudden scream. I saw a teenage girl in a bandana and hiking boots point a finger downward at something on the opposite side of the ledge where Philip had been lying. Her female companion leaned over the barrier, her hand flying to her mouth. I battled through traffic toward the sidewalk and raced toward the ledge.

I looked down.

I squinted into the sunlight, blinded by the reflected

glare of the river, but not so blinded that I couldn't make out the body of Philip Blackmore spread-eagled on the paved walkway twenty feet below me.

Mom had obviously forgotten to mention a further consequence of excessive drinking.

It could kill you.

CHAPTER 12

And when I looked again," I explained an hour later, "he'd disappeared. That's when I ran to the ledge and . . . and saw what had happened."

Officer Agripino Piccione used the blunt end of his pen to scratch the place where the wild hairs of his eyebrows intersected over the root of his nose. "And what you tink happened?"

"He fell!" Duncan's hand was a comforting pressure on my shoulder as he stood beside me in the cool shade of the Uffizi's arcade. "He drank too much too quickly at a wine bar, and when it caught up to him, I think he passed out, and . . . and fell off the ledge."

Piccione flipped backward through the pages of his notepad. "How many people dis make who fall dead on you tour?" he asked tiredly.

"Four dead. One missing. But this was an accident. I saw it myself."

"You tink *Signora* Root, someone push her," he said, consulting his notes. "You no tink Blackmore pushed?"

"I didn't see anyone standing near him who *could* have pushed him in the few seconds when I wasn't looking at him." I eyed him, aghast. "*Uff da*. Do *you* think someone pushed him?"

"*Ooff da*? What you mean, *ooff da*?"

"It's a Norwegian idiom," Duncan informed him. "Loosely translated it means holy cow, holy smoke, holy cats, holy moly, holy mackerel, holy shit, or holy crap."

I stared at Duncan. Holy moly? No self-respecting Norwegian would ever say holy moly.

Piccione frowned. "How you use in sentence?"

Okay. Had I missed something? I replayed the scene in my head. No. I was sure no one had been around Philip. His fall had been an accident. But why did his death suddenly seem to smack of Jeannette Bowles's? "By any chance, have you seen the videotapes from the Duomo yet?" I asked Piccione. "I know you're busy investigating all these other incidents, but I should think if you'd get on those tapes, they might provide a huge break in the case."

"*Signorina* Andrew, I conduct investigation. *Si?*" Ignoring my question, he turned to Duncan. "Why you no see anyting?"

Duncan nodded toward the lines of people still jammed together beneath the arcade. "I'd gotten held up trying to extricate my companions from the unrelenting clutches of the clothes and art hawkers. You want a friendly suggestion? Get rid of them. They're a nuisance."

"I make note of dat and give to prime minister. I'm sure, how you say, he get right on it." Piccione slapped his notepad shut. "How much longer you people be in Florence?"

"We leave for Montecatini tomorrow morning," Duncan replied.

"Better for me you leave today. You people big trouble."

Testiness sharpened Duncan's voice. "You indicated you might want to question some of the guests about Ms. Root's death later this evening. Have you changed your mind?"

"We wait for autopsy report, den decide. I tell dem be quick so you leave soon." He nodded toward a nearby police car, where Marla and Gillian were crying hysterically and Mom was huddled over them, trying to lend comfort. "What you want do wit *signoras*?"

"Ms. Michaels has a minor heart condition, and Ms. Jones has severe hypertension, so it wouldn't hurt to have them checked out by a professional," said Duncan. "Can one of your officers give them a ride to the hospital?"

"*Si*." A digital tone sang out from the cell phone holster on Piccione's belt. "*Pronto*," he answered, striding away from us. I gazed up at Duncan.

"Do you want me to ride with Marla and Gillian to the hospital?"

"I'll go. That's my job. And maybe you wouldn't mind if your mom came, too." He bobbed his head toward the police car. "She's calmed the ladies down considerably in the past hour. Look at the three of them. I think they've become fast friends." His eyes grew distant, his voice wistful. "Your mother reminds me of my aunt Carolyn. I don't know what we would have done without her support after my sister died. She was a regular Rock of Gibraltar."

"I'm so sorry about your sister, Duncan," I offered in a small voice.

He shrugged. "You think you've dealt with the worst of it, but the emotions seem to keep cropping up, and then you have to deal with it all over again." On a whim he unzipped a security pocket on his shirt and removed a micro address book. Flipping to a page toward the middle of the book, he studied it intently. "I still have her name penciled in under L. Address. Phone number."

He held the book up for my perusal. I squinted at the name printed in tiny block letters. MOLLY LAZARUS.

"I've tried to erase it a few times, but I can't bring myself to do it." He touched a hesitant fingertip to the page. "It'd be too much like saying . . . she never existed. As long as she's still in my book, I figure—"

He cleared his throat self-consciously and threw a distracted yet composed look back toward the police car and nodded. "Your mother obviously has the touch, Emily. I'd hate to ruin her efforts by separating her from Gillian and Marla."

I watched the divas sobbing into Mom's ample breast and realized how satisfied this must be making her feel. She was being helpful. Doing something positive. Making a difference. This might go down as the highlight of her trip. "I expect she'll want to go with you, but you have to promise me you won't let her out of your sight. You'll be there with her at the hospital, then escort her back to the hotel?"

He raised his fingers in the air in a familiar salute. "Scout's honor."

"I don't want her left by herself until they find Gabriel Fox."

Duncan eyed me curiously. "Why ever not?"

I hesitated. Did I dare trust him with my theory? What the heck? I was offering theories to everyone. Why not him? "Okay, it might sound a little off-the-wall, but—"

"Four dead," Officer Piccione announced as he rejoined us. He shoved his cell phone back into the holster on his belt and trained his black eyes on my face. "None missing."

"You found Gabriel Fox?" I croaked.

"At Fiumicino Airport in Rome. You right, signorina

Andrew," he said with grudging respect. "Signor Fox, we find him trying to leave country."

Curiosity seekers crowded the balustrade to watch a black bag containing the body of Philip Blackmore being lifted onto a gurney and deposited in the rear of a modified station wagon. The divas, along with Duncan and Mom, had been carted off to the hospital, and Officer Piccione and his minions had already departed. But the crime scene people had taken a long time with the body, so I'd stayed behind to watch the proceedings from the street above. I realized my presence did Philip Blackmore no good now, but being here while they fussed over his body made me feel as though I was paying my respects to him in some small way. This wasn't part of my escort duties. I figured it was simply part of being a decent human being.

Before he'd left, Officer Piccione had informed us that the Rome police would be detaining Gabriel Fox for questioning about his disappearance from Pisa. *Questioning*, he emphasized. There was no law against leaving a tour group early. But I suspected there probably *was* a law about skipping out on a tour after you'd murdered three of the guests. Odds were, if Fox wasn't dead, he was guilty. I still didn't know what would possess him to commit triple murder, but—

Chirrup chirrup. Chirrup chirrup. Chirrup chirrup.

Everyone around me went for their phones, but it was mine ringing. "Hello?"

"I got that information you was asking about," Nana said. "You want it now or later?"

"Now is fine. But hold on a minute." I squirmed through the glut of onlookers to a quieter spot near the columns of the arcade. "Where are you calling from?"

"A phone outside the cybercafe. I bought me one a them

phone cards, but it's taken me five tries to get the call through. It's easier hackin' into the National Security Agency."

A chill stiffened my spine. I was going to pretend she hadn't said that. "Okay, Nana, what do you have for me?" I thought I caught a glimpse of Fred's hat in the crowd by the balustrade, but when I blinked, it disappeared.

"I done what you said, dear. I found some news articles and interviews in the archives a some trade magazines, and you'll never guess what Sylvia Root done before she began her literary agency. She was a romance author! Pretty successful, too. Wrote what they called erotic series romance under the name Elizabeth Hampton."

"No kidding?" Is that what she'd been trying to hide when we'd had lunch together two days ago?

"No kiddin'. Some articles said she had the talent to become more popular than some famous romance author by the name a Barbara Cartland, because Sylvia was a lot more racy. One article claimed she was perched on the edge a romantic stardom. And then, it all went bust."

"What happened?"

"Some fella reviewed her books and said such bad things about 'em, she couldn't write no more. He said her characters were dim-witted. Her plots were half-witted. Her dialogue was dull-witted. Her prose was heavy-handed, half-baked, and— Wait a minute. I got it written down here. Oh, yeah. And 'hebetudinous.' Isn't that a fancy word? And it's not even hyphenated. So the upshot was, Sylvia lost all her confidence, went into seclusion, came down with a case a what they call writer's block, and never wrote another word."

"All because of one reviewer?"

"All because a Gabriel Fox. He was the fella what done the reviewin.'"

"Gabriel Fox? Oh, my God! He'd mentioned at lunch the other day that he'd begun his career reviewing pulp fiction. But I never dreamed that one of the authors he'd reviewed was Sylvia." No wonder she'd been carrying a grudge against him. No wonder she'd been uncivil to him from the moment they'd met. He'd ruined her writing career! She knew how vicious he could be because she'd already been victimized by him.

"The thing is, dear, Sylvia probably made more money as an agent than she ever would have as a writer, so maybe she shoulda thanked him for the review instead a holdin' a grudge."

Nana had a point, but I doubt Sylvia would have agreed. "You're a genius, Nana. Thank you."

"I'm not done yet. I didn't have no luck hackin' into Hightower's internal memos, so I done the next best thing. I stuck my nose into one a them publishin'-related chat rooms and learned plenty. Someone whose screen name was SLUSHGAL said it wasn't no secret about the bad blood between Philip Blackmore and Gabriel Fox. She said Blackmore warned Fox at the weekly staff meetin's that if he didn't start actin' like a team player, Fox could edit all the literary novels he wanted, but it wouldn't be at Hightower Books. Blackmore called him a pseudointellectual boor and said if Hightower didn't change its publishin' direction, they was gonna sink, and sink fast, but Fox couldn't see past his own elitist nose to realize the good it would do the company. So SLUSHGAL says Fox tried to form employee opposition to the move to romance, but he didn't get no support. It made Blackmore so angry, though, he gave Fox both romance divas to edit as a kind a punishment. Fox wasn't real high in Blackmore's good graces, but I guess for the tour, at least, they tried to put on a good front."

"How did SLUSHGAL know all this?"

"She wouldn't tell me, but I bet you anythin' she works at Hightower, or used to. She knew too many a them fancy publishin' words not to be in the business herself."

Philip's irritation with Gabriel made sense now. No wonder he'd fired him. No wonder he hadn't been concerned about his whereabouts. He must have thought Gabriel was trying to sabotage the whole tour. And when I thought about it, I realized his assumption wasn't far off the mark. Two deaths of aspiring writers and one of a literary agent. I hadn't been able to see the connection before, but I was beginning to see it now.

"And one last thing, dear. I found a website for that Bowles woman and links to some a the New England resorts where she was wined and dined. She spent a fair amount a time at the Mount Washington Hotel. She liked the climbin' around there and even done volunteer rescue work on weekends. Made me think her lawsuit mighta had somethin' to do with her rescue work, so I hooked into another link that listed all the climbin' accidents that ever happened on Mount Washington, but I didn't find Jeannette's name nowhere. Awful sad stories though. Forest rangers gettin' froze to death in the winter. Lightnin' strikes killin' hikers. A young honeymoon couple dyin' in a landslide."

Honeymoon couple? That was so sad. So untimely. And so like what had happened to Duncan's sister. I frowned. I supposed people died on their honeymoons all the time, but still— "What can you tell me about the honeymoon couple?"

"There was a real long article on that one. The husband was a famous English mountain climber by the name a Robert Adcock. He'd even conquered Mount Everest. A real expert. But he went where he shouldn't and took his

wife with him. I guess they was buried for days before anyone found 'em."

"Did they list a name for the wife by any chance?"

"Molly, was her name. Molly Adcock. You there, Emily?
I can't hear you breathin'."

Molly Adcock? Born, Molly Lazarus? Was that possible?
Good Lord, had Nana stumbled upon an obituary for
Duncan's sister? I tried to ignore the goose bumps racing
up my arms. "I'm here, Nana. Where are you off to now?"

"Me and George are goin' back to the hotel." A meaningful pause. "Your mother's still there with you, isn't she?"

"Um, actually, she's in the hospital."

"The hospital? Oh no. I told George somethin' like this
might happen. Your mother can be such a trial. Go ahead
and tell me, dear. I won't hold it against you. What'd you
do to her that landed her in the hospital?"

"Me? Nothing! She's not hurt. She's on a goodwill mis-
sion. But you don't need to know the details now. I'll tell
you later." Why ruin an afternoon of carnal bliss with more
bad news?

"Well, I'm proud a you for restrainin' yourself, Emily. I
don't know if I coulda done it. You have any idea when
your mother might be back?"

"I guess that depends on how efficient the Italian medical system is. But if their medical system is run anything
like their phone system, I wouldn't expect her back for several hours."

"That's what I wanted to hear. Back to the hotel,
George," I heard her say as she hung up. "Pronto."

When I walked back to the stone rail overlooking the
river, the vehicle containing Philip Blackmore's body had
already departed, so other than two laborers who were
spreading some kind of powder onto the stained pavement,
there was no evidence that a man had lost his life here

today. It made me realize how little I knew about Philip Blackmore. Was he married? Did he have children? Was his George Hamilton tan the real McCoy or was it the result of weekly visits to a local tanning salon? Poor Philip. Duncan, or perhaps someone from Landmark Destinations' main office, would be making all the necessary phone calls back to the States about now. Which reminded me. I had a phone call of my own to make.

I found the number for the Florence police station in my guidebook and punched it up. I told the person who answered that I had information to give Officer Agripino Piccione about a case he was working on, and I'd appreciate it if he could call me back as soon as possible. I left my name and cell phone number, but as I signed off, I wondered if Piccione would receive the message at all. The only words of English the person I'd spoken to seemed to know were, "Yes," and "Excuse me," which didn't leave me very hopeful. But as I headed back through the arcade of the Uffizi, I counseled myself not to be so negative. I mean, Italians probably knew a lot more English than they let on. So I'd probably hear from Piccione within the hour.

By ten minutes of eight that night, he still hadn't gotten back to me, and my two follow-up calls to the station had gained me nothing other than inane conversations with people who spoke even less English than the first person I'd spoken to. The other troubling thing was, Mom wasn't back from the hospital yet. Of course, neither was Marla, Gillian, or Duncan, but that didn't make me feel any less anxious.

I hadn't told anyone about Philip Blackmore's death, thinking it would be more appropriate for Duncan to make the announcement at the meeting tonight, but as the minutes ticked by, and people kept gathering in the lobby to await the contest results, I got worried that if no one showed up by eight, I might have to take matters into my own hands and do some explaining about what happened today. Not something I was looking forward to, especially since one of the words I'd have to use in the explanation would be the dreaded noun, "morgue."

I paced in front of the staircase, checking my watch and the front door every thirty seconds. Bodies were jammed shoulder to shoulder in the lobby, on the vinyl sofas, on the coffee tables, on the floor. People laughing. People talking. Even some of my group had come to hear the announcement. The Teigs. The Stolees. Lucille Rassmuson. Osmond Chelsvig. Alice Tjarks. "Shouldn't someone be getting this show on the road?" Keely asked from her perch on the sofa. "It's five minutes of eight. I want to hear the results."

"None of our luminaries are here," Brandy Ann yelled above the din. "Shouldn't they be here by now?"

"Does anyone know what room Philip Blackmore is in?" Amanda asked. "I could run up and get him."

I checked my watch: 7:57. Okay. Like it or not, I had to say something. "About the results of the contest," I said, skirting the edge of the group. "We ran into a rather significant problem today that might delay—"

"I'm here!" Mom announced as she barreled through the front door, red-faced and breathless. "I'm sorry I'm late, but I'll run upstairs to get the results and be right back. I know you're all champing at the bit, so I'll be quick. Just hang on." She charged past me without saying a word. I gave chase, catching up with her by the stairwell.

"Mom! What's going on?"

She peered up the length of the stairwell, at the risers that were covered with a spanking new rubber runner. "Oh, my goodness! Did the Dicks find time to do that this afternoon? What a nice job. I'll have to compliment them when I see them. I guess it must be safe to take the stairs now."

"Mom! Where *is* everyone?"

She looked beyond me to the waiting crowd. "I don't really have time for this now, Emily, but the big news is, I talked to the president of Hightower Publications on Duncan's phone from the hospital, and you'll never guess. He put me in charge!"

"Of what?"

"Of everything. I believe his exact words were, 'The show must go on.' He refused to serve up any more disappointment to the guests, so the tour is continuing, and I'm calling the shots. Isn't this exciting?"

Mom was in charge? Oh, God. What was wrong with this picture?

"We can talk later, Emily. I have to get those contest results before the natives get too restless." Up the stairs she bounded, leaving me to stare after her. Mom was in charge?

"*Buona sera,* pretty."

I let out a little yelp at the sound of Duncan's voice behind me.

"Sorry," he apologized. "I didn't mean to frighten you."

"Where have you guys been?" I asked, motioning him into the hallway around the corner so he could explain in relative privacy.

He braced a shoulder against the wall and brushed a wisp of hair off my cheek. "Socialized medicine. It takes forever. They're keeping Marla and Gillian overnight for observation. Have you told anyone about Philip yet?"

"I figured that was your job."

"Good girl." He smiled at me with his eyes, then let out a sigh that smacked of utter weariness. "I'll break the news after your mother announces the winner of the contest. God, can anything else go wrong on this trip?"

I winced involuntarily. "Is that a rhetorical question, or do you really want to know?"

"Never mind. Pretend I didn't ask." He checked his watch. "You didn't hear from Officer Piccione this afternoon, did you? I'd like the final word about whether he's intending to question the group about Sylvia's death. When he receives her autopsy results, I suspect he'll decide further questioning won't be necessary. But I'd like to know for sure."

That gave me a jolt. "What do you expect him to find in the autopsy results?"

He snapped his fingers. "That's right. You weren't at dinner last night. You didn't see—"

"That's it, ladies," Jackie's voice rang out from the hall to my left. "Quick like bunnies. We don't want to miss the big moment."

I glanced down the shadowed corridor to find Jackie herding two elderly women in leopard skin pants and tank tops toward us. Their hair was Howdy-Doody orange, styled into manly buzz cuts, and from their ears hung long clusters of beads that rattled softly as they scurried in our direction. Good God, where had she picked up these two—

OH MY GOD! IT WAS THE SEVERID TWINS!

They stumbled past in strappy high-heeled sandals with toe thongs. They winked at me with thickly mascaraed eyes and waved with glittery fingernails that were as gold as their earrings. "We'd stop to talk," said Barbro—

"But we don't want to miss the big moment," Britha finished for her, hastening toward the lobby.

EH! I gripped Jackie's arm as she sashayed by in a pink leather miniskirt. "What did you do to them?"

"Don't they look adorable?"

"Sure! If you like geriatric butch!"

"And I took them shopping afterward," she said proudly.

Duncan cleared his throat and made an awkward gesture toward the lobby. "Will you excuse me? I should probably make my presence known in there."

"What were you thinking?" I raved at Jackie as I peered around the corner at the twins. "I can't take them back to Iowa like that! They'll be laughed out of town. Banished from political caucuses. Excommunicated from their church. Lutherans don't do orange hair!"

On the other hand, their hair had turned out nothing like mine, so maybe it wasn't so bad after all. I perked up. "What happened to the idea of having their hair cut exactly like mine?"

"Bad timing. Donatella's was closed, so we had to find another salon. But it was the coolest place, Emily. They had manicurists, pedicurists, body waxers, masseurs, stylists, color experts. When the twins saw the list of services, they decided to go the whole nine yards."

I slanted a final woeful look at them. "Do they realize their hair is the color of Raggedy Ann and Andy's?"

"Patrizio said that was *the* color this summer and it would look *splendido* with their blue eyes."

"Are you sure Patrizio wasn't trying to use up product to beat the expiration date?"

Jackie appeared shocked. "You can be *so* cynical. Patrizio would never do that. He was much too soulful." She fanned her hand in front of her face. "Not to mention he had abs you could have grated cheese on. Unh."

I paused. "How do you know what his abs look like?"

"That was the cool part. It was straight out of a Fellini movie. If you paid a little extra, you could have all your services performed by employees— Are you ready for this? In the nude!"

A memory fluttered in my brain. "Excuse me?"

"I thought the ladies would be horrified, but they really got into it. They even took pictures! You know, Emily, they're really quite liberal for Lutherans."

I clapped my hands over my face.

"I'm gonna take the idea back to Tom, but you wait. There's probably some kind of blue law that forbids cutting hair in the buff in Binghamton. The guy who owns this salon is making a bundle though. The main salon is in Florence, but he has franchises in Milan, Paris, and Lucerne. Hey, maybe Etienne has had his locks chopped there."

Lucerne? Hair cutting in the nude? Oh, my God. This couldn't be the same guy who'd tried to hit on Nana in Switzerland, could it? I shot a look up at Jackie. "Did you happen to speak to the owner?"

"Nope. But Patrizio pointed him out to me. Funny-looking little guy actually."

I recalled a faint image. "Hair like a cactus? Face like a ferret? Knees like old potatoes?"

Jackie's mouth dropped. "Euw. Scary. How'd you know that?"

"By any chance, was the salon named . . . Nunzio?"

She sucked in her breath and inched backward as if I were an apparition. "Okay, Emily, cut it out. You're really starting to creep me out."

It *was* the same guy! Wow, there were apparently a lot more business opportunities for perverts here in Europe than back in the States.

I heard a muffled thud and a yelp from the stairwell and dashed around the corner to find Mom stumbling awkwardly down the stairs despite the new runner. She held up her hand to ward me off. "I'm all right, Emily. It's the risers. I think they're just too far apart. Must be hard to measure things right when you're using that durned metric system."

My panic subsiding, I helped her the rest of the way down the stairs and into the lobby area, where we were greeted by applause, whistles, and a feeling of general anxiety. Duncan reached out a hand to Mom, guiding her into the middle of the crowd where she could command center stage. "Mrs. Andrew is here to announce your contest winner."

Heads turned right and left in surprise. "But where are Marla and Gillian and Philip Blackmore?" someone called out. "Shouldn't they be the ones to announce the winner?"

"Mrs. Andrew is in charge," Duncan replied smoothly, "so please give her your full attention." A space opened up for him so he could sit on the floor. I stood on the outer fringe of the group, marking the agonized anticipation on the faces of Amanda, Brandy Ann, Keely, Fred, and all the other contest entrants. Jackie slid by me in her pink leather miniskirt and curled up uncomfortably on the floor beside the twins. Mom scooted her wire-rims higher up on her nose and smiled at the crowd.

"I want to tell you what an honor it's been for me to judge your wonderful proposals and ideas. We have some very talented writers in our little group here, and I think you all deserve a round of applause."

Raucous clapping erupted, interspersed with a few abbreviated hoots. Mom quieted them down with the panache of a symphony conductor. "Look at all of you. So anxious to learn the identity of the next rising star in the romance world. Who will it be?" She bobbed her head at the people around her, squinting at their name tags.

"Elaine Lewis? Amanda Morning? Fred Arp? Lucille Rassmuson?"

Lucille waved her hand to object. "Yoo-hoo! Margaret! I didn't enter the contest. We're just here to see who wins. But we have eight-thirty dinner reservations, so could you get cracking?"

"You betcha. Sorry." Mom removed a slip of paper from her pocket and snapped it open. "To remind you now, the winner will receive a one-book publishing contract with Hightower Books and an advance of ten thousand dollars." Her words were breathy with excitement. "I'm so nervous! Okay, I don't want to keep you waiting any longer. The winner is—" She squinted at the name tags, building up the drama, then suddenly lowered her paper. "I'm sorry, but before I announce the winner, could I trouble you to arrange yourselves in alphabetical order? I can help if you like. It shouldn't take too long. It's so much more orderly that way. Can I have all the A's in the far left corner, please?"

Groans. Hisses. *Oh, Lord.*

Nana rounded the corner of the stairwell at that moment, cheeks pink and eyes glowing despite the fact that her hair was even wilder than it had been this morning. I knew this look. I'd *lived* this look. And I realized it could only mean one thing.

She'd finally "done it," and done it right. Aw, that was so sweet!

George shambled along slowly behind her, head drooping, shoulders sagging—a black eye patch slanted across his face. *Eye patch?*

OH, MY GOD! SHE'D POKED HIS EYE OUT!

"Mrs. Andrew doesn't really need you in alphabetical order!" Duncan instructed as he catapulted himself to his feet.

"Yes, I do," she countered.

"Stay where you are," Duncan pleaded. I dashed over to George, peering nose to nose with him.

"Oh, God, I'm so sorry! I never should have left the two of you alone together."

George smiled at me with his little gap-toothed grin and slid his arm around Nana's waist. "Ith's nuthin.'"

I dried my face with the back of my hand. Nana offered me a tissue.

"George," I reasoned. "Have you looked at yourself in the mirror? You only have one eye!"

Nana tugged on the seam of my top and bent her head close to me. "He's got two eyes, dear, but the patch is the surprise I was tellin' you about. The barbarian stuff wasn't workin' out real good, so he thought a some other romantic hero he could be."

I gave him a critical look. "A World War II vet with a lazy eye?"

"A pirate, Emily. And it worked out so good, he's decided to stay in character. He got some real nice bargains on leather eye patches at the open-air market. In seven designer colors."

"All right!" I heard Mom concede from the lobby. "Have it your way! But I still think it would work better if you were in alphabetical order."

"Get on with it, Margaret!" Dick Stolee yelled as he focused his camcorder on her. I herded Nana and George closer to the group. Mom snapped her paper in front of her again.

"Very well then. The winner of the Passion and Pasta romantic book contest is . . . contestant number twenty-four!"

Heads spun every which way. People looked confused. Befuddled. From her perch on the sofa, Keely popped a bubble and shouted, "No one ever told us what our contestant numbers were. Don't you have a list that matches names with entry numbers?"

Groans. Grumbling. Impatient sighs.

Mom snapped her fingers and looked suddenly enlightened as she slipped her hand into her other pocket and extracted a second piece of paper. "Okay, I have it now. The winner of the Passion and Pasta contest is . . ."

The crowd leaned forward. Brandy Ann pinched her eyes shut. Amanda crossed her fingers in the air. Keely cracked her gum. Fred clutched the chin straps of his hat. Dick Teig burped.

" . . . Jackie Thum!"

that was assumed to be a self-portrait of the sculptor him

CHAPTER 13

A piercing shriek ripped through the lobby as my miniskirted ex-husband leaped to her feet. "I won! Oh, my God! I won! I'm an author! I'm going to be famous! I'm going to be rich!" She hopped giddily up and down, then bent down to yank Britha and Barbro off the floor to hop with her.

"Well, would you lookit that," said Nana, staring at the trio. "You have any notion she entered that contest?"

I shook my head in slow motion, too stunned for words.

"That Jackie's sure got a lot a talent," Nana philosophized. "Maybe you shoulda stayed married to her."

A smattering of applause trickled through the room as Jackie curtsied and bowed. "Jackie Thum," she burbled, wishboning her arms in victory. "Romance author! But tell me honestly. Do you think I should have a pen name? Something more literary? What about Jackie with a 'qu' instead of a 'k'?"

"What about Jackie O?" Grace Stolee suggested.

Spirited applause from the Iowa contingent for Grace's suggestion.

"I kinda like Yora Fink," Keely offered, sneering.

Scattered applause. A few hisses.

"I knew some Finks in Minnesota," Nana whispered to me. "Nice Scandinavian family. You s'pose they're any relation?"

I wandered over to Jackie. As she settled the twins back onto the floor, I muttered in an undertone, "I thought you said you didn't read romance novels."

She shrugged prettily. "I lied."

"So what about your plans to become a tour guide escort? That's why you're on this trip! That's why you bought the little minirecorder. That's what you want to become!"

She retrieved her minirecorder from her shoulder bag and slapped it into my hand. "Here. You can have this. I won't be needing it anymore. No offense, Emily, but your job is a drag. I don't think I'd last more than a day. And let's be honest. Don't you think I'm better suited to stardom than servitude?"

I gave my eyes a major roll as Duncan took the floor again. "Congratulations to Jackie on her win," he said in a mellow voice. "I'm sure we'll all look forward to seeing her name in print."

Considering the disappointed scowls on most of the faces in the room, I wouldn't bet the farm on it.

"How about teasing us a little with the book's plot," he coaxed.

Jackie gnawed on her lower lip for a moment. "Umm, okay. It's the story of a small-town woman's desperate search to find love again after her husband dumps her for another man in the cutthroat world of Broadway theater. Kinda like *Midnight Cowboy* meets *A Chorus Line*."

I hung my head and covered my eyes. *Oh, God.*

"Sounds as though it has best seller written all over it. Good luck with your new career." He took a deep breath, a pained look creeping into his rugged features. "Our next order of business is one that I regret having to share with you." His voice dropped an octave. "I'm sorry to report that Philip Blackmore was involved in a freak accident this afternoon. On his way to lunch, he apparently lost his balance and fell onto the embankment near the Ponte Vecchio. I wish I could tell you that this particular story has a happy ending, but it doesn't. Philip Blackmore died from his injuries at approximately one o'clock this afternoon."

Gasps. Cries. Shocked whispers.

"Marla and Gillian were with him, and they're fine," he continued, "but they were so traumatized, they're being held for observation at the local hospital."

Silence overtook shock. Alarm filled eyes. Uneasiness weighted shoulders. People looked at Duncan and at each other, fearful and wary.

"This is too weird for words," Keely called out. "Passion and Pasta Tour my ass. It's more like the Passion and *Perish* Tour. What about the lectures we were promised? The insider tips from the experts? The chance to talk one-on-one with people who could get us published? The only thing you've been consistent about delivering so far are dead bodies!"

"Yeah," Amanda agreed. "This tour is bogus. I want a full refund!"

"I want a refund, and I want to go home!" Brandy Ann chimed in, starting a chain reaction that boiled over into shouts, snarls, and verbal chaos. I took a step back from the crowd. Whoa! I was sure glad I wasn't in charge right now.

This was scary. I watched Duncan very carefully to see how he'd handle the situation.

He cocked his head as if listening to something, snatched his cell phone from its holster, and pressed it to his ear. Ah, yes. The beauty of the mobile phone—allowing you the opportunity to be interrupted at the most inconvenient times of your life.

He said something into the phone, then glanced in my direction, motioning to someone behind me. I turned around.

There was no one behind me.

Unh-oh. I was getting a bad feeling about this. I looked back to find him gesturing to me more furiously. "It's the police!" he shouted above the din. "You need to take over! I can't hear what the guy is saying!"

WAS HE NUTS? I didn't know how to control an angry mob! But that did give me an idea. I pressed the record lever of Jackie's tape recorder. "Memo to Mr. Erickson: It might be wise to include a section on mob control in the next printing of the official *Escort's Manual.*" Hey, this was a pretty nifty little gadget!

The noise level rose to near deafening. Duncan shouted for calm, but when everyone ignored him, it reminded me that I *did* know something about mob control. I mean, I babysat my five nephews on a regular basis. I knew a lot!

Suddenly empowered, I let fly a shrill teakettle whistle that had people cupping their hands over their ears to prevent their eardrums from popping. I might not have Nana's expertise at Tae Kwon Do, but my whistle was so devastating, I could probably register it as a deadly weapon.

As I assumed the reins of command, Duncan retreated to the front desk area to resume his conversation with the

Florence police. "Okay," I addressed the crowd when they removed their hands from their ears. "We need to take a vote."

That's all it took for Osmond Chelsvig to pop up with his new camcorder and begin to record the proceedings.

"I need a show of hands. How many people would like to continue the tour despite what's happened?"

Every member of the Iowa contingent shot a hand into the air, which wasn't surprising. They were so accustomed to people dying on tour that I suspected it didn't faze them anymore. "Twelve votes to continue. And how many people would like to throw in the towel and go home?"

Everyone else's hand shot upward. I sighed. "It looks like the majority of you would like to go home."

"You didn't ask for abstentions," Osmond said from behind his camera.

I directed a long, narrow look into his lens. "Are there any abstentions?" I asked stiffly.

"I abstain!" Jackie waved her arm over her head. "I don't know if I'd be better off continuing the tour or flying home early to finish my book. How long do you think it'll take me to finish? Eh! What if I can't complete the manuscript on time? Do you think they'll give me an extension? What if I can't handle the pressure? Oh, God. What have I done? What was I thinking? I HATE DEADLINES!"

"I think there's been bad karma on this tour ever since it began!" Fred jumped in. "Fires. Dead bodies. Who's gonna be next? I don't want to wait around to find out!"

I'd had this same discussion on our Swiss trip last year. On that occasion, the guests had decided to head for home before more disaster struck. But in this instance, the circumstances were entirely different, so knowing what I knew now, I felt confident trying to put a few minds at ease and possibly salvaging the trip. "I can just about guarantee you that no one else on this trip is going to fall down a flight of stairs and die," I stated with some authority.

"How do you know that?" Brandy Ann demanded.

"Because Gabriel Fox was caught trying to leave the country this morning. He's in the custody of the Rome police at the moment, and I suspect when they're through interrogating him, they're going to learn that *he's* the person responsible for all these so-called accidental deaths."

A collective gasp went around the room. "Gabriel Fox?" Mom repeated. "Oh, my goodness, Emily. Are you saying he's a murderer? But he's much too well groomed to be a criminal."

"Yeah!" Keely seconded. "Why are you picking on Gabriel? Just because he skipped out on this dopey gig doesn't mean he killed anyone."

"Did any of you know how much he really didn't want to be here?" I questioned. "Gabriel Fox despised romantic novels! He considered them so far beneath him that he conducted his own private war against them at Hightower. He couldn't stand the thought of not editing literary novels anymore, so when Philip Blackmore shoved romance down his throat, I suspect he planned his revenge by trying to rid the world of anyone who ever aspired to add her voice to the genre. He killed quietly and ruthlessly and was clever enough to make it look like an accident! All of you writers were in danger, and you'd still be in danger if he hadn't run off after killing Sylvia."

More gasps. "Why'd he kill Sylvia?" Amanda called out. "She wasn't a romance writer."

"She used to be! Years ago. She wrote under the name

Elizabeth Hampton and was making quite a name for herself until Gabriel Fox reviewed her work and said things so scathing, her confidence shattered, and she never wrote another word. He ruined her writing career! But she kept that part of her life a secret, so he never knew the reason she despised him so much."

"If that was the case, how come she didn't kill *him*?" Lucille Rassmuson objected. "If a fella ruined my career, that's what I'd want to do."

Nods. Whispers of assent.

"If she killed him, she wouldn't be able to antagonize him anymore, and I think making his life miserable was one of her greatest pleasures. On the other hand, by killing her, he'd be eliminating another person who was promoting the romance genre, and that's exactly what he wanted to do. Sylvia would never stop selling romances to Philip Blackmore if she lived, and Philip Blackmore would never stop shoving every last one of them down Gabriel's throat. He probably thought he *had* to kill her."

"How did he kill her if he was in Pisa?" Brandy Ann questioned.

"He did the same thing I did yesterday. He took the train back to Florence and caught her unawares last night."

More nods. Soft chatter. Less fear.

"Did that Fawkth fella kill Philip Blackmore and make it look like an ac*th*ident too?" George inquired.

I shook my head. "Philip's fall really was an accident. I saw the whole thing."

"So you think we'd be safe if we continued the trip?" a blonde woman asked in a tentative voice.

"I *know* you'd be safe," I assured her. "How could you not be safe? They've caught the killer." I smiled at the relief on the faces before me and felt a modest surge of pride that my sleuthing efforts might have saved the trip from a premature end. Was I getting good at this job or what? Alice Tjarks stood up and aimed her camcorder at me.

"Folks back home might be interested in how you figured out what's been happening here, Emily. You want to go through the details again so I can get it recorded? I bet the fellers at KORN radio might even want to interview you when we get home. They could make you out a real hero."

I blushed at the suggestion and felt my neck grow warm as a few scattered claps erupted into a round of enthusiastic applause. Oh, wow. I smiled, and bowed, and curtsied, and blushed some more. This was just like being onstage. Only this was a lot better because I wouldn't have to wake up to any bad reviews in the morning paper.

"Tell us how you figured everything out," Dick Teig urged when the applause died down. I heard a little *whir* as Osmond adjusted the zoom lens on his camcorder.

"You really want to hear all that?" I asked.

"Speech!" yelled Dick Stolee.

"Speech!" yelled Alice Tjarks.

I gave my shoulders a humble shrug. "Okay, if that's what you want. Um, I first started to become suspicious—"

"The word's just in from the surveillance tapes," Duncan interrupted as he came up behind me. He listened intently to the person on the other end of the line, then uttered a few words of Italian into the phone and held it away from his ear before announcing, "Jeannette Bowles wasn't pushed from the top of the Duomo."

Murmurs. Muttering. Gasps.

"The tape shows that she was backed against the gallery railing, shooting a picture of something above her head. Those of you who climbed to the top know it can be pretty windy up there, and the weather conditions proved fatal for Jeannette."

The wind blew her off? Oh, man, there should be signs warning about that.

"Some of you may have noticed that she was wearing a scarf around her neck two days ago. The video shows a wind gust ripping the scarf from her throat and carrying it over the rail. When she spun around to catch it, she found herself immobilized because the back of her dress was snagged on the railing. But she lunged for the scarf anyway and was too off-balance to stop herself when she leaned too far over. It all happened in a matter of seconds. She didn't even have time to scream."

My breath caught in my throat. Jeannette Bowles died not because Gabriel Fox pushed her but because she was wearing my coral sweaterdress with the decorative shoulder strap? Oh, my God! Would she still be alive if my dress had been constructed from polyester instead of the more snag-prone cotton knit? Could I be charged with negligent homicide because I'd exercised my preference for breathable fabrics?

"Are you saying Gabriel Fox didn't have anything to do with that Bowles woman's death?" Dick Teig asked.

Duncan shook his head. "He was nowhere around her when she fell."

Dick turned to Osmond. "Don't erase that tape. If Fox decides to sue Emily's ass for slander, you could make a bundle."

"Wouldn't that be more defamation of character?" Helen asked.

"No, no," Lucille corrected. "It would be a clear case of libel."

"But Gabriel Fox *has* to be the killer," I blubbered. "He had the opportunity. He had the motive!"

"Didn't no one try to help that woman unsnag her dress?" Nana asked.

Duncan shook his head. "She was all alone in that section of the gallery for several minutes while people attended to the man who was suffering from heat exhaustion. A man in a safari hat."

Safari hat? All eyes flew to Fred, who suddenly looked as if he'd like to disappear through a hole in the floor.

"It wasn't heat exhaustion," he said grudgingly. "It was a panic attack. And it was all their fault!" He stabbed his finger at Brandy Ann and Amanda. "I told them I didn't like heights. I told them I'd do better visiting museums, but nooo, they had to climb to the highest point in the whole damn city!"

"Hey, you didn't have to come with us!" Amanda yelled.

"And then what would I have done? Wandered around Florence all by myself? What fun is that? I'm always by myself!" He dropped his head to stare self-consciously at the floor. "I . . . I kinda liked being part of a group."

Poor Fred. A victim of peer pressure even at his age.

"What about Sylvia?" Keely called out. "Was Gabriel Fox anywhere around her when she fell down the stairs?"

Duncan waved his phone in the air. "He was on a train to Rome when she fell. And according to the autopsy results, Sylvia Root's blood alcohol level was soaring at the time of her death, so that, combined with the condition of the stairs and the fact that her foot was caught in the hem of her pants, paints a rather accurate picture of the incident. The police will be filing no criminal action in the case. It's been ruled an accident."

"She got so pickled at the restaurant last night, I don't see how she made it *up* the stairs in the first place!" Lucille Rassmuson charged.

"But she wasn't a mean drunk," Grace Stolee admitted. "She told some funny stories at dinner. At least, I think they were funny. She was slurring her words so badly, I couldn't catch some of the punch lines."

"Sylvia was drunk last night?" I exclaimed.

"Stinking drunk," Dick Teig called out.

I heaved an agitated sigh. You'd think maybe someone could have *mentioned* that to me?

Chirrup chirrup. Chirrup chirrup. Chirrup chirrup.

Suppressing a scream, I snatched my phone from my bag. "What?"

A crackle, followed by a surprised, "Emily?"

"Ohhh, hi, sweetie." I regarded the multitude of unblinking eyes staring back at me. "Um, this isn't really a good time for me." I angled away from the crowd.

"I won't keep you, darling. I'm on the train headed for—*KRRRRKKK.* I thought I'd—*KRRRKKK.*"

"Etienne?" I sighed my frustration. "Hello?"

Behind me, I heard a loud crack of bubble gum followed by Keely's voice. "So let me get this straight. Gabriel Fox didn't kill anyone. None of us were in danger of being murdered by him. Sylvia Root died because she was drunk, and Jeannette Bowles died because she was klutzy. What about the first woman who died? Cassandra."

"That was ruled an accident from the beginning," Duncan said.

"So Emily's theory was a bunch of crap?" Keely asked.

"Emily's theory was well thought out," Duncan replied, "but I suspect, in this case, she was wrong."

I spun around and gave him a frustrated look. Well, maybe my theory wouldn't have been so wrong if I'd had all the information! "Etienne?" I said into the phone, turning away again.

" . . . teasing about having money left to buy a train ticket," I heard him say.

"Did you end up losing all your money at the casino?" I asked, wondering if Switzerland might have an organization that was the equivalent of Gamblers Anonymous. "No, no. My luck held. I told you, darling, at the gaming table, I can't seem to lose."

"Did you win enough to buy a plane ticket to Iowa?"

"More than enough. How does seven hundred thousand sound to you?"

Delete three zeroes. Divide by two. "Three hundred fifty dollars? I don't know if that'll get you all the way to Iowa, but it might if you try Priceline dot com. You can get some real bargains with them."

"Not lire, darling. I did the conversion for you. Seven hundred thousand American dollars."

"EXCUSE ME?"

A female voice whined loudly behind me. "So if all these deaths were really just accidents, do you think we're safe to continue the tour?"

"That would be my recommendation," Duncan replied. "Marla and Gillian will rejoin us tomorrow, then the rest of Italy awaits. I'd hate to say good-bye to all of you before I had a chance to finish what I started." He brushed lightly against my back, sending a jolt of electricity up my spine.

"Seven hundred thousand *dollars*?" I sputtered into the phone.

Etienne laughed in his beautiful French/German/Italian accent. "That's why I— *KKRRRKK.*"

I sprinted toward the front desk to see if the reception was any better over there. "Etienne? Can you hear me?"

"We'll be checking out tomorrow at ten o'clock," Duncan announced, as people unfolded their limbs and eased to their feet, "so be down here in the lobby ready to board the bus by 9:50. The memorial service that Philip Blackmore arranged for Sylvia will be held at eight o'clock tomorrow morning in one of the minor chapels of the Duomo, so those of you who'd like to pay your respects to all our recently departed guests can do so then."

I clutched the phone in my hands and strangled it. "Can you hear me now?" I screamed at it.

Guests wandered past me, giving me odd looks as they made their way back to their rooms. I saw several people in the Iowa contingent congratulate Jackie, then a group of them headed out the front door. I pressed the phone to my ear again, relieved when I heard the faint tones of Etienne's voice coming through the line.

" . . . birthday gathering jogged my memory and reminded me what I should have asked you in Ireland last month. I don't know how I—*KKRRRK*—as important as this, but I need to know, darling. Will you—*KRRRRRRKKKKK!*"

"Yes!" I shouted into the phone. "I will! Whatever you're asking me! The answer is yes!"

KRRRRRRRKKKKK!

"Damn!" I screamed. I squeezed the phone. I punched buttons. I shook it in my fist. I pressed it to my ear again.

KRRRRRRRKKKKK!

"Bad connection?" asked Duncan, sauntering over to me.

"He's on a train," I said, refusing to give up. "Maybe he's going through a tunnel or something."

He leaned casually against the front desk, regarding me with his dark eyes. "If he's on his way back to Lucerne, he's a fool."

"He's Swiss. He's very efficient and . . . and duty-bound." But no matter what he was, he wasn't on the other end of the phone line anymore. I stuffed the phone back into my bag. "He'll call back," I said cheerily, hiding my disappointment.

The corners of Duncan's mouth lifted imperceptibly. "Of course he will. In the meantime, how about having a drink with me?"

I was a woman who loved men in all their various sizes, shapes, and incarnations, but at the moment, Duncan Lazarus was not the man I wanted to be around. "Thanks for the offer, but I really should start throwing things back into my suitcase."

His eyes sparkled with amusement. "That's right. I've seen the size of your suitcase. You probably should have started yesterday. I don't suppose you need any help? I'm a natural at organizing, folding and . . . filling empty spaces."

I narrowed one eye at him. "It seems you're a natural at just about everything."

"Not everything. Apparently I need to work on my technique for convincing beautiful women that I'm a good catch. You suppose my antenna is defective? I always seem to fall for the ones who are taken. But like I said before, we still have a lot of days left on this tour. I'm not prepared to give up quite yet."

Oh, God. Why me? I scanned the now empty lobby, shaking my head in disbelief and thinking that I could actually feel egg dripping from my face. "I can't believe how off base I was about everything."

"You had at least one thing right. Gabriel Fox didn't want romances shoved down his throat anymore. That's why he ditched us in Pisa. He told the Rome police he refused to demean himself by returning to Florence to judge Philip Blackmore's imbecilic contest. And he implied he'd rather chew razor blades than spend more time with that, and I quote, 'crazed flock of wannabe writers,' unquote. So he decided to fly back to the States instead."

"Can he be charged with anything?"

"He's guilty of chickening out, which isn't a crime. It's a personality flaw, not even prosecutable in Italy." He bent his head and said in a whisper so close to my ear, I could feel his breath, "It's a common frailty among people who aren't from Iowa."

CHAPTER 14

I returned to my room, wondering if anyone would miss me if I flew home, too. I mean, with the way this trip was going, I doubted I'd miss myself! I'd maligned Gabriel Fox to the point where he could sue me. I'd sent Nana on a wild-goose chase over the Internet when she could have been canoodling. I'd wasted an entire day tailing people when I could have been shopping. I'd prompted Jackie to parade around as a poorly dressed transvestite stalker. I'd labeled every accident a capital crime and ended up looking like the tour escort who'd cried wolf. And I didn't even want to get started on my love life. I was having "connection interruptus" with the man I wanted and "connection overloadus" with the man I didn't. AARGH! Maybe I could just lock myself in the bathroom and turn on the shower. That could put a quick end to my misery.

I walked to the bathroom and inspected the folding door. The lock was broken, so it wouldn't stay shut. Great. With my luck the water would all leak out before I could drown myself, and I'd end up having to pay for flood damage.

Wallowing in self-pity, I grabbed my suitcase and swung it onto the bed, then plopped down beside it, burying my face in the crook of my elbow. Maybe I should have taken Duncan up on his offer. I could use a drink. I could use a lot of drinks. But I knew that kind of remedy wouldn't work. I was too hard-core Midwestern to resort to drowning my sorrows in a bottle. I needed to look for a silver lining rather than drink myself into oblivion. Philip Blackmore had tried that, and look where it had gotten him.

Giving myself an invisible slap upside the head, I forced myself to a sitting position and took mental stock of the situation. Okay, I might have ended up with egg all over my face, but the good news was, there was no killer on the tour. Duh! How could I feel bad about that? The deaths had all been accidental, so if people started watching out where they stepped, maybe we could continue the rest of the tour without incident.

I felt a sudden release of tension in my muscles.

As for being sued, if no one told Gabriel Fox about what I'd said, he'd have no reason to sue me, right? I pondered that. No one would tell him, would they? Gillian and Marla hadn't heard my accusation, and Jackie surely wouldn't rat on me. So what were the chances that anyone else on this tour would ever have contact with him again? Slim to none, I'd guess.

A hint of a smile pulled at the corners of my mouth.

As for the other stuff, Nana always enjoyed surfing the Internet, Jackie loved playing dress-up, I still had loads of time to shop, and Etienne— My brain executed a mental somersault. Oh, my God! Etienne was rich! What had he said? Seven hundred thousand American dollars? Why, that was—I added three zeroes and multplied by two— that was like 1.4 *billion* lire! Wow!

A full-blown smile raced across my lips. Okay, this wasn't so bad. This wasn't bad at all!

Chirrup chirrup. Chirrup chirrup. Chirrup chirrup.

I dived for my cell phone. "Etienne? I was just thinking about—"

"*Signorina* Andrew?" said the voice on the other end. "Dis Officer Agripino Piccione. *Devo scusarmi.* Our phone line no good today. I have message you want speak wit me."

I paused, swallowing my disappointment. "I did want to speak to you. Earlier. I had information about Gabriel Fox I wanted to share with you, but since the information isn't relevant anymore, I guess I don't need to talk to you after all. Sorry to have bothered you."

"*Bene, bene.* No boder. *Signor* Lazarus, is he at hotel wit you? His line busy but I need speak wit him *pronto.*"

"He was here a little while ago. Do you want me to try and find him for you?"

"*Si.* You find him, you have him call me. You no find him, you tell guests we question dem eight o'clock tomorrow morning at you hotel. *All* guests. In lobby."

Unh-oh. "Um—eight o'clock could be a problem. We have a memorial service scheduled for eight o'clock tomorrow morning at the Duomo. Could you possibly come at say, nine-thirty?"

Silence. "We come eight o'clock, *Signorina* Andrew. You tell guests."

"But . . . wait a minute! Why do you need to question the guests? I thought you'd ruled Sylvia Root's death an accident."

"Not Sylvia Root's det we question. Philip Blackmore. We no tink he die from accident. He have high level *alcool* in blood. We tink someone do dis him."

"Al—what?"

"How you say. Alcohol."

"That's right. I told you earlier, I watched Philip Blackmore knock back three glasses of Merlot at a wine bar this afternoon. We all saw him get drunk. I feel badly that none of us was brave enough to stop him, but you don't tell people like Philip Blackmore that he's over his limit. I mean, can you imagine what—"

"No *vino! Alcool!* The alcohol. It poison him."

I breathed heavily into the phone. "He drank too much Merlot. You just said that!" I wondered if I'd be better off escorting tours in say, the Mid-Atlantic states.

"Alcohol! Other alcohol—"

I waited for him to continue. "Hello?" Dead air space. "Officer Piccione?" I waited some more. "Hello?"

Silence.

I suspected this was the reason Italians drank so much. Not as an alternative to bad water, but to help them forget the frustration of their lousy phone system.

I set my phone on the bed and stared at it. Philip Blackmore died from alcohol poisoning? How did a two-hundred-pound man suffer alcohol poisoning from three glasses of wine? I'd seen how three quick drinks had impaired his judgment, but poison him? That didn't seem possible. Unless—

I jackknifed upward. Unless the wine had been some dangerously potent brand. I'd heard an Italian drink called *grappa* could knock you off your feet in no time flat, but Philip hadn't been drinking *grappa*. He'd been drinking Merlot.

Or had he?

I pinched my eyes shut and reconstructed the scene at the wine bar. Philip had chugged one glass of red wine, then trundled off to buy himself another. He'd downed that one in short order, then asked Duncan to get him a refill. The glasses had looked like Merlot, but could they have been something else? Had he been drinking this other alcohol that Piccione had mentioned? Or could someone have introduced it into the wine without Philip's knowledge?

My eyes flew open.

Oh, my God. Someone could have tampered with Philip's drink. But the only person who had the opportunity was . . . *Duncan.*

I sat very still for a heartbeat, disbelieving that Duncan Lazarus was capable of murder. No! I refused to accept that. Not only was Duncan not the murdering type, what possible reason would he have to kill Philip Blackmore? The publishing mogul and the tour guide? There was no connection there. I inhaled a calming breath.

Was there?

I pressed the heels of my palms into my eyes. NO! I wasn't going to do this again! I was too suspicious for my own good. There was no evidence to support the accusation that Duncan had killed Philip. Buying a man a drink *did not* earn him killer status.

Except that Piccione had said someone had poisoned Philip. And that meant I'd seen an accident that had been no accident at all.

I'd seen an accident that had been a murder.

Oh, God! I sprang to my feet, worrying my bottom lip as I paced alongside the bed. What if there was a link between the two men? But what could it be? Something personal? Something business-related? Something family-related?

That thought gave me pause.

Duncan's sister?

But it was so far-fetched! What connection could Philip Blackmore possibly have to a young woman who may have died in a mountain-climbing accident? I mean, I suspected the closest Philip Blackmore had ever come to hiking up a mountain was publishing a book about it!

I stopped in my tracks as a recent memory jogged loose in my brain. *Oh, my God!*

In the next instant I was riffling through my tour papers, throwing aside itineraries, medical forms and Landmark brochures, until I found what I was looking for—a paperbound booklet giving a complete and illustrated history of Hightower Books, from its inception in 1950 until the present. I flipped through the high-gloss pages, hoping the section I needed would be in there. And in one of the back appendices, there it was. A listing of every book and best seller ever published by Hightower Books.

Please, let me be right. Please, let me be right.

I frantically scanned the titles, decade by decade, and when I got to the nineties, I hit pay dirt.

Number one on the best-seller list eleven years ago was *The Thrill of Off-Trail Hiking*. The book Nana said George had read and taken to Yosemite with him. The book he'd dismissed as being too dangerous to try. The book endorsed by a bevy of expert climbers, one of whom, I suspected, was an Englishman named Robert Adcock, who'd endangered himself and his wife by going off trail, and who'd died because of it—because of the book published by Philip Blackmore.

That was it! That was the connection. It *had* to be. Duncan blamed Philip for his sister's death, and he'd gotten even by poisoning him.

OH MY GOD! Okay, I might be wrong, and I might be sending the police on a wild-goose chase, and I might end up with egg all over my face again, but I couldn't sit on what I knew. I had to tell someone.

I rooted through my shoulder bag for my Florence guidebook and punched in the digits for the Florence police office.

Dead air. Static. More dead air. If I hadn't liked my new hairdo so much, I might have plucked every hair out of my head in frustration.

I resumed pacing and worried my lip some more. Okay, now what? I . . . I should call Duncan. No matter what else happened, he needed to be told about the police coming to the hotel tomorrow morning so he could alert the guests to stay here rather than attend the memorial service. I just hoped when he learned the police were going to conduct an interrogation that he wouldn't try to skip town. I guess if he did, we'd know for sure he was guilty.

Heart pounding, I punched in Duncan's number.

BZZ. BZZ. BZZ. BZZ.

Busy signal. Oh, God. I was almost relieved! But I wondered where he was and who he was talking to . . . and what I was supposed to do now.

Section 2E of my *Escort's Manual* stated that no matter the situation, the savvy tour escort always prioritized her agenda and took care of first things first.

Okay. I could do that. I scanned the room, visualizing what I needed, then began gathering things into a pile. Post-it notes. Pen. Pocketknife. List of guests with corresponding room numbers. Cell phone.

I think that covered it. Noting the first name on the list, I headed up the central staircase to the third floor and stopped in the deserted hallway before Duncan's room, but I didn't knock. Nope. My days of being cornered by crazed killers were over. No way was I going to place myself in harm's way again. I wasn't a total moron. I was an Iowan. I was raised to learn from my mistakes.

I punched in Duncan's cell phone number again.

BZZ. BZZ. BZZ. BZZ.

I pressed my ear to the door.

Silence.

If he was in his room, I'd be able to hear him talking, but I couldn't hear a thing, which meant his room was empty. He was out. So if I left a note on his door, he'd see it when he got back and could take care of the business at hand without having to talk to me. Yeah. I liked that idea. It sounded much more safe to me than blurting out in the panic of the moment, "You did it!" and being targeted as the next victim to get clobbered.

I scribbled a note in my tiniest writing telling him about the change of plans and indicating that I'd tell the Iowa group to save him the trouble. I slapped the note onto the door and with my knees a little wobbly from nerves, sprinted back down the stairs to the second floor. Okay. That had gone well. With relief adding a little spring to my step, I checked my list again and began knocking on doors.

No answer at Mom and Nana's room. I left a note.

No answer at the Teigs' or Stolees'. That's right. They had dinner reservations. I left a note.

No answer at Alice Tjarks's room. Another note.

I rapped on door number five, relieved to have one of the Severid twins, minus her name tag, gaudy earrings, and high-heeled sandals, answer on the first knock. "I bet I know why you're here," she said, inviting me inside. "I bet you want your clothes back. We have everything folded for you and ready to go into your suitcase. We were planning to bring them down to you when we finished packing, but you're just too efficient. You beat us to it. You were so nice to let us borrow your lovely things, Emily. We're going to give you very high marks on your evaluation, aren't we, Barbro?"

"With all our praise, you'll get a raise!"

I looked from one to the other, marking which twin was which. I also noted their room was even more shabby than mine, with holes in the carpet, wide strips of paint peeling off the wall, and no lighting other than the dull fixture overhead. The only furniture in the room other than the two beds was a small desk in the corner. The only decorative accent in sight was the standard liter of foul-tasting bottled water perched on the desk. *Uff da.* I hoped they were assigned the presidential suite at the hotel in Montecatini to make up for their experience here. They'd been so sweet not to be in my face about the accommodations. I really owed them.

"Actually, ladies, I'm not here to pick up my clothes. I'm here for another reason." At which point I explained about my recent call from Officer Piccione and how it affected tomorrow's schedule.

"Why are the police going to interrogate us about Philip Blackmore's death?" asked Britha. "Didn't you say you saw the whole thing? That his fall was an accident?"

I smiled wanly. "I don't seem to be right all the time."

"Well, it's too bad we'll have to miss the memorial service," Britha fretted. "We attended every funeral service Papa ever officiated, didn't we, Barbro? He delivered real good eulogies. Always brought a tear to my eye."

Barbro nodded agreement. "Folks died. We cried."

"He gave a real memorable one for Harvey Gasser. Do you remember Harvey, Emily? He was the swine farmer off Route 221 who raised that thousand-pound pig. Trouble was, the family brought the pig to the funeral with them and caused all sorts of seating problems. No one wanted to sit with the pig, so it got a pew all by itself, and then there weren't enough seats for the rest of the friends and relatives. Some folks got pretty irritated because they had to stand, but if you ask me, the pig really needed its own pew. I mean, it was big as a VW bus."

I nodded, slightly glassy-eyed. "I'm sorry I missed that one."

Britha smiled. "I think it was before your time anyway, dear. Don't you think so, Barbro?"

"It happened back in '69. His wife had been a friend of mine."

I stared at Barbro Severid, suppressing a sudden urge to scream. "I have been *so* curious about this. I really have to ask. Have you ever been involved in a conversation where you didn't feel the need to rhyme all your words?"

"Of course, I have!" Barbro said, laughing. "Some words are simply impossible to rhyme. Like silver. And tsetse. And gazebo. Although you can try placebo with gazebo, but, it's hard to gracefully slip 'placebo' into a conversation. What are some of the others, Brit? Oh yeah, panda."

Britha Severid began ticking off words on her gold-lacquered fingers. "Xylophone. That's a real hard one. So she usually tries to direct her musical conversations to string instruments. Harps. Fiddles. The percussions and winds can be real stinkers."

"You try thinking of a word that rhymes with piccolo," Barbro challenged me. "You'll get a migraine trying."

"I can think of a word that rhymes with tuba," I enthused. "Tuba's a wind instrument. How about scuba?"

Britha ignored me as she continued her litany. "Chocolate. Celery. Oxygen. She tried using toxin with oxygen once, but it really wasn't a good fit."

"Cathedral," said Barbro. "Phenomenon. Four-syllable words are especially difficult."

Cuba. Aruba. Hey, two more words that rhyme with tuba! I was pretty good at this!

Britha started in on her other hand. "Breakfast. Modem. Anemone."

Oh, God. Now I'd gone and done it. I'd opened Pandora's box. "Are these all your new clothes?" I interrupted, walking over to one of the beds.

The twins rushed over to the bed, where their new togs were laid out in all their garish splendor. "Jackie was so sweet to take us shopping today," one of them said. "She's quite the fashion plate. She even took time to show us how to transform our makeup from daywear to eveningwear."

"Is that the eveningwear you have on now?" I asked, wincing at the peacock blue shading and thick liner above their eyes.

"Heavens no. This is daywear. Eveningwear is a lot more dramatic."

EH! I studied the clothing on the bed. The metallic gold tank tops. The zebra-striped vests. The black leather pants. The see-through blouses and mesh sweaters. I couldn't help being amazed that with all the exclusive clothing shops in Florence, Jackie had still managed to find a Frederick's of Hollywood. But I had to hand it to her. There wasn't a thing here that wouldn't look dynamite with orange hair. She really did have great color sense.

"We've run into a small problem though," Britha said to me. Or was it Barbro? Now that she'd dropped the rhyming gig, I couldn't tell. "The tags are still attached to everything, and we don't have any scissors. We could try gnawing them off, but our dentist says that's very bad for your teeth."

"As it happens," I said, retrieving my Swiss Army knife from the pocket of my capri pants, "you're in luck. Compliments of Nana. She bought this for me in

Switzerland last year. It performs twenty-nine functions." I held it out for their perusal. "Thirty if you count throwing it at someone."

"It has a hole in it," Barbro observed. Or maybe it was Britha. Geesch, where were their name tags? "Is it broken?"

I touched the hole fondly. "There used to be a little clock in that hole, but it got broken, so I pried it out. The rest of the gizmos work all right though."

I plucked the miniature scissors out of the housing and with the twins' help, began snipping tags from all their new purchases. There was quite a pile when we finished, which indicated a fact of which I'd been totally unaware.

Writing sentiments for greeting cards must be a lucrative business. Britha and Barbro Severid had spent a fortune.

"What color eye shadow would complement this?" one of them asked as she danced around the floor with an alligator jacket.

Hunh. I didn't think Lutherans were allowed to dance. No, wait. That was the Baptists. Catholics could dance, they just couldn't have sex until they were married. I didn't know how the Baptists felt about sex before marriage, but I'd guess they'd say it was permissible as long as you didn't assume any upright position that could be misconstrued as a rumba.

I gathered the tags off the bed and was about to trash them in the cylinder by the desk when something at the bottom of the wastebasket caught my eye. A bottle. The same bottle that had fallen through their plastic sack at the top of the Duomo.

Only now the bottle was empty.

I glanced in the twins' direction. Jackie obviously hadn't pierced their ears, so how had they used up an entire bottle of rubbing alcohol in two days' time? Maybe they'd spilled it. Or more logically, maybe they'd decided to take sponge baths instead of hassling with the inadequate shower facilities. I remembered Mom giving me sponge baths with rubbing alcohol and water when I'd been feverish as a child. But it seemed they advised against that these days because of the toxicity, or something like that.

I held onto the tags, eyeing the bottle more closely. The label screamed *91%* in large blue numbers. Pretty strong solution. I usually bought the 70 percent solution to use as an astringent, but unlike the twins' bottle, my sixteen-ounce bottle seemed to last forever.

Shrugging, I dumped the tags into the cylinder, my eyes suddenly freezing in their sockets as I watched them fall onto the bottle. *Emily, you dolt!* The "other" alcohol that had poisoned Philip Blackmore. Had it been rubbing alcohol? Was that what Officer Piccione had been trying to say? Oh, my God! But . . . but the twins hadn't been anywhere near Philip at the wine bar. How could they have—

I tried to visualize every detail at the wine bar again. I could see Philip in his well-worn pink polo shirt. His deep tan. His silver hair. His hand clutching the stem of his wineglass. His—

In my mind's eye, I telescoped closer, noticing something I hadn't noticed before.

Uff da! It was so clever. So perfect. So devious! I regarded the twins, my heart about to explode in my chest, my mouth dry as sandpaper. Oh, God. They weren't sweet little old ladies. They were cold-blooded murderers! At least, one of them was, and I was pretty sure which one.

Mom had pretty much told me two days ago, but I hadn't picked up on the clue. I COULD BE SO DENSE!

With Slinkies for legs, I leaned casually against the desk, struggling to continue smiling. "Wasn't that great about Jackie winning the contest?" I asked, as they continued to fuss with their new outfits. "She never even gave a hint that she could write. Mom mentioned the other day that one of you wrote a book once. Is that true?"

The twin who wasn't dancing with the alligator jacket turned abruptly to look at me. "Your mother told you about my book? How could she know that? I've never told anyone about that." She paused thoughtfully, and in that instant, I could almost see the lightbulb flickering on over her head. She stabbed a finger at her sister. "*You* told her, didn't you, Britha? Margaret Andrew volunteers at the library with you. You gave away the secret I asked you never to tell anyone!"

Britha clutched the alligator jacket contritely to her chest. "I'm sorry! But you wrote it so long ago, I didn't think you cared anymore."

"Of course, I care! I'm extremely sensitive about my failures. How would you like me to run around giving away all *your* secrets?"

Britha contemplated that for a moment. "Actually, I don't think I have any."

"Are you sure?" Barbro asked, frowning. "What about the time you Vaselined the collection plate at the ten o'clock service. Are you still keeping that a secret?"

"I did that? I thought you did that."

"I think *both* of you are keeping secrets," I broke in. "Tell me, how surprised were you to discover Philip Blackmore was on this trip with you? Quite a coincidence, hunh? The editor who rejected your stewardess novel years ago appearing in the flesh. That's the connection, isn't it? Gabriel Fox ruined Sylvia Root's career with his harsh comments. Were Philip Blackmore's comments about your manuscript so devastating that even after all these years, you had to get even?"

Barbro's face seamed with a woeful expression. Her

voice grew soft. "His comments weren't *all* devastating. He told me I'd selected an excellent weight typing paper for the manuscript."

Oh, that's right. He'd mentioned he always liked to say something positive about a writer's work. "But you never wrote another word of fiction! He ruined your budding career." I drilled her with a somber look. "That's why you killed him." I paused. Damn! I promised myself I wasn't going to do that anymore!

Barbro did a double take. "I did?"

"Yes, you did. And I'll tell you exactly how you did it." I retrieved the empty bottle of rubbing alcohol from the wastebasket and held it in the air as exhibit A. "You emptied the contents of this bottle—which is highly toxic if swallowed—into one of Philip Blackmore's bottles of drinking water."

Barbro stared at me, wide-eyed. "How did I do that?"

"You . . . you sneaked into his room, dumped some of the good water down the sink, and replaced it with the isopropyl alcohol." I recalled his violent reaction to the water earlier in the day. He'd spat it out because of its taste, but he hadn't been tasting sewage. He'd been tasting isopropyl alcohol! *Uff da.* He'd still be alive if he hadn't forced himself to finish it.

Barbro seemed intrigued. "How did I get into his room?"

"The same way my mother got into mine when I wasn't there. She grabbed the key off the board when the front desk was unattended and let herself in."

Barbro broke out in a wide smile. "I'm very cunning, aren't I? But tell me, Emily, are you sure it was me? To tell you the truth, I don't remember doing any of that."

Britha sucked in her breath. "Oh, no! First, Mumma, now you. Stage one dementia!"

Barbro appeared disoriented, but I wasn't going to let that fool me. In the past year, I'd dealt with killers more clever than Barbro Severid. "Philip Blackmore ruined your life, and you never forgave him, did you? You wanted the fame and fortune that bestsellerdom would bring you, but instead you had to settle for the anonymity of penning greeting card sentiments in a small town in Iowa. He destroyed your dreams. Dashed your hopes. And you hated him for it. So you killed him." I narrowed an eye at her. "I know it's none of my business, but how's the money in the greeting card business? I bet you make a decent wage, don't you?"

Barbro tilted her head to observe me from another angle. "If my recollection is right, Emily, I think I've enjoyed writing greeting cards. No pressure. Few deadlines. And I've gained celebrity in a behind-the-scenes kind of way. Did you know I penned the saying 'Have a nice day'?"

"Mom mentioned that! Do you know how many languages it's been translated into? Do you receive royalties on foreign translations?"

But Barbro wasn't paying attention to me any longer. She was staring at my cell phone on the bed. "I suppose you'll have to call the police to report what I've done. I just wish I could remember all the details so I could give them a full confession."

Aw, that was so sweet!

"They won't prosecute if she's suffering from dementia, will they?" Britha asked me.

Barbro eyed her sister. "Why did we buy rubbing alcohol in the first place? I wanted to buy insect repellent, but you insisted we buy alcohol. Why was that?"

"We could use the rubbing alcohol to treat the bug bites if we got any," Britha explained. "And the alcohol was cheaper than the fly dope, remember?"

"What I remember is, we couldn't read any of the labels to figure out which bottles were the antibug ones. You just went straight for the rubbing alcohol."

Britha shrugged. "It's always a good idea to have a strong medicinal disinfectant at hand. It also comes in handy for removing adhesive from fabric and ugly water spots from mirrors."

"But the bottle is empty. I didn't use it up. Did you?"

Unease flitted across Britha's face. "I told you yesterday. I knocked the bottle over and accidentally spilled it."

"Where?" Barbro shot back.

"On . . . on the bathroom floor!"

"Liar!" Barbro gasped. "There was a full bottle sitting on the shelf over the sink when I got up to use the john last night!"

Unh-oh. Could it be Britha who was suffering the stage one dementia?

"Oh, my stars!" screamed Barbro. "It was you! You did it! You've broken the Sixth Commandment!"

"I have not!" Britha screamed back. "I would never commit adultery!"

Oops. Wrong Commandment.

"The Fourth Commandment!" cried Barbro.

"I always obeyed our parents!" Britha flung back.

I rolled my eyes. Catholics might be notoriously unschooled in Bible verse, but we made up songs to help us remember the Commandments. "Try Fifth Commandment," I urged Barbro.

"You've broken the Fifth Commandment!" she wailed. "You killed Philip Blackmore!"

"I did not! You have no evidence. You can't prove a thing! All you have to go on is what Emily says, and she thinks *everyone* is guilty!"

"That's not true!" I protested. "I never accused Nana. Or

Mom. Or George. Or Jackie." But hold on. Barbro was claiming that Britha killed Philip Blackmore? That made no sense. That made no sense at all.

I raised a finger in the air. "Excuse me? Why would Britha want to kill Philip? I don't quite understand the motive."

Barbro made a wild gesture toward her sister. "Because he . . . !" She hesitated. "Because she . . . !" She lowered her arm and stared curiously at her sister. "Darned if I know. Why'd you do it, Brit?"

Britha Severid's face flushed red as a cinnamon bear. Her eyes popped wide. Her mouth started to twitch. She glowered at her sister and screeched in a voice like an insane Teletubby, "Because of you! I did it because of you!"

Barbro looked stricken. "Oh, my Lord! What have you done? You didn't have to kill him because of me! I haven't suffered mental distress because of his rejection. He didn't ruin my life!"

"*Your* life? You idiot! He ruined *my* life!"

Okay, now I was *really* confused.

"What do you mean he ruined your life?" Barbro challenged. "You didn't send a manuscript to him. He didn't reject you!"

"But he rejected *you*, didn't he?" Britha crowed. "And then I had to *live* with you all these years! Do you know what it's been like? Listening to you try to rhyme every *goddamn* word in the dictionary?"

Barbro clapped her hand over her mouth. "Blasphemy!" she scolded. "Third Commandment! Third Commandment!" She looked at me for confirmation. I shook my head and held up two fingers. "Second Commandment! Second Commandment!"

"You couldn't just talk like everyone else, could you?" Britha reproached. "Noooo. You had to rhyme everything.

Mumma and Papa thought you were so cute. Well, you're *not* cute! You're a raving lunatic! An aberration! A freak of nature! And Philip Blackmore made you that way! If he'd bought your book, you might have ended up normal. But you're not normal, and it's all his fault! He's to blame. I'm not sorry I killed him! He deserved to die for the living *hell* you've put me through all these years!"

Britha regarded her sister with a menacing look. "I almost got away with it. In fact, I could still get away with it if I play my cards right."

Barbro wagged her finger at her sister. "Please don't pout, but gambling's out."

"Why did I kill Philip Blackmore?" Britha screamed insanely. "I should have killed you!"

Dropping her alligator jacket to the floor, she launched herself at Barbro. BOOM! They fell to the floor in a heap, legs kicking, arms swinging.

Oh, God! I stared in horror as they rolled around on the floor like mud wrestlers, their hands locked around each other's throats. I hoped they were both taking daily doses of Fosamax. We didn't need any broken hips on this trip.

"Stop that!" I instructed, rushing over to where they were grappling on the carpet. "You're going to hurt each other!"

"Get off—!" choked one twin.

"Can't breathe!" the other gasped.

I darted a look from one flushed face to the other. Gee. It would be nice if I could tell them apart.

BRRRRRRRRRRRRRRRRRG! BRRRRRRRRRRRRRRRRG! BRRRRRRRRRRRRRRRRG!

I startled at the sound. Oh, my God! What was that? The fire alarm?

BRRRRRRRRRRRRRRRRRG! BRRRRRRRRRRRRRRRRRG! BRRRRRRRRRRRRRRRRG!

I looked down at the twins. Oh, this was handy. Nothing like an unscheduled fire to speed up the strangulation process.

I made a megaphone of my hands and yelled down at them, "You need to stop this right now! THE HOTEL IS ON FIRE!"

"*Grrrrrrh,*" choked out one twin.

"*Arrrrrrh,*" choked out the other.

BRRRRRRRRRRRRRRRRG! BRRRRRRRRRRRRRRRRG! BRRRRRRRRRRRRRRRRG!

Oh, honestly! I dropped to my knees and seized their forearms, trying to pry them apart. "Let go! Come on now. Britha. Barbro. WE NEED TO GET OUT OF HERE!"

Thwack! An errant hand smacked me in the mouth. "Ow!" I cried, my hand flying to my lip. "That hurt!"

BAM! Another hand cracked me on the nose. "OW!" My eyes stung with tears. My lip seeped blood. I dodged another flailing arm and jumped to my feet. Okay, now I was *pissed.*

BRRRRRRRRRRRRRRRRG! BRRRRRRRRRRRRRRRRG! BRRRRRRRRRRRRRRRRG!

There was only one solution. I had to take out the bad twin. The question was—Which one was Britha?

I shifted my gaze back and forth. They were identical except for one thing. One characteristic. One feature. Something so ordinary that no one ever noticed. Boy, they sure looked absolutely identical to me. WHAT WAS IT?

I grinned with sudden inspiration.

I spied their camera on the desk and raced toward it. I powered it up and pressed the button Nana had shown me in Pisa. Tiny images appeared on the display screen. Statues. Bridges. Fountains.

"*Gaaaaaa . . . !*" croaked one twin.

"*Euwwww . . . !*" croaked the other.

I punched faster. A bunch of holes poked into a piece of stone. What the—? Oh, yeah. Those were the holes in the cathedral in Pisa that the day-vil kept screwing with. Wow. That made a really boring picture. *Punch, punch, punch.* People. The Duomo. Aha! The photo I'd taken on the gallery of the Duomo. The twins with their name tags. And the closeup shot showing every hair, every pore, every detail.

BRRRRRRRRRRRRRRG! BRRRRRRRRRRRRRRRG! BRRRRRRRRRRRRRRRG!

I searched up, down, left, right. Their eyes. Their mouths. Their— A slight inconsistency caught my eye. It looked like a mere speck on the screen, but this could be it. A difference so small, so insignificant, that no one ever noticed. I squinted more closely. This *was* it! It had to be!

I looked desperately around the room. A weapon. I needed a weapon! My gaze fell on the liter of bottled water on the desk. Aha!

I raced toward where the twins were entwined on the floor. One on top, one below. Damn. It was hard to see anything with them in this configuration. "Excuse me, ladies, could I trouble you to roll over a little?"

"She . . . !"

"I . . . !"

With a grunt and a growl they rolled onto their sides like chickens on a spit.

"Thank you. That's perfect." I checked out one twin. I checked out the other. Nodding, I raised my liter of bottled water like a baseball bat. "I'm really sorry to have to do this, ladies, but if we don't get out of here, we're going to be toast."

I swung downward, delivering a walloping blow to the back of Britha Severid's head. THUNK!

She startled. She gasped. She wilted into unconsciousness.

Her hands fell away from her sister's throat, freeing her.

I separated the two women, praying my hunch had been right.

"Did you kill her?" the conscious twin blurted out, rubbing her throat.

I gave her an odd look. "Of course, I didn't kill her. I just—" Oh, God! I couldn't have whacked the wrong one, could I?

"Roses are red, violets are blue," I shouted over the racket of the fire alarm.

"I'm still alive, all thanks to you!"

I smiled at Barbro Severid. Oh, yeah. Right twin.

CHAPTER 15

So I borrowed a lesson from you with the fire alarm and decided that was the best way to gather everyone into the lobby to tell them about the change of plans tomorrow." Duncan caressed the stem of his wineglass as if it were an intimate part of the female body, but I tried hard not to make anything of it.

The hour was just shy of midnight, and we were at an open-air restaurant in the Piazza della Repubblica, surrounded by white linen-draped tables, singing waiters, and hundreds of twinkling minilights. The police had come and gone, taking Britha Severid with them. Mom and Nana were taking Barbro under their dual wings, lending comfort and support. Nana was pretty excited about her new role, saying it was almost as good as attending a wake. I figured if she was forced to spend more time with Barbro, maybe George would have a better chance of survival.

"I'm glad the fire was only a false alarm," I said, taking a sip of my wine. "But I have to admit, it came at a good time. It kind of got my adrenaline pumping."

Duncan traced a fingertip along the back of my hand. "That old adrenaline," he said in a husky voice. "Hard to keep it from pumping sometimes. I'm curious. Are the tours you escort always this . . . eventful?"

I thought about that for a moment. "Yeah. I think they are."

"And where is it you'll be escorting your next tour?"

"Hawaii. Over Halloween. It's a cruise of the islands."

"Sounds wonderful. I'll be sure to stay at the opposite end of the world."

"These situations are not my fault!"

He elevated one skeptical eyebrow at me. "What I want to know is, how did Britha do it? When did she lace his water with the alcohol?"

"From what Barbro was able to figure out, Britha must have pocketed Philip's duplicate key when she got back from dinner last night, then entered his room this morning just after breakfast while he was waiting in line to take the elevator. The elevator was so slow, it gave her plenty of time. Barbro was taking her turn in the bathroom, so the coast was clear."

"I guess a man needs to watch himself around women from Iowa. There's more to them than meets the eye."

I leaned back in my chair, searching his face with my eyes. "What's going to happen to Britha? Will they test her mental competency? Try her here? Send her back home?"

Duncan shook his head. "I hate to admit it, but I don't know much about the criminal justice system here. Nothing like this has ever happened on one of my tours before. But we can pay a visit to the police station tomorrow before we go. They should be able to answer some of our questions. Will that work for you?"

I nodded my thanks. Okay, Duncan Lazarus wasn't a killer. He was a very nice, very intelligent, very sexy man.

And I was going to be spending ten more days with him. Oh, God.

He grinned widely. "Now, would you like to tell me how you knew which twin to clobber with your bottled water? How could you tell them apart? They look exactly alike."

"Mmm, not exactly. One *teensy* feature is different."

"And that is . . . ?"

I tugged on my ear. He looked confused. "Carol Burnett used to do that at the end of her variety show," he commented. "I caught all the reruns when I visited my grandparents in the States."

I rolled my eyes and tugged again.

"Their ears are different?" he asked tentatively.

"Their lobes. Britha's lobes are attached. Barbro's are *de*tached."

"Detached from what?"

I smiled coyly. "Britha's lobes don't drop away from her ear. They form a continuous curve. They're attached. Barbro's, on the other hand, form a little teardrop of skin that hangs slightly below the ear. The lobes are *de*tached. Britha's earring fell off at the top of the Duomo, and that's why. She didn't have as much lobe to attach a clip-on to."

"And people never noticed the difference between them because—?"

"Because it was only a minor irregularity and most probably because . . . they always wore earrings!"

"And you observed this how?"

My smile widened. "From a photo I took of them. Digital cameras are amazing."

As a chorus of violins struck up a tune from the front of the restaurant, Duncan shook his head, laughing. "Brilliant. Absolutely brilliant. But I have some bad news for you." He circled his hand around mine, his thumb resting on the pulse point at my wrist. "The hotel is going to charge you for that bottle of water you used on Britha. You apparently cracked the plastic. The water all leaked out."

"No problem. I saved lots of money on the leather jacket I didn't buy." I bowed my head, hesitant to ask this next question, but needing some kind of closure. "I don't mean to pry, Duncan, and I know it's painful for you to talk about, so I apologize, but would you mind telling me"—I lifted my eyes to his—"what was your sister's married name?"

He regarded me askance. "O'Grady. Molly O'Grady. She met a black-haired Irishman at Trinity College in Dublin and knew instantly that she'd found her soulmate. Funny how some people just know."

I shivered at the look he gave me. "How did she die?" I asked gently.

"A boating accident in Venice. I still have trouble conducting tours there, but I'm coping."

Chirrup chirrup. Chirrup chirrup. Chirrup chirrup.

Duncan pointed to my shoulder bag. "That's yours. I decided to go incommunicado for once."

"Hello?" I said into my phone.

I heard a spate of soft, sensuous Italian being spoken into my ear. I felt an awkward smile play across my lips. "Etienne? Where are you?"

I listened intently, trying to hear him over the melodic voices that had joined forces with the violins. "Right. I thought that's what probably happened. A tunnel." I listened some more. "Unh-huh. This . . . this is a good time." I flashed Duncan an uneasy smile. My heart thumped. My stomach churned. My blood pounded in my ears. This was it. This was really it!

I listened to the words pouring from Etienne's mouth in his beautiful French/German/Italian accent. Apologies. Sweet nothings. *That's it. So far, so good. Keep going.* A little

ore buildup and finally the question I'd been waiting to
ear for so long.

I bit my tongue until he was finished. I inhaled a deep
reath. I forced a half smile at Duncan, then responded to
tienne's question in a slightly different way than I'd imag-
ed.

"YOU WANT ME TO WHAT?"

POCKET BOOKS
PROUDLY PRESENTS

HULA DONE IT?

MADDY HUNTER

Available in paperback Summer 2005
from Pocket Books

Turn the page for a preview of
Hula Done It? . . .

The Hawaiian islanders weren't as predictable as the English, and it was this unpredictability that Captain Cook and his crew found so confounding. There was no rhyme or reason behind the natives' selfless gift-giving one day and their crazed hostility the next."

Professor Dorian Smoker glanced toward the back of the cruise ship's lecture room for the umpteenth time, his pale blue eyes flickering with an uneasiness that seemed unwarranted for a man recognized as the world's leading authority on Captain James Cook. What in the heck was back there that he found so disturbing?

I glanced subtly over my shoulder to find people packed into the room like proverbial sardines. I wasn't surprised to find standing room only. Professor Smoker was the academic headliner for our Hawaiian Island cruise, which advertised excursions to the sites visited by Captain Cook on his final sea voyage. The audience was filled with bespectacled, erudite types with name tags that identified them as members of organizations I'd never heard of: the Sandwich Island Society, the World Navigators Club, Haute Cuisine International.

I wasn't sure why the Haute Cuisine people were here, but intuition told me they'd probably confused Captain Cook with Mr. Food or the Galloping Gourmet and were expecting a guy in an apron and chef's hat to wow them with food preparation and tasty free samples. Instead, a man in a navy cardigan and baggy Dockers had mesmerized them with tales of an eighteenth-century English explorer.

And I do mean *mesmerized*. Even the guests who were obviously sitting in on the wrong lecture made no attempt to leave. As physically unremarkable as Professor Smoker was, once he started speaking, he oozed such magnetism that he held all of us spellbound. His knowledge gave him an intellectual swagger and confidence that made him appear taller, leaner, stronger. Without having to rely on a form-fitting costume donned in a phone booth, Professor Dorian Smoker suddenly became the sexiest man on the planet—not bad for a fifty-something academic with a slight paunch, bad posture, scruffy beard, and thinning gray hair.

But I still wondered about the odd glint in his eyes. Was it alarm or a piece of fuzz caught behind a contact lens?

"Five days after the Captain was slain by the islanders, one of King Terreeoboo's chiefs returned Cook's body to the crew of the *Resolution*," Smoker continued. "Or more correctly, they returned a jumble of bones that included the Captain's hands, skull, legs, lower jaw, and feet. The thigh bones and arms were never recovered."

My grandmother, whose name tag was crammed with microscopic text that read: *Marion Sippel—Windsor City Bank Travel Club; Windsor City, Iowa; Birthplace of America's First Pork Fritter Finger*, looked up from the ragged sheet of paper she was studying and leaned over to whisper in my ear. "If they'd waked him at Heavenly Host there wouldn't a been no public viewin'. It's one a them rules a thumb. You gotta have a body to be eligible for the open casket option."

Smoker sipped a mouthful of water before allowing his

gaze to drift slowly over his audience. "Captain Cook's remains were committed to the deep on February 22, 1779, and on the following day, under the command of Warrant Officer William Bligh, who would gain infamy years later aboard the mutinous ship, *Bounty*, the *Resolution* set sail for England. After a return voyage of eight months the ship arrived back in the Thames, having suffered the deaths of a score of crew members, the ship's surgeon, and Captain James Cook himself. Cook's wife, Elizabeth, survived him by fifty-six years."

"I hope I don't survive your grampa by fifty-six years," Nana whispered. "That'd make me"—she moved her lips and pinched her eyes shut in a quick calculation—"a hundred and thirty-two. We're talkin' brain cells like leaf lettuce."

Nana watched a lot of specials on the Discovery channel, so she was current with all the latest geriatric news.

"Excuse me, Professor." Tilly Hovick raised her walking stick in the air to attract his attention. Tilly was a retired university professor who'd become fast friends with Nana on our trip to Ireland. She stood nearly six feet tall in her stocking feet, was thin as a torch light, and had an affinity for wearing pleated woolen skirts and matching berets, though as a concession to the tropical climate, she'd reverted to cotton blends with coordinating visors. "You're familiar with the *Resolution*'s crew roster. Was there a seaman aboard by the name of Griffin Ring?"

Dorian Smoker lifted his brow in surprise. A curious smile touched his lips. "There was indeed a crewman by that name aboard the *Resolution*. Ordinary Seaman, Griffin Ring. A rather taciturn fellow with a dubious background that scholars later discovered may have involved the suspicious death of a relative and the theft of a family heirloom before he embarked on the expedition. But no formal charges were ever drawn up because he died shortly after returning to England. His name is absent from most primary sources, so he remains something of a mystery in the annals of navigational history." Smoker's eyebrow arched upward at Tilly. "Do you mind my asking what interest you have in Ring? He's mentioned so sparingly in the literature, how do you know his name?"

Tilly extracted a plastic storage bag from her canvas tote. Inside was a book the size of a Harlequin romance which she removed from the plastic and held up for Smoker's observation. It was bound in discolored leather that still showed patches of burnt sienna, was thick as a deck of playing cards, and looked like something straight out of the Old Curiosity Shop. "I found this in a hidden compartment of an antique chest I recently inherited. It appears to be the handwritten journal of Griffin Ring, Ordinary Seaman aboard the sloop, *Resolution*. From what I've read, it documents the events of Cook's last journey of discovery in the South Pacific. You're the expert, Professor. What would you have to do to determine if this journal is authentic or a masterful hoax?"

The room erupted in a low-level buzz. Heads turned. Chairs creaked. All eyes riveted on Tilly and the slim book she clutched in her hand. Professor Smoker inhaled a deep breath then nodded to a young woman in the front row who stood up to address us.

"Professor Smoker thanks you for attending today's lecture." Her voice projected into every corner of the room without effort. Good lungs. Great diaphragm. I suspected she'd had professional voice training, or lived in a family where she'd had to yell a lot. She was in her mid-twenties with a foot of coarse brown hair caught in a scrunchy at the base of her skull. Her smile was subdued, her tone no-nonsense, and she wore serious, elliptical-shaped eyeglasses that appeared to add ten years to her age and twenty points to her IQ. "Please check the schedule in tomorrow's *Compass* for the time and location of our next session. Apparently, we're going to be a moveable feast. And if you have questions about—"

"I've got a question," a man at the back of the room called out. "Where's the Coconut Palms Café? The ice cream social begins in ten minutes and they're serving thirty-two different flavors. That's one more than Baskin-Robbins!"

"I know where it is," another man replied. "Five decks up. And it's all you can eat!"

That started another buzz that led to serial chair-scraping and a mass exodus of people through the two exit doors. But who could blame them? One more flavor than Baskin-Robbins. Even I was curious.

Nana tugged on my arm. "I need two M&M's for the scavenger hunt. You think they might have M&M's at the ice cream social?"

"What kind do you need? Peanut, almond, crispy, peanut butter, or plain?"

She consulted her list. "Blue."

Professor Smoker left his podium and sauntered in our direction. "Would you mind if I took a closer look at your journal, Mrs."—he eyed Tilly's name tag—"Hovick?"

"Professor Hovick," she corrected, giving his hand a firm shake. "Iowa State University. Retired."

The degree of respect in his eyes inched upward, like water on the indicator level of a twelve-cup coffee maker. "History?"

"Anthropology. And these are my traveling companions, Marion Sippel and her granddaughter, Emily."

Smoker nodded to each of us before beckoning to the young woman who had announced the end of the lecture.

"Let me introduce you to Bailey Howard." He graced her with an appreciative smile as she joined us. "My brilliant graduate assistant who has single-handedly rescued me from drowning in a sea of memoranda, e-mail, and otherwise useless bureaucratic spam. It'll be a sad day when she graduates. I'll be lost without her organizational skills."

Bailey angled her mouth into a crooked smile, looking uncomfortable with the compliment. She shrugged one shoulder. "I'm a Virgo," she said without bombast. "We have an obsessive need to create order out of chaos."

Hey! I had that need, too! Especially when it came to nail polish and shoes. But I was a Libra, not a Virgo. Must mean my birthday fell on the cusp.

Smoker laughed. "Bailey knows nearly as much about Captain Cook as I do. In a few years, I suspect she'll be applying for my position. But in the meantime"—he extended a polite hand toward Tilly's book—"I should very much like to peruse your journal. You found it in an antique chest, you say?"

Tilly handed over the journal. "An antique bachelor's chest willed to me from a cousin who lived in England for many years. Marion's grandson found the hidden compartment quite by accident when they were visiting last week. He was pretending the chest was the control panel for the Starship Enterprise, and when he turned a knob to reverse engines, the compartment opened up. A charming youngster, young David," she said stiffly. "So"—she searched momentarily for the right adjective—"energetic."

Nana shook her head. "In the last year he's went from action figures, to farm machinery, to spaceships. His mother thinks he's got Attention Deficit Disorder. Or Hyperactivity Disorder. Or Attention Deficit Hyperactivity Disorder. I think he's showin' real good signs that he's normal. You got grandkids, Professor?"

Smoker opened the journal, his eyes skimming the first page. "I've never married," he said off-handedly. "I'm afraid I've made my career my life. This journal is in extraordinary condition for a book that's over two hundred years old. Excellent ink pigment. Minimal deterioration of the paper. Legible handwriting. It's almost too good to be true."

"My sentiments entirely," Tilly agreed. "Not to mention that your typical seaman in the eighteenth century couldn't write." She cocked her head to regard the journal from another angle. "And yet, if you read a few pages of what Ring has penned, you find a certain element of authenticity about it."

"The twentieth century gave rise to forgers who knew their profession well," Smoker asserted. "I'd need to read the complete journal before I could make any kind of determination, but at first blush, Professor Hovick, I'd deem it a well-crafted hoax." He closed the book and attempted to hand it back, but Tilly merely stared at it.

"I feared as much. But still . . ." She leaned on her walking stick, her eyes registering a sudden decision. "I invite you to read the complete journal then."

The book seemed to weigh more heavily in Smoker's hand. "It could take days. Are you comfortable entrusting it to me for that long?"

She nodded assent. "However long it takes, Professor. If you're able to resolve its true origin, I expect it will be well worth the wait."

"I can't promise any startling results, but please consider it on my front burner. What's your cabin number, Professor Hovick? I'll get back to you as soon as possible."

While Tilly and Dorian Smoker exchanged cabin numbers, I observed two young women standing by the door at the back of the room, watching us and each other with icy glares. One was tall and shapely, with a curtain of dark hair framing her face. The other was tanned and blond, with some kind of colorful tattoo hugging her shoulder. The brunette wore a skimpy pink halter top and belted white short-shorts that exposed her navel. The blonde was equally naked in a black bikini top and matching micro-miniskirt that was the size of a candy wrapper. Looked like they were both modeling the latest in Dallas Cowboys cheerleader cruise wear. Who knew? Maybe they were expecting a football game to break out somewhere.

"You don't got a business card I can have, do you, Professor?" Nana asked Smoker as she eyed her crumpled list again. "It's on account a the scavenger hunt. We're s'posed to ask perfect strangers to give us really stupid stuff, and that's s'posed to break the ice."

He smiled as he slipped the journal back into the plastic storage bag that Tilly handed him. "You're in luck, Mrs. Sippel." He reached into the pocket of his shirt and removed a leather case that was slightly bigger than a credit card. "I always carry extra when I'm lecturing. You never know who might want to visit my website, or make a contribution to the university." He plucked a white card from the stack and offered it to Nana. "Will that do?"

"You bet," said Nana, giving it a quick glance before stashing it in the oversized leather pocketbook that was her signature piece. "You don't happen to have a couple a blue M&M's on you, do you?"

"Afraid not. You might try a vending machine."

"Have they got vendin' machines on board? I haven't seen none, but then, I haven't been lookin'. Good idea." She looked suddenly worried. "I only got a few more hours before the hunt ends, and if I can find three more things, I got a good chance a winnin' the grand prize."

"Which is?" asked Smoker.

Nana read from her paper. " 'A priceless memento that celebrates the uniqueness of the Hawaiian Islands.' I'm thinkin' maybe a free ticket to that luau they're offerin' on Maui."

Better that than a book contract with a five figure advance. A little chill tickled my spine. Been there. Done that.

Bailey Howard tapped her watch to catch Smoker's attention. "It's about that time, Professor. We're supposed to vacate the room by 4:00."

Smoker gave us a devilish wink. "You see what I mean about her being organized and efficient? She'll be dean of the College of Arts and Letters before long. Ladies, it's been a pleasure meeting you." He shook hands with all of us before graciously pointing us in the direction of the door, which, I figured, was our cue to leave.

Gathering up our belongings, we ambled toward the exit, only to have the two cheerleaders charge past us toward the front of the room, eyes locked, teeth set, like defensive backs in blitz formation. "You s'pose it's the professor's birthday?" Nana asked, peeking over her shoulder at the women.

"Why do you ask?" I peeked too, watching the two beauties greet Smoker in the same way cannibals might greet a wayward traveler.

"Them two girls look like they just popped outta one a them X-rated birthday cakes. You s'pose they got a naughty bakery on board?" She paused in thought. "I wonder if they do special orders?"

Whether it was his birthday or not, the good professor certainly looked surprised, but not in a good way.

Tilly stopped us once we exited into the corridor. She nodded back toward the lecture room, a knowing look in her eye. "I saw this all the time when I was teaching. Sexual misconduct is rampant in academia, especially with the more high-profile professors. He's probably slept with both those young women."

"No," exclaimed Nana.

"Yes," assured Tilly. "A man doesn't have to be good-looking for a woman to find him sexually attractive. They've conducted studies. Position. Authority. Knowledge. To a woman, these are much more powerful aphrodisiacs than good looks."

"Who done that study?" asked Nana. "Someone at ISU?"

"I read it in *Cosmo*. The sad thing is, those girls probably signed up for the cruise hoping to surprise Smoker, and instead, they ended up surprising each other. It has to be a devastating blow to learn you're not the one and only." Tilly shook her head. "He'd better be prepared to do some fast talking. You know what they say, 'Hell hath no fury . . . '"

"Blue M&M's," said Nana. "Which way to the Coconut Palms Café? It's located aft, but I don't know if that's left or right."

I didn't know either, but I did know one thing. If what Tilly said was true, I was glad not to be in Dorian Smoker's shoes right now.

The *Aloha Princess* boasted thirteen decks, three swimming pools, two five-star restaurants, a miniature golf course, a climbing wall, a world-class fitness center, an exotic spa, and thirty-two kinds of ice cream, but nowhere within its luxurious chrome and glass interior was there a blue M&M to be found. Striking out at the Coconut Palms Café, we ventured to the casino on deck 6, where we ran into the rest of the scavenger-hunting Iowa contingent—

their voices raised in complaint as they brandished their ragged lists.

"They've got no vending machines on this boat," sniped Bernice Zwerg in a voice that scratched like coarse-grade steel wool. "How are we supposed to get our hands on those over-priced packets of M&M's without vending machines?" Bernice had undergone emergency bunion surgery on both feet last June, but she'd bounced back well enough to book a last minute reservation on our cruise. Lucky me.

We were gathered near the front of the casino, opposite the glassed-in cashier windows, where a coin-counting machine rattled and chimed like a race-car engine. Reflective disco balls hung from the ceiling. Slot machines hunkered in military formation on the floor. Gaming tables flanked the perimeter. Digital sound effects rang out like a chorus of off-key kazoos. Hoots. Hollers. Screams. Laughter.

"Did anyone try the General Store on deck five?" asked Dick Teig, hitching up the belt of his size 52 waist Italian knit trousers. I'd discovered a killer in Italy. Dick had discovered couture. "They should have M&M's in the candy section."

"Osmond and I checked," announced Alice Tjarks in her KORN radio voice. "All they have is Skittles." She waved into the lens of Osmond Chelsvig's four-month-old camcorder then gave him a big 'I'm on vacation' smile.

"Skittles?" asked Helen Teig, Dick's wife. "I love Skittles. Did you buy any?"

"At three dollars a bag?" Alice shot back. "Who's got money like that?"

"I do," said Nana. "But I'd rather spend it on them midget Tootsie Rolls. The fresh ones don't even stick to my dentures."

Ding ding ding ding ding. A victorious shriek echoed out from the depths of the casino. I nodded to Nana and Tilly, indicating that I was ready to head out and explore some more. I'd had enough of the casino's gaming tables and slot machines. Gaming tables reminded me of *chemin de fer*. *Chemin de fer* reminded me of Italy. And Italy reminded me of Etienne, who'd won an unexpected fortune while visiting his family and had gotten his memory jogged enough to ask me . . .

My heart started thumping in my ears.

. . . to have the gall to ask me . . .

My face grew hot.

. . . to have the absolute *effrontery* to . . . to . . .

AAARGH! I was *not* going to think about Etienne right now. I refused to let him spoil my holiday. But I needed to get out of the casino, and fast.

Inhaling a calming breath, I headed out the door, with Nana and Tilly hot on my heels. "Where to, ladies?" I asked, digging a floor plan of the ship out of my shoulder bag. "A spin around the promenade deck, which is . . . let's see . . . one deck down? Or would you prefer a round of miniature golf on the putting green on deck thirteen?"

"I've never played miniature golf," Tilly admitted. "The closest I've come to it is playing croquet with a tribe of Pygmies in the Andaman Islands."

"I'd like to hit the spa and borrow a rock like Bernice done," Nana said. "And while I'm there, I'm gonna sign up for one a them Ionithermie treatments. It costs a hundred and twenty dollars, but the flyer promises you can lose up to eight inches in the first session."

"Eight inches of what?" I asked, wondering if this was the right advertising ploy to attract your more squeamish male guest.

"Cellulite. They plaster you in seaweed and wire you up

like the Frankenstein monster, and that's s'posed to detox-ify your fat cells and firm you up real good."

"I underwent a similar ritual in New Guinea," Tilly recalled as we approached the elevator. "Only they plas-tered me in jungle foliage instead of sea vegetation, and I wasn't sure if their goal was to cleanse me or eat me. Cannibals can be quite easily misunderstood."

When the door to the elevator slid open, we stepped into a glass cylinder that was reminiscent of a laboratory test tube. It overlooked the atrium at the center of the ship—a huge, unexpected column of open space between decks 4 and 11 that was rimmed by tiers of balconies and overhung by a crystal chandelier that looked like a giant upside-down Sno-Cone. I punched the button for deck 11 then clung to the safety rail as we glided upward on the barest whisper of air. "I'll be," Nana marveled, her nose pressed to the elevator glass. "This is like bein' inside a hypodermic needle."

I looked down at the elegant champagne bar on deck 4, where a staircase of illuminated acrylic risers spiraled toward the next floor. That would be the perfect place to have the group pose for pictures on Halloween night, when we were all expected to dress in costume for the mas-querade gala. I hadn't decided on a costume yet, but I fig-ured I could rent one at the clothing shop on deck 5. They were supposed to have a good selection in a variety of sizes.

"It's breathtaking, isn't it?" mused Tilly as we peered outward through the ship's glass walls. The gleaming waters of the Pacific Ocean appeared calm as bath water. There was no land in sight, only blue sky and open sea. "Balboa first named this ocean the South Sea, but Magellan changed the name to the Pacific, no doubt for the calm waters that greeted him after a harrowing passage around the tip of South America. Can you feel the stillness, ladies? The wonderful calm? This must be the same calm that Magellan felt."

A bell *pinged*. The elevator door *shushed* open.

"MAN OVERBOARD!" shrieked a woman as she banged through the door from the outside deck. "Man overboard! Help me! Somebody help me! PLEASE!"

Only when I stepped outside the elevator did I realize the woman was Bailey Howard.

THE BRUSH-OFF

Reyn Marten Sawyer is content running her salon out of her restored historic house—at least until her mentor, the Hairdressing King of San Antonio, is found murdered with one of Reyn's hairbrushes. Now Reyn has a murder to solve while tangling with the dangerously sexy detective handling the case.

LAURA BRADLEY

"A hilarious debut.... Fans of cozies, screwball comedies, and Sarah Stroymeyer's *Bubbles Yablonsky* mystery series will savor this fun...ride."

—*Publishers Weekly*

POCKET BOOKS
A Division of Simon & Schuster
A VIACOM COMPANY

Available from Pocket Books

09855

POCKET BOOKS MYSTERIES
are to die for!

Curl up with a cozy...

POCKET BOOKS
A Division of Simon & Schuster
A VIACOM COMPANY

Available from Pocket Books   09856